Fetching Dreams

MARY BLECKWEHL

IMMORTAL WORKS

Salt Lake City

D1496335

Immortal Works LLC
1505 Glenrose Drive
Salt Lake City, Utah 84104
Tel: (385) 202-0116

© 2023 Mary Bleckwehl
marybleckwehl.com

Cover Art by Ashley Literski
http://strangedevotion.wixsite.com/strangedesigns

ISBN 978-1-953491-55-8 (Paperback)
ASIN B0C4K2ZTMQ (Kindle Edition)

For those who seek a purpose—MB

FOREWORD

Dear readers,

I admire this incredible work by Mary Bleckwehl for it combines an insightful and realistic story about the challenges of accessing water for everyday use in developing countries with the empowerment of two young girls from opposite cultures who are searching for purpose. As you read, you'll be taken on a journey to a remote village in Western Kenya and get a glimpse of the daily lives of young girls and boys, the challenges they face and how culturally assigned roles determine their participation at home, school and community.

I was born and raised in a rural village in Kenya, not so different from Neyah's. This story elicited great childhood memories-the joys, the food, my own family relationships, school and community life. Although access to clean water is still a problem for millions around the world, there is hope. I worked for a nonprofit organization that leads the global charge for bringing clean water and sanitation efforts to those who need it most. Through cooperative efforts there is good reason to believe the water crisis can be solved. I see that ray of hope shining through in this book.

Fetching Dreams is a mine of information and a source of inspiration for young children looking for purpose and significance. It will fire young people's imaginations and show how global friendships can be world changers, one project and one place at a time. Read it, enjoy it, learn from it and thank the author for writing this captivating story.

—Rose Ringeera, Doctoral Candidate, U.S. International University Africa, Nairobi, Kenya

PROLOGUE: LETSOKOANE VILLAGE, AFRICA

My baby sister looked like a broken doll. She didn't quite fit into the wooden box Bosco found in the scrap pile, so Papa tilted Lulu's head to the side to squeeze her in. I reached into the box and poked her belly. Lulu always giggled at that. Instead of bouncing back, her belly stayed dented in like an extra belly button.

"Neyah, sing the lullaby your sister liked." Papa's voice sounded small as a field mouse.

Mama moaned.

As I sang, Bosco took off his dirty shirt and wrapped it around the box. Gently laying her in the hole Papa dug, he pushed dirt over the box and patted it into a mound. It looked like my brother had just planted something. I glanced at the yellow water container by my feet and got this crazy urge to pour water on Lulu to see if she would somehow come alive again. But I could not waste the water. We needed it for the goats.

WAITING AT THE WATER HOLE

The decaying carcass barely resembled what it once was. It lay stuck under some downed weeds in the murky water a few meters from Neyah. A slight woman, who had a sleeping baby strapped to her back, set her cracked water pot down and grabbed a thick stick. Tugging what remained of the stringy body from the waterhole, she tossed it into the bushes. Something about its nose seemed familiar to Neyah. She wondered if it was the dog her twin brothers, Kato and Hassan, secretly fed in the village.

The putrid smell crawled up Neyah's nostrils, threatening her eyes. As she inched closer to her turn to dip water from the mudhole, Neyah spun away so the stench hit the back of her shaved head instead of her nose. Her belly rumbled. The bowl of leftover ugali Mama warmed for her breakfast hadn't been enough, or was the stench from the rotting dog causing her belly to twist and moan?

Twelve-year-old Neyah could handle the smell and the hunger pain. But the wait drove her crazy. She tapped her toes. Impatience screamed inside her head. After walking over an hour to get to the water hole, she stood in line for two hours for a chance to gather the precious water her family needed. For eight years she'd carried water, which meant hundreds of hours of waiting and weeks of missed school.

At least I can go to school later today, she thought with a smile.

A snake slithered into the water. Neyah shifted weight from one bare foot to the other. She hadn't inherited Bibi's patience. Her grandmother, Bibi, was Papa's mother, and shared Neyah's sleeping hut in their village compound. Bibi's real name was Subira, which meant patience, because she was born under a peaceful sky. However, Neyah, like her mother, lacked patience. Her parents gifted her with a name that meant "full of purpose" since she came into the world when the corn sprouted.

Smiling at a crane freely gliding overhead, Neyah considered her namesake, her purpose. What could it be? She wished it to be something surprising and significant.

Staring at the scene before her, Neyah pondered how to make waiting more bearable. Count the birds? The clouds? Or the babies in their mamas' sling?

Neyah studied a sleepy infant whose bottom looked as though he might break through the thin fabric. The sling's worn floral pattern was barely visible. Neyah wondered how many babies the sling had carried over the years.

Neyah shifted her attention to the animals that came to drink. She longed to touch them, to whisper her dreams into their ears. A strange kind of kinship with these creatures made the treks tolerable, almost enticing. A few scraggly donkeys and an alert impala drank quietly across the waterhole. Cattle wandered as though searching for an old friend. A colorful bird hitched a ride on a cow's head. Between drinks, animals lifted their heads and stared at the fetchers.

Maybe, Neyah thought, *I'll be an impala in my next life, swift and free to go when and where I choose. Except, I'll need to watch for hungry lions.*

As Neyah advanced in the slow line, she considered the girl in front of her. Layila lived in her village and had missed school today too. Neyah wondered if the American girl she wrote to missed school when she fetched water. She sent Abby her first pen pal letter weeks ago. Neyah thought about what she had written.

Hello to new friend Abby in US America I am Neyah I live in Africa It is August I like to write but do not like to talk I am 12 years now and just started third term I walk to school if drought or floods are not here I like school much I have a big dream to go every day and be a doctor someday like Mama says but next five days I miss school to fetch water I like new words I like Mr. Sahli He be good teacher with big waist and big laugh and big teeth and one eye that does not look at me He tell us stop writing now It be your turn.

Neyah Jabari
Saramba Primary School
Kenya

Neyah's mind wandered. Perhaps she would soon receive a letter from Abby.

Turning her attention back to Layila, Neyah recognized her four plastic containers. Originally, they held cooking or motor oil, but after getting scrubbed clean, they were sold at the market to women looking to buy a container to fetch water in. Neyah watched Layila pour water into the container's tiny opening with her rusty cup. It took time, but every drop counted.

Patience. Bibi's voice crept into Neyah's ears.

No one talked here for good reason. Neyah glanced left, then right. The risk of attracting the attention of crocodiles living nearby loomed large. Shivering, Neyah thought of cousin Winna, who lost her foot to a hungry croc and nearly bled to death last year. Winna no longer fetched water. Instead, she hobbled to school every day with two walking sticks and a missing foot.

Layila finally filled her containers. She handed her dipping can to Neyah, who waded into the familiar cool mud. As the mud oozed between her toes, she hoped the snake she saw earlier had slinked somewhere other than under her feet. The floral pattern of her faded skirt slow-danced on the surface and finally sank as it took on water.

The taste of dust sat on Neyah's tongue. Swishing away the dead snails and floating insects, she filled the cap of her can and lifted it to her mouth. The cool water soothed her dry throat. Filling the cap twice more, she closed her eyes and enjoyed the satisfying drink each time she tipped her head back to swallow. Then she got to work.

Neyah dipped and poured the brown liquid into her five-gallon jerry can. After securing the cap, she dragged her faded yellow container out of the mud. It stunk. Now she stunk. This was a swamp. The cattle and other animals bathed in it; they used it as a toilet. Neyah knew all this.

Closing her eyes for a second, Neyah steadied her vessel and mentally prepared to hoist the forty pounds of water onto her head. Bending one knee and readying her leg, she sucked in air and lifted the jerry can onto her thigh. Tipping one corner of it off her leg, Neyah slid a hand under the heavy can. She guided it upward to just the right spot on her head in one synchronous motion as she stretched to a balanced stand. Turning, she nearly tripped over a very pregnant woman struggling to position a pot on her own head. Neyah's jerry can wobbled, but her strong arms held on.

The pregnant woman grimaced before stepping onto the path. Her four small children followed. Neyah followed, watching their small feet slap the ground all the way home.

2

A DELIVERY FROM BOSCO THE GREAT

Relieved to be home, Neyah set her jerry can down and massaged her neck. Now she could go to school! Her best friend, Malaika, would hopefully be there along with exciting new words and her enthusiastic teacher, Mr. Sahli.

"You are just in time," Neyah's mother, Sara, called. "Bring the water near my fire."

Neyah hauled it across the dirt and gave the jerry can a pat.

Bibi sat in her usual spot: a tree stump worn smooth from years of sitting. Neyah ran to greet her grandmother with a late morning hug and sank to the dusty ground in front of her.

Neyah murmured as Bibi rubbed the tension from her shoulders. Fetching water gave her a variety of aches.

"Hello, Mama! Hello, Bibi!" called Bosco. Neyah's ten-year-old brother had arrived home early from school to herd the goats and cows, ensuring they had water and the best patch of grass.

"Jambo, Bosco," said Mama. "Find the ugali left from last evening for you and Neyah."

Squatting low in front of his sister, Bosco peered up into her face and smiled the every-tooth-showing smile he was famous for. "Hello, Neyah!"

Ignoring her brother's teasing face, Neyah surveyed Mama's pot of ugali as if it held great intrigue. Surprised to see small chunks of beef jerky in the cake-like porridge Mama made from ground maize and hot water, she snatched a piece of the smoky meat and popped it in her mouth. A delicacy from the last cow slaughtered in the village, its smoky flavor mingled with the ugali and made for a rare treat. As the burst of flavor dissolved on her taste buds, she noticed more of the beef strips curing over Mama's fire. Her grateful eyes met Mama's eyes. She knew it took time for Mama to cut the meat into long, thick strings.

"Mmm," Bibi murmured. "Something special is cooking!"

Poking a forked branch under the ashes of her fire, Mama uncovered another strip of warmed beef. She brushed the dusty flecks of ash from it before cutting it into sections with a machete and burying them in another bowl of ugali. She carefully placed the bowl into Bibi's shaky hands and patted her mother-in-law's shoulder.

"Here is your something special, Bibi. It may be the last beef for a while."

Neyah pivoted toward her hut, savoring the beef flavor. Bosco followed in his daily challenge of getting her to talk. "The Great Bosco might have something for you from Mr. Sahli!" His sing-song voice made Neyah giggle inside.

Neyah stopped and reached for Bosco's backpack, but he twisted away, still grinning from ear to ear. He threw his hands jubilantly toward the sky. "Guess what it is!"

"Homework," Neyah stated in a way that said, *That is all it ever is.*

"Yes, and something else you will like!" His teasing smile both amused and infuriated her.

Curious, Neyah wondered if it could be her first pen pal letter. Or maybe nothing. Bosco sometimes made things up just to get her to talk. She placed her hands on her hips, waiting for Bosco to hand it over.

"You need to guess!"

She took a step toward Bosco, attempting to grab him, but he jumped back, hoping for a game of "bet you can't catch me." He scampered around one of the two family huts.

Bibi stated the obvious. "Bosco, you are a tease."

"Here it is!" Doing his best to taunt his sister, a grinning Bosco held up the "something else" between his thumb and pointer finger and waved it back and forth.

The size of the envelope caused Neyah to catch her breath. The attractive package looked nearly as blue as the midday sky over Kenya. Abby's letter? It had to be. She lunged at Bosco. With a wide-eyed grin of satisfaction and shrieking laughter, he ducked and ran off with the envelope firmly in his grasp.

After two laps around the small thatched hut, Mama's voice broke off the chase. "Does the Great Bosco hear those thirsty cows bellowing?" She tried to hide the smile tugging at her lips. "You need to take them now before they drop dead."

After one more lap, Bosco tossed the envelope at Neyah. She snatched it from the dusty ground, folded it with care, and stuffed it into her pocket.

"Aw! You are not going to read it to me?" Bosco never gave up easily. "Mr. Sahli said it is your first letter from America."

"Bosco, there is no time for reading or chasing," Mama said sternly. "Come eat or you will starve until dinner. Neyah, help Bibi to the toilet when she finishes her ugali and tea. Once you eat, you need to head out on your next fetching."

Neyah's forehead crinkled. Next fetching? Maybe Mama forgot this was her school day.

Not much louder than a whisper, Neyah worked up the courage to speak. "Mama, today is my half-school day."

"Did you say something, child?"

Neyah took a breath. "I go to school today."

"Not when we need water for the cows, fields, and my ugali."

Arguing with Mama never worked, so Neyah didn't bother. Her neck hurt from the weight of carrying the water, and she didn't feel like eating. But when the smell of beef wafted by, she picked up a bowl. Savoring each bite, she thought about missing school again. She ached to learn new vocabulary words, perform a science experiment, and see Mr. Sahli's artful handwriting.

"Water is life," Bibi said after returning from the toilet. Neyah had heard this announcement from Bibi many times and knew it wouldn't be the last.

Reluctantly, Neyah left the family compound to fetch another round of water. Her feet dragged in the dust. She wished the water hole sat right beside her hut instead of six kilometers away.

The American letter rustled in her pocket as Neyah walked, inviting her to open it. Hurrying far outside the village to a hidden spot, she couldn't wait any longer. She sat to read cross-legged on a large stone that was partially hidden by prickly bushes. After pulling the pretty blue envelope from her torn pocket, Neyah started reading.

Hi! I'm your pen pal from Cedar Grove, Minnesota. I just started seventh grade. Mr. Simon, my Social Studies teacher, said he was in the Peace Corps with your teacher. I guess they decided our classes should team up to write letters for our cultural exchange unit. He handed us our first letters today. I'm matched with you! Thanks for your letter. This is going to be a little weird writing to someone I haven't met! The only letters I've written are to my grandparents in Nebraska.

You're the same age as—

A hit from behind caught Neyah off guard.

"Ahhh!" She screamed for her life. "Bandits!"

Neyah rolled into the barbed growth while the letter flew up and out of sight. She heard the thin fabric of her dress rip where the sharp barbs caught it and felt the prickly branches bite into her left arm. Her fear temporarily deadened the pain and yanked her to her feet to face her attacker.

For the first time, Bosco's laughter felt like a relief. The bandit was her brother.

"You are supposed to be fetching water!" he tried to scold her the way Mama would.

"And *you* are supposed to be herding cattle!" She tried matching his tone, but her voice shook. Blood trickled onto her hand from a spot where her arm had been cut by the branch.

"So, now you talk!" Bosco yelled in an accusing tone. He pulled his filthy bandana from his neck, wiped Neyah's arm, and stuffed it into her pocket.

"Sorry about your arm."

Motioning toward her letter, Bosco asked in a milder tone, "Will you read it to me later?"

Hesitating, Neyah nodded.

Bosco picked the letter from the dust and handed it to his sister. For once, he appeared serious. "Do not sit and read here! The next attacker might be a real bandit."

AFTER DINNER, Neyah helped her tired Mama clean the bowls before scurrying to the two-roomed hut she and Bibi shared with Bosco and Paul. Kneeling on her mat, she examined the cuts on her arm.

"Here I am!" cried Bosco, as he crawled into the hut and snuggled up next to her. "Where is the letter?"

Neyah shook her head and pulled out the letter. She had secretly hoped Bosco had forgotten.

You're the same age as me. I'll be 13 pretty soon and I go to Rosa Parks Middle School. I play soccer (I'm slow but I try!). I'm in orchestra too, but my favorite school activity is art club every Tuesday after school.

Andrew is my brother. He's eleven and a SUPER pain! Well, not all the time, just when he's eavesdropping on me and my friends, and sneaking my candy!

Millie is my six-year-old sister. I love her to pieces. She makes up ballet moves while I practice my violin. Then there are my parents, of course. Dad doesn't live with us right now because my parents aren't talking. Something about Dad getting fired and him feeling like he's let us down. It's a bummer because Mom and Dad make a good team and are best friends. I can tell Mom misses him. Dad makes us laugh and loves horses as much as I do. In fact, he just signed me up for riding lessons! Do you ride?

I haven't been to Africa. It sounds like the weather there is as bad as Minnesota-in a different way, of course! We have snow blizzards that cancel school sometimes. But my grandparents are taking us to Hawaii over spring break. No snow there!

Hold on—I need to look up Africa and find you.

Wow! Africa has a lot of countries! I printed the map and circled you in Kenya. Now you're on my bulletin board!

Good morning! I started this last night but fell asleep with the pen in my hand—weird! That's never happened before. This letter writing is the best homework ever! Love it!! In case you haven't noticed, I like to use ! a lot. I'm a pretty excited person and like to talk. The only way to show it in a letter is with the ! Woohoo!!!!!!!

No fetching water for me, but I'm going to use some right now to shower before the bus comes. I ride the bus now since Dad isn't here to take me to school. By the way, I have a secret plan to help my parents get back together. Stay tuned!

Your turn! Your new friend, Abby Larson.

P.S. You like words and I like to draw. We make a good team. Here's a photo of my bedroom and my school picture. My hair was kind of weird that day!! Bye!

Bosco giggled. "It is not just her hair that is weird. Look at all that stuff she has!"

Neyah shrugged.

Glancing at his sister's arm, Bosco wrinkled his forehead. "What did Mama say about your scraped arm?"

"I told her the truth."

Bosco whispered, "You told Mama you stopped to read on a rock and that I pushed you off?"

Neyah couldn't believe that Bosco "the Great" actually looked nervous.

"I said I tripped and landed in a prickly bush."

Bosco's shoulders relaxed. He watched Neyah fold her letter. "I like hearing your voice. And you are a good reader."

Neyah smiled bashfully.

"Why do you not talk much?"

Biting her lip, Neyah felt the sting of tears in her eyes.

Bosco shrugged. "See you in the morning!"

Neyah gave a limp wave and turned to help Bibi to the toilet.

Once she settled into her hut, Neyah tore pages from her journal and began her next letter to Abby. Before the African sun dropped below the horizon, she took one last glance at the words she'd written. Words on paper comforted her. Neat, silent words.

3

PAPA IS SICK

Dear Abby I live in village in Kenya country of big sky and land I like night sky where bright stars speckle it like spots on chickens I pretend stars are nests and I be great bush bird I would fly from one to other to meet you How many days to your home

I go to school and secondhand market and water hole Thank you for picture I never seen girl with white hair I don't have picture I have short black hair so bugs don't make nest I live with Mama Papa Bibi and four brothers Bosco 10 Paul 9 and Kato and Hassan, both be 7 Bosco teases to make me talk Paul be nice brother with so much hope and tells good story but his writing like chicken scratching in dirt Kato and Hassan be born on same day and have big smiles Mama be hard worker and tell us our chores Papa be kind man and take care of family like sky and wind watch over land

Sometimes I wish I be boy and get chance for school every day and my letters would be 100% But I be girl and fetch water many times a day from water hole six km walk How many trips you go for water What is PS and shower and orchestra I like learn new words You be my new teacher on

paper Is your bus ride dangerous I walk five km to Saramba
Primary on days I go to school.

> *Your turn*
> *Neyah Jabari*

6:15 a.m.

"Goodbye Neyah. Do not spill any water today," called Paul. "I will be thirsty when I get home."

"Hey, favorite sister!" teased Bosco. "Are you going to say goodbye to me, your favorite brother?"

Neyah said nothing. His teasing irked her, but not as much as missing school. It would be a week before she'd be able to go.

Standing barefoot in the September morning air, Neyah clutched her yellow water can and welcomed the cool soil between her toes. Soon enough, the scorching sun would heat the ground.

As her brothers headed down the dark road out of their sub-Saharan village, she watched their canvas backpacks bounce up and down. Since the sun hadn't found the horizon yet, Neyah soon lost sight of them and their pale blue school shirts. She hoped Bosco would remember to get her homework and give her pen pal letter to the headmaster.

Neyah envied her brothers. Off they went while she stayed to fetch water. She wanted to throw down her yellow water can, grab her own school bag, and catch up with them. She kicked at her faded schoolbag. Her brothers received a new backpack from the mission each year. Mama made her bag from two squares of an old dress. Neyah thought it looked old from the first day she used it.

Frustration whirled inside her head. *It is not fair! The boys are learning to read and write, and I am learning to balance a container on my head.*

Neyah let the water can slip from her hand as she whispered, "I will be more than a water carrier someday."

Bibi, sitting nearby on the old tree stump, smiled in agreement.

"Neyah! You need to get going before the heat beats you!" Her mother's impatient voice startled Neyah from her daydreams and brought her back to reality. "I went to the water hole myself this morning and have better things to do than tell you about our fetching needs."

Mama sat near her hut cleaning pots in the morning darkness. Neyah smiled affectionately at her thin twenty-nine-year-old Mama, who was muttering her morning prayers.

"I pray for swift healing for my husband, Haji. I pray for healthy cattle and rain for our fields. I pray for the souls of my baby girls, Lulu, Zora, and Samira..."

As Mama prayed, Neyah gazed beyond her family compound to the beauty of the wide valley. Her family, one of the fifty-some families who made up the remote village of Letsokoane, descended from ancestral tribes and did mixed farming to survive. The area was a dry, desolate part of western Kenya, dotted with small rural villages among the hills and valleys. Residents struggled to compete with the weather and still provide for their families by planting and harvesting most of their food.

"The milking cows need water, Neyah. And I will have nothing to cook ugali and make tea if you do not bring water before dinner."

Neyah wanted to protest. *I am not going to the water hole anymore, Mama! I am going to fetch from the open well instead because it is only a kilometer away. If I do that, I will have time to get two or three fetchings in and still get to school.*

But the small girl with skin like polished black satin said nothing; she seldom spoke. Even if she wanted to talk, she didn't want to upset Mama. Neyah knew Papa's recent ailment kept him from fieldwork. Soon her mother would be off to hoe the maize and beans herself. And ever since Lulu's death at the open well, Mama forbade her to go anywhere near it.

Neyah stared at her water can before giving it a swift kick that sent it spinning. The chickens scattered to escape the yellow tornado. The can scooted across the packed earth before tipping over at the feet of her frail and nearly blind grandmother.

Bibi leaned forward from the stump she sat on and picked up the sacred, yellow jerry can. Once it looked new and bright like the noonday sun over Kenya, but now it appeared faded to a cloudy pale. Stained and dented, the molded plastic container carried water just the same. Bibi handed it to Neyah and squeezed her hand. "It is a good day to fetch, Neyah."

Neyah accepted the can from Bibi and ran behind her hut, where she plopped herself onto a cracked plastic carton. Wrestling her word journal from her worn smock pocket, she flipped it to yesterday's entry. She felt sad about missing the opportunity to write the words herself. Relying on Paul's poor writing maddened her.

She read his crooked letters.

Watering hole (*noun*) 1. A small, natural depression where water collects.

2. a pool where animals drink.

Neyah added a third definition with a dull pencil she kept inside her journal.

3. a place where I walk and wait and wonder.

"NEYAH!" Mama's shout made her jump. "The other women and girls just left, so catch up! I do not like you walking alone. There have been three attacks by crazy men this month."

Neyah grasped the water can handle. Even empty, the can felt like a great stone weighing her down.

"How is Papa?"

"You are talking to the ground, Neyah."

She took a deep breath and lifted her head. "How is Papa?"

"Weak." Mama swept small rocks away from her fire. "However, Uncle Aman brought some healing herbs."

Neyah's furrowed brow told Mama she wondered where the herbs came from.

"From the village medicine man," Mama said. "He traveled miles into the forest to collect them from shrubs only he knows about."

"Will they help Papa?"

Mama's face looked doubtful, but Bibi's words assured Neyah.

"He will be healed!" Bibi smiled joyfully. "When that day comes, our family will show appreciation by giving a goat. It will earn us a trip to this special forest to learn what herb mix healed him. That is the way."

Satisfied, Neyah said, "Tell Papa I will give him the first drink of water when I get back."

"I will, sweet girl," said Mama. "Someday you will make a fine doctor, caring for people the way you care for Papa. Now go. Walk safe. I am headed to the market to sell eggs."

Neyah worried about Papa. He slept most of the day. She walked to his hut to say goodbye but halted when she heard the angry voice of Zuberi inside.

Why is that mean man bothering Papa? Neyah wondered.

The whole village knew Zuberi. He only came around to bully others into thinking his way and to make trouble.

"Haji, she is almost a woman," Zuberi said. "It is time you sell her. A man's honor is in his cattle, and you will get many fine cattle in exchange for your daughter's hand in marriage. I know a man named Silas who could use another wife. Let me know when you are ready to deal."

Neyah backed away. *Sell me? Papa would never do that.*

Not trusting her voice, Neyah hugged Bibi tighter than usual before leaving to fetch.

"Water is life," said Bibi.

Maybe, thought Neyah, but it can't be the only thing.

She made her way out of Letsokoane on the one dirt road winding through the village from end to end. The distant voices of the women and girls who left before her drifted to her. Birds sang while the breeze tickled her neck. Shuffling by the bush where her school uniform lay drying, Neyah passed other family compounds. She caught the scent of fresh manure mixed with smoky cooking fires and weak tea. A neighbor's hungry pig scooted out of her way.

Two curious goats stopped their wandering and watched Neyah leave. One followed as if knowing she headed toward water.

"Liza, go back!" The goat bleated its disapproval over having to stay behind.

Village cattle were often kept in the boma, an enclosure for livestock at the center of each family compound. However, Neyah's family boma, shared with several other families, showed gaps in the crude stick fence. This meant curious goats, skittish chickens, and skinny cows often escaped and strayed at will.

As Neyah walked, the angry words Zuberi spoke to Papa floated back to her. Why didn't Bibi say something? She must have heard him.

Neyah knew of the custom of trading daughters for cattle. But Papa loved her, and he knew of her plans to be a doctor. That meant Zuberi wasted his time talking to Papa, Neyah decided, as she turned her eyes to the beaten path.

Before Neyah stepped into the clearing, she stopped and twirled with her water can held at arm's length as if it were a dance partner. She took a moment to look back at her village and sighed. No banks or grocery stores, no electricity or clinic, and no water source.

However, something important waited to blossom in Letsokoane, including a dreamer.

4

MALAIKA, MORE THAN A FRIEND

Although Neyah knew walking in a group made fetching safer, she made no attempt to catch up to the others. She found solace in being alone with the lingering moon, and the words she rarely spoke aloud.

She softly recited a poem she wrote for her English lesson.

> *Words and time will lead me*
> *To the place where I should be*
> *Today it is called a dream*
> *Tomorrow reality*

No one heard except the cool African breeze swirling the dust in front of the girl's bare feet. And maybe the masked weaver singing in the lucky bean tree.

Neyah's eyes followed her small feet in the dim morning light. The ground beneath her remained cracked from lack of rain. The short rainy season in the Great Rift Valley was weeks away. Neyah shivered at the thought of the dry season soon to follow the rain. She didn't know which was worse. The rainy season attracted mosquitoes that caused malaria, and the dry season caused a drought that made animals and people vulnerable. Two uncles and a neighbor died during last year's drought. Her twin brothers' favorite goats, Alice and Tumaini, didn't make it either.

On the days Neyah walked to school after fetching water, she set a fast pace. But today Mama needed her all day for chores, so why hurry? Neyah knew she'd only have to wait once she reached the water hole.

With the thick tree groves behind her, Neyah wove through the tall, grassy plain. Stretching her neck to catch sight of the other fetchers from her village, Neyah's imagination wandered. She became anxious, worrying every tree and bush might be hiding a bandit ready to grab her. *Mama was right; I should have left with the other carriers.*

To keep her mind off bandits, she thought of her first trek with Mama to this water hole. She had asked Mama why they needed to find a new source of water. Neyah recalled Mama's sad response. "Because we can never go back to that horrible well where we lost Lulu." Neyah still recalled the blue, patterned dress Mama had worn as she led the way with no Lulu bouncing in the sling.

Tears slipped down Neyah's face, and her cadence slowed as she softly sang Lamtietie Damtietie. It was Lulu's favorite lullaby–the one Mama didn't allow her to sing anymore.

The sweet words about hushing a baby asleep tugged at her heart as it always had.

Neyah frowned as she listened to her singing voice. Her brothers howled and covered their ears with leaves when they heard her sing. Bosco had told her, "You sound like a monkey squealing!"

I have too many brothers, thought Neyah. She needed a sister to sing with her and help carry water. She needed Lulu. Lulu had loved her singing.

The slight African girl suddenly stopped singing and rubbed her stomach. Lately, the belly pains felt worse. With no toilet in the bush, Neyah stepped behind some tall grass and squatted.

Returning to the path, she kept silent. The path leading from the steep ravine loomed ahead. It might be embarrassing if anyone coming up the ravine heard her monkey voice. And Mama had warned her about this spot where bandits sometimes hid. There was no need to give them notice of her presence by singing.

"Hyena!" A screamed explosion from several meters away sent Neyah's body tripping backward into a full sprawl. Her eyes zeroed in on the animal's foaming mouth at the same time she realized it was her best friend, Malaika, who gave the ear-piercing warning cry.

"Neyah!" Malaika screamed. Her outburst sent the hyena scampering into the bush.

Out of breath from her climb up the steep ravine path, Malaika ran to Neyah's side. "Neyah, are you all right? Sorry if I scared you. Me and my loud mouth!"

Neyah gulped in air. "Your loud mouth just saved me." Neyah tried to relax her breathing. "I hate hyenas."

"Me too, and that one is sick. Get up. He may still be around."

"I doubt it. Your scream probably scared every bush animal to the other side of Africa."

Malaika laughed. "Come on, friend!"

Malaika bounced along, causing her empty jerry can and perfectly plaited hair braids to swing side to side.

"Saida fetched for our goats this morning while I wove reed sleeping mats," said Malaika. "We need more water though, so here I am!"

Neyah marveled at her friend's constant enthusiasm and

soon forgot about the hyena. Malaika didn't seem to mind lugging water. *Maybe she was born under the same happy moon as Bibi*, Neyah thought.

"I wish we lived in the same village, Neyah. We would have so much fun jumping rope and doing homework."

Neyah nodded. She felt her shyness melt a bit in the company of her friend. If her friend lived in her village, it might feel like having a sister again!

Their two villages were close, with a deep ditch separating them. Neyah imagined sprouting wings to soar over the divide to Malaika's village. With so many chores, who knew if they'd have much time to spend together, but it felt great to dream!

Malaika led the way on the beaten path, chattering non-stop with Neyah following at her heels. Created over time by villagers walking and compacting it into a rock-hard surface, the trail felt as smooth as a paved highway in most places. Even the torrential floods during rainy seasons seldom destroyed the paths.

Neyah glanced at the side of the path and took care to keep her feet away.

"Malaika, watch out for the poison ivy growing among the brush."

"Yes, we do not need to have our feet itch and burn like they are on fire!"

The bright floral skirt Malaika wore led the way. It swayed back and forth like a field of flowers dancing in the breeze. Neyah knew Malaika's city grandmother often gave her new clothes. She wished for just one flowered skirt as she glanced down at her shapeless smock. Even though Neyah wouldn't trade her Bibi for anyone, she longed for a grandmother who could buy her a new dress.

"Neyah, what did you write for Mr. Sahli's ten-year question?"

"I missed that day."

"Then you can tell me! What do you want to be doing in ten years?"

Neyah pondered the question. No one had asked her this before.

Softly she answered, "Maybe a doctor."

"Really? How come?"

"Mama says our village needs a doctor." Neyah wasn't sure of all a doctor did. She enjoyed the discoveries of science though, and Mr. Sahli insisted doctors were good scientists.

"Great! I will come to you when I have babies. You can tell me what to do with them!"

Both girls giggled.

"Guess what I want to do?" Malaika didn't wait for Neyah's reply. "I want to be a famous piano player. Bibi told me she is giving me her piano."

Neyah didn't care what Malaika did as long as she would still be her friend.

"Hey, guess what else!"

"You do not have to carry water anymore."

"No!" laughed Malaika. "Not that. I will be carrying water until I am a famous piano player. Guess again!"

"Your Mama is having another baby?"

"Wrong again!" Malaika giggled.

"I give up."

"I am going to Kapenguria to visit Bibi! And you will never believe this! Her water comes right into her water bowl from a pipe. And it is a different color than our water!"

Neyah looked doubtful. "What do you mean? Water is not a rainbow."

"I do not know what color it is exactly, but Bibi wrote a letter and told me it is not brown like ours. She said she can see right through it! Neyah! Imagine that! You should come with me to see it!"

Neyah let Malaika go on about her Bibi's city water while she fantasized about someday living where a pipe brought water right into her hut. Maybe her writing friend, Abby, knew about this water you could see through.

Malaika and Neyah joined a swarm of other girls and women at the small water hole. They waved at girls they recognized and knew they were also missing school. Neyah wondered if they sometimes wished they were boys.

The water carriers formed two lines and took turns kneeling at the water's edge between tall weeds. An elderly woman finished filling her clay pot. Instead of a cover, she stuffed leaves into the opening.

Malaika whispered, "She will never get that on her head," and stepped forward to help heave it to her bare head.

"How do people get those heavy pots home without spilling?"

Neyah shook her head, thankful for her plastic container.

Malaika elbowed Neyah with a teasing grin. "Now your favorite part. Waiting."

Neyah grimaced. She watched a one-armed girl.

Malaika noticed the girl too and shivered. "Maybe a crocodile got her. My grandmother says they do not mean to eat you, but they do. It could happen to anyone here."

Neyah glanced around. No crocodiles. Only two little boys peeing in the water. She shook off the scary thought of a crocodile attack and turned to watch wobbly toddlers playing in a puddle. One happily scooped water into a dented teakettle and practiced carrying it on her head.

Watching a young mother dip water into her vessel with nothing but her hands, Neyah let her mind drift to school. Right now, I could be in school learning how to make Papa better or how to build a well. She fantasized about discovering water in Letsokoane and buying a flowered skirt in the market until she saw a pair of feet in front of her. Gnarled from walking barefoot over rocks and roots, the feet struggled to hold the old woman up. Another woman's open sores on both feet caused Neyah to shudder.

Her eyes traveled from feet to bellies. Close to a dozen women with swollen bellies with babies inside waited in line. Young girls, not much older than Neyah, already had a baby. Their knees quivered under the weight of balancing water on their head and a baby on their back. Neyah feared this could be her in a few years. She forced her thoughts back to flowered dresses and city water.

Neyah tapped her foot. *Patience. I hear you, Bibi. I do.*

She recited facts in her head while she searched the faces of those waiting. She wondered what they were thinking about.

From a burlap bag tied around her waist, Malaika tugged her flatbread smeared with wild berries. "I made it," Malaika whispered. She handed a chunk to Neyah. "Eat it before the flies do."

Hungry flies swarmed in the warmth of the day, bent on getting a taste. Some sat on children's runny noses and crawled in the corners of their eyes and around babies' mouths.

Finally, Neyah and Malaika took their turn drawing water. After filling her five-gallon can and lugging it from the water, Malaika wiped the mud from her hands with dry grass. She grunted as she heaved the yellow container onto her head. Neyah did the same, straining to get hers centered.

Back on the trail, Malaika bubbled with chatter again. "We are getting good at balancing! Remember when we used to strap the jerry can to our backs?"

Neyah grunted. The forty pounds of water overwhelmed her featherweight frame. Her head caved into her neck.

"And the time you slipped, and the can crashed against a rock causing the cover to pop off?" Malaika paired her words with labored breathing. Her water can weighed over a third of her body weight.

"I lost it all," Neyah panted.

Ahead of them, a girl wearing a patched dress slipped on loose gravel. Pinned under the weight of her water, it took two women with heavy loads of their own, to lift her.

"When is your next day in school, Neyah?" Malaika struggled to both breathe and talk.

"Tuesday." Neyah adjusted her grip on the jerry can. She concentrated on keeping evenly balanced to avoid a fall into the thorns.

"Me too! What writing lesson are you on?"

"The persuasive essay," Neyah replied between grunts.

"Oh, I finished that one. I wrote a letter to my grandmother and persuaded her to let me visit. What is yours about?"

"Not sure."

Neyah winced at holding the truth from her best friend. Neyah knew exactly what she wanted to write her persuasive essay about. Her future as well as the future of her entire village was at stake. She had to persuade someone to do something about it. She just wasn't sure how.

The girls talked less and less as the unforgiving sun and water weight drained their energy. Taking a rest under the umbrella canopy of an acacia tree, they were thankful for the break from the midmorning heat. A steady stream of women and girls passed with arms held high to steady their load.

Reluctantly, Neyah stood. "Mama is waiting."

They reached the flats where a small patch of maize grew. The tall stalks provided welcomed shade. When they approached the cutoff, angry voices caused everyone within listening distance to halt.

"Crazy drunken bandits!"

"Leave her alone!"

"Stop it! Nooo!"

Neyah and Malaika huddled together and strained to see two men swatting a woman with thorny branches.

"Ouch! What do you want, crazy man?"

"You. We want you."

After a lot of kicking and scuffling, another woman shouted, "I have something better. Food. Here. Take it. There is more here than you need for a week."

The offer of food seemed to satisfy the men. They stumbled off the path and into the brush, muttering obscenities as they fought over the bread.

HAVING RETURNED WITH HER WATER, Neyah set her jerry can near the fire and rubbed her aching neck. From Mama and Papa's hut, she heard angry voices.

"Why are you considering this now?" Mama asked. "You need to only think about getting better!"

Papa's voice exploded. "I will get well, but Zuberi is right. I am responsible for this family and make the decisions. Neyah will make a fine wife and will bring us ten healthy cows!"

Neyah clenched her fists. The idea of being sold to a man churned her stomach.

Storming out of the hut, Mama nearly stumbled over the water Neyah had brought home.

Following a moment of awkward silence, Mama asked, "Any problems at the water hole this morning?"

Shocked by what she just heard from Papa, Neyah could only shake her head.

"Good. Eat before you fetch more water."

5

TEAM NEYAH AND ABBY

Nearing the end of their hour trek to the one-room building called Saramba Primary School, Neyah and her four brothers rounded the last curve. The five-kilometer climb up the hilly trail overworked Neyah's legs, but not her mind. Excitement surged as she thought about the chance of a full day in school.

"How many days since you have been in school, Neyah?" Paul asked between coughing fits.

"Six." Neyah tilted her head up to view the tin-roofed school constructed of handmade bricks. Students hung from the window openings and waved. She saw Headmaster Omar Sahli in his colorful dashiki shirt and giggled at his booming voice.

"There is Neyah, our science girl!" Mr. Sahli called out with his famous belly laugh.

Mr. Sahli loved teaching science more than anything else and, therefore, felt a connection to this girl who loved science. He set his large hands gently on her shoulders and smiled. "You're going to learn so much today, Neyah Jabari." His left eye drifted to the outer corner but the right one aimed straight at her eyes.

Neyah smiled back at the large man, a former Peace Corps volunteer who came to Kenya nine years ago, fell in love with the people and a local woman, and never left.

"A letter from our pen pals came last week. The translator just finished yours."

Too excited to thank him, Neyah grabbed the letter and ran into the school. She threw her school bag on the heap of others by the back wall. Hurrying to the bench she shared with Malaika, Neyah tore the letter open.

Malaika threw her arms around Neyah. "You are here!"

"Yes, and I got another letter!"

Malaika's eyes popped with excitement. "I wanted to do pen pals but signed up too late."

"You can read my letter with me."

"Sure! But first I have to tell the boys about the baby warthog I found running through my hut!"

The new words on the blackboard stared at Neyah. She wanted to get them in her journal before the science lesson began, but temptation over her new Abby letter won out.

Dear Neyah,

I'm waiting for our internet to come back so I can google how far a kilometer is. Oh! here it's back. All I can say is—WHAT!?! You walk like seven miles a day for water?! And three miles each way to school? I'm sorry, but I would die, pass out, ride a horse (my first choice actually!), get a bike, take a taxi, anything!

What do you carry the water in?

By the way, my hair isn't white, we call it blonde-and it's my best feature I think!!

I can't believe you don't have a picture of yourself. Do your parents have cell phones? That's where most of the pictures of me are—on my parents' phones I mean. I get my own when I turn 13. I cannot wait!! Think of the pictures I can take with Jazzy—she's the horse I take riding lessons on. Today was my fourth lesson, and we learned to trot! I feel like a different person when I ride! Ah! So great! ~~I can take lots of pictures of me with my horse when I get my phone. I get a phone when I am 13!~~ Sorry, I just reread my letter and for some reason said the same thing again. Duh! Mom says I'm repeating things a lot lately.

I like the idea of being your teacher of new words. So, this is what I know: A **SHOWER** is what I use to wash my body. I turn this part (called a faucet) and voila! This means no water fetching for me! We have 3 bathrooms so plenty of water!!

ORCHESTRA is like a band of stringed instruments. I play the violin. Here's a picture of me practicing with my brother Andrew bugging me, so I know what you mean about brothers! I don't know what I'd do with four!

Andrew's helping me with "the plan" for getting Mom and Dad back together so he's a good egg. You need a sister though—they're so sweet.

Your friend in the U.S., Abby Larson

P.S. means postscript (I had to ask mom). It's something you add to a letter after you sign off-if you have something more to say, which I always do! I love to talk in case you can't tell!! How about you? And, who is Bibi? Maybe you can draw a picture of your family.

One more thing. Step 1 of my plan to get my parents back together is a success! I sent Mom and Dad a separate invitation to a candlelight Italian dinner I made (okay, it was just ravioli from a can and breadsticks). Instead of eating with me (which is what each of them THOUGHT was the plan), it was just the two of them WITH ROMANTIC CANDLES! I *think they liked it! They honeymooned in Italy so I thought Italian food might be the ticket! Anyway, I didn't hear any yelling, and Mom couldn't stop singing afterward.*

I like solving problems, so I think we (and by we, I mean Team Neyah and Abby!) have to solve your water problem. I'll talk to Mr. Simons tomorrow about it. But I have a ginormous headache so bye bye!

Your turn!

DING DING! The school bell rang across the valley.

Just in time, thought Neyah, as she finished reading Abby's letter. She tucked it into her school bag and headed outdoors for the morning gathering with Team Neyah and Abby on her mind.

"Winna and Nilsa, it's your turn to hold the flag," Mr. Sahli announced.

As the faded Kenyan flag fluttered in the breeze, nearly seventy students from ages six to fourteen sang the national anthem in Swahili. "Ee Mungu, nguyu yetu." O God of all creation. Mr. Sahli's deep baritone voice blended with the young voices blanketing the hillside with the tender hope of future generations of Kenyans.

After the song, Mr. Sahli handed the only four history books the school owned to the boys standing near him. "Levi, Bosco, Devison, and Samuel will read about our capital city of Nairobi.

Devison began. "Nairobi became Kenya's capital in 1963. It has modern skyscrapers with electric lights and water. It also has shantytowns without modern conveniences."

History lessons usually bored Neyah. They told of stuff that already happened. She wanted to hear about the future, not the past. But today, Neyah thought about Abby. Maybe she lived in a skyscraper. Someday she wanted to visit Abby and her American city.

Once the history reading ended, Mr. Sahli spoke. "Good reading, boys. Every country has a capital city where the government people meet to make laws. Every community is responsible for rules and helping people too, just like in your village."

He took a deep breath and smiled into the faces before him. "Usually we have math first, but today's science lesson will take extra time, so we'll start with science. Let's go inside!"

Students hustled through the doorway and to their seats. One hundred twenty-nine students were enrolled this year at Saramba. The building only provided seating for seventy children. Occasionally students doubled up on the wooden benches or sat against the wall. Today, absences were high which meant finding a seat wasn't a problem.

Mr. Sahli walked to the ancient blackboard, cracked from one end to the other, and began writing. Other than the tapping of his chalk on the board and a few birds chirping in the rafters, quiet filled the room.

Neyah leaned her elbows on the desktop that was attached to her bench and let her eyes take a tour of her schoolroom. She felt at home here. Worn but useful weather and multiplication charts covered holes in the wall. Old maps of places she never heard of bordered the windows. Noticing a new poster of African wildlife hanging from the ceiling, she recalled Mr. Sahli's lesson about animal migrations. Neyah hoped to see one someday.

She spied an old clock leaning against the wall; it only had an hour hand. Mr. Sahli liked teaching students how to tell time. Neyah didn't know why. No one she knew owned a clock.

When the tapping of chalk ended, Moswen shouted. "WHAT?"

His loud voice and a collective gasp from students abruptly

ended Neyah's visual tour. She silently read the words her teacher wrote on the faded board:

The water you are drinking may kill you.

As if the written words weren't shocking enough, Mr. Sahli read them aloud.

"That is not true. I am still alive!" Moswen's outburst got a few laughs.

"I will watch for you to raise your hand next time, Moswen."

We are going to talk about water? Neyah sighed. Even though she loved science, Neyah didn't want to hear about water. She got enough of it at home.

We are out of water.

Neyah, you cannot go to school because we need more water.

Mr. Sahli continued. "Today we are going to use an instrument called a microscope to discover what's in the water we drink. I borrowed it from a friend in Morocco where I grew up." He pointed to the top of the strange device. "Here is the powerful lens you will look through. It magnifies organisms in the water that our eyes can't see on their own. The word, magnify, means to make something appear larger. Your new words are on the board. While you write, I'll get the microscope set up."

Microscope (*noun*) an instrument having a magnifying lens for inspecting objects too small to be seen by the unaided eye.

Magnify (*verb*) make something appear larger than it is.

Neyah proudly gazed at her handwriting before glancing across the room to Paul. She didn't have a cure for his cough, but maybe she could help him with his horrible handwriting.

Still admiring her words, Neyah heard Mr. Sahli's soft voice in her ear. "Words on paper are nice, but words spoken are important too." Neyah's face grew warm. Why was everyone trying to get her to talk?

6

A SHOCKING SCIENCE LESSON

M r. Sahli poured cloudy water from a gourd flask into a bowl. "I asked Bosco to bring in a drinking water sample to view under the microscope. Asante, Bosco, for remembering!"

Neyah steamed in silence. *Bosco never told me this! And why didn't Mr. Sahli ask **me** to bring a water sample? I'm the one who does the fetching.*

Neyah frowned at Bosco. He responded by sticking his tongue out at her through a teasing smile.

Mr. Sahli rubbed his brown hand over his smooth head the way he often did when he talked. Flashing his wide smile, he gave directions. "You'll each observe the water sample and record observations. We'll discuss what we see and why it's important. While you're waiting for your turn, work with your math group on tomorrow's assignment, and practice your handwriting. Palms up if you understand."

All palms flipped up.

The first to peer into the microscope, Malaika screeched. "EEEW! What are those wiggly things?" Her body squirmed to imitate what she saw.

"Just observe and record, Malaika," said Mr. Sahli. "If you have comments, they go on your science report."

While Neyah worked with her math group, Devison, the school genius, stared at her. She tried ignoring him. During handwriting practice, she snuck a peek, and he still stared. It was getting harder to ignore him. She was relieved when it was finally her turn to wait in the microscope line.

When Neyah peered through the microscope and saw the wiggly things, she put her hand to her belly. Were these things swimming around in her belly right now?

It took time for each student to look through the single microscope. Mr. Sahli asked, "What does a good scientist do when they observe a specimen like this?"

"They puke their guts out!" blurted Nathanial. Moswen laughed.

"I'll ask again, and this time, I remind you to think like a scientist and wait to be called on before speaking. What does a scientist do when they make an observation?"

Devison raised his hand.

Anticipating Devison's response, Malaika rolled her eyes in Neyah's direction. Neyah covered her mouth to stifle a laugh.

Students called him Devi, which he hated. At age fourteen, Devison was the oldest student in the school and probably the smartest one in the county. Instead of playing at break time, he studied the chemistry periodic chart or read the history textbook. While others thought this odd, Neyah admired his passion for learning.

Devison spoke in his usual loud, measured manner. "Observation is the first step of the scientific method. The next steps are to propose a hypothesis and perform an experiment to test the hypothesis and, finally, analyze the data to decide whether to accept or reject the hypothesis." When he finished, he smiled at Neyah.

Neyah squeezed her eyes shut. *Why is he looking at me?*

Neyah couldn't help but feel a little jealous of Devi's knowledge. To be a doctor, maybe she needed to know what Devi knew.

"Asante, Devison. You are right. Scientists use the scientific method, and since we have already observed, does anyone have a hypothesis to share? A conclusion about what you observed?"

"Worms and dirt!" Bosco called out. "We drink worms and dirt."

Ignoring Bosco's lack of self-control, Mr. Sahli wrote his hypothesis on the worn blackboard.

Other than Paul's hacking cough, the room remained quiet until the headmaster explained.

"Yes, Bosco, there's dirt in the water. And little creatures or microorganisms called bacteria resembling tiny worms swim in it. Whether we get water from the watering hole or a filtered faucet in Nairobi, all water contains some of these little wiggly fellows."

A murmur of surprise trickled throughout the room.

Malaika leaned toward Neyah's ear. "My Bibi does *not* have worms in her water."

Mr. Sahli took his time unfolding two pictures. "Some are good bacteria like this photo. They help our insides stay healthy. Some are bad and look like this."

Again, Bosco didn't wait to raise his hand. "What do the bad ones do?"

"They can cause illness. The illness can make our stomachs hurt and cause diarrhea. This leads to dehydration."

Mr. Sahli started writing on the board.

Neyah enjoyed this part, seeing her teacher's decorative writing slowly reveal a new word.

Dehydration (*noun*) condition resulting from excessive water loss.

"I drink a lot and never get sick!" Bosco announced proudly and grinned widely at his friends.

"You're lucky, Bosco. Now, let's see if you can practice your self-control and wait to be called on."

Bosco's chin dipped, and he nodded sheepishly.

"Drinking doesn't cause sickness. Dehydration does. Our bodies have blood and other fluids keeping us alive. The bad bacteria in the water cause us to lose that fluid. This may result in serious diseases we can die from, like typhoid fever and cholera."

Mr. Sahli paused and scanned the faces of the students. "I'm sure many of you have noticed Sampson's absence."

Mr. Sahli's voice dropped low. "I'm sorry to tell you. Sampson died last night."

Other than a few low moans, silence filled the room. Death announcements weren't uncommon in school.

The teacher took a deep breath and continued. "He died from dehydration, probably cholera."

Papa, thought Neyah. *Is he dying?*

Mr. Sahli continued. "We all get sick now and then, right? Vomiting, fevers, diarrhea. How many of you know someone who died and not because they were old?"

One hand crept up. Two more. Soon, nearly everyone in the room had their hand up.

Neyah finally raised hers. Two of her baby cousins. The young father and his son from the neighboring compound.

"There's a good chance these people would still be alive if they drank water without bad bacteria," stated Mr. Sahli.

Kato raised his hand. "Does the water Bosco brought have good or bad wigglies in it?"

Mr. Sahli paused. "Both."

Neyah closed her eyes. That water came from the jerry can she or Mama carried.

"What do they do exactly? The bad ones?" asked Cheiru, one of the few girls in school.

Mr. Sahli unfolded three more large pictures. One showed a skinny worm nearly a meter long sticking from a person's lower leg.

Neyah gasped. Some students twisted away. Malaika covered her mouth and made a gagging sound.

"This is a parasite called a guinea worm. It can grow inside our intestines and crawl out through the skin. The parasite is one of the deadliest organisms found in dirty water."

A collective groan filled the room.

The next picture showed a teenage girl with sunken eyes and bones showing through her thin skin. Mr. Sahli explained how she suffered from cholera. The third photo showed a young boy. "This twelve-year-old boy contracted typhoid, lost half his body weight, and experienced seizures."

Mr. Sahli's eyes swept the room. No one blinked. He continued to share numbing data.

"Three to four million people a year die from contaminated water. Most live in Africa. And most are children."

Her teacher's words sent Neyah's head into a spin. She felt nauseous and needed a drink of water, but the thought of taking one from the outdoor barrel made her feel worse. She glanced out the door. A stray dog drank from the barrel. The dog looked filthy, and his ribs showed through his scabby hair.

For the first time, Neyah wished she'd stayed home. This lesson had turned into one she never wanted to learn. She couldn't remember a time when someone in her family didn't feel ill. She suffered from stomach problems herself. The twins got headaches and diarrhea often. Neyah glanced at Paul in time to see him wipe his drippy nose on his sleeve. His raspy cough sounded worse. Was all this illness from the water she fetched?

Neyah peeked at Valencia from the corner of her eye. The twenty-year-old volunteered as a water carrier, making nearly a dozen trips a day to the spring above the school. It was less than a hundred-meter climb up the hill, but Valencia's legs were twisted and stiff. Her birth defect affected every limb. A short and stubby left arm hung limp and useless. Her "good" arm connected to a twisted hand with claw-like fingers that looked like they'd been chewed on.

Valencia dragged the water can with a rope tied around her waist to fetch water for the school. After clawing her way up the steep grade on her hands and knees, she struggled to open the cover with her good hand. She filled the container from the trickling crack in the rock and slid back down.

As if reading Neyah's mind, Devison asked, "What about our water?"

All eyes landed on the outdoor barrel. They watched Valencia chase the stray off with a branch.

"Does our water contain parasites that can grow inside us like those in your picture?"

Before Mr. Sahli could respond, Samara ran outside. Many groaned and cradled their stomachs while hearing Samara vomit.

Mr. Sahli cleared his throat and made an announcement. "Dear scientists, we'll take our morning break, and then I promise to share some good news about water when we return!"

Neyah spent her break indoors writing missed lessons.

"Neyah," Mr. Sahli said, "play and exercise are as important as missed lessons."

"I get exercise, sir."

"When you talk to the desk, it's difficult to understand you."

Lifting her head and focusing on his good eye, she said, "I walk many kilometers a day. I do not need more exercise. Thank you."

Mr. Sahli nodded. "All right. Come out when you're done."

Neyah felt eyes on her. She turned and noticed Valencia huddled in the corner like a frightened animal. Neyah set her pencil down. She only knew one thing about Valencia. She was an orphan. Valencia's parents got swept away in a flood, forcing her to drop out of school and care for her grandmother.

"Are you all right?"

Valencia drew her knees to her chest. Tears filled her dark eyes.

"No one drank my water today."

"I would like some."

Valencia hopped up and filled a cup for Neyah. As she drank the cool water, Neyah tried not to think about the possibility of bad wigglies swimming in it.

"Asante."

Valencia smiled. "The same to you."

After the break, Mr. Sahli's words reassured the students. "The water Valencia brings us is from a spring. Spring water is generally clean. Do not be afraid of drinking it."

Valencia and Neyah exchanged smiles.

"Now, let's get back to our lesson. In the scientific method, the next step is to test our hypothesis. Every time we drink contaminated water, cook with it, wash our dishes with it, we're testing this hypothesis."

"And the data shows?" Devison asked.

Mr. Sahli pressed his lips together. "We need to do something."

Neyah's throat felt tight. Her heart thumped. Urgency motivated her to speak.

"People who get sick from water-do they all die?" Barely

audible, Neyah's tiny voice caused everyone to turn toward the girl who had never spoken in class before.

Mr. Sahli tried to mask his sense of shock.

"No, not everyone dies."

It was all Neyah needed to hear. Papa wouldn't die, not from the water she carried. Her family already lost little Lulu, a tragedy Neyah tried not to think about. Water had caused that sad tragedy even though the little one never drank a drop.

The headmaster continued, "Dear scientists, remember this. We need water to live, so don't stop drinking it! We are out of time today, but tomorrow we'll talk about the secret of how to make water safer to drink!"

Mr. Sahli always ended lessons with a sense of hope. Smiling widely, he dramatically pointed to his slogan nailed to the wall. Every student except Neyah joined him in reading it. "Knowledge is just another word unless you do something with it."

Waving at students as they headed home, the headmaster spoke aloud to himself. "She finally talked in class. Neyah finally talked." He returned to his desk and whistled as he prepared lessons for the following day.

7

LOOKING FOR A PURPOSE

Hello Abby I wash face and eat my ugali Now I write to you on paper from mission church I like your questions I do not have a cellular but two men in village do They talk in it to buy goat or cows I don't understand how phone makes photos Mr. Sahli show me photo of computer I write INTERNET in my word journal He tell me internet is computer machine and I can ask it anything and see everything in world Internet sound like magic machine

I had three sisters Two died when they try to be born before me The other is Lulu She died not long ago Mama say to me to never talk of it It makes her sad

I like your USA name A first gift Kenya parents give child is noble name I wear this name all my life It be tradition that our name binds us with days our ancestors walked and days we walk ahead Mama's mother was Neyah and now I be Neyah It stand for purpose of life I dream to know my purpose What be your purpose Mr. Sahli say Abby means papa's delight That be reason your papa like you so much I know my papa love me much but I hear him talk of selling me as wife to get cattle in trade This be tradition but I not like it for me I only tell you I am frightened about it

I do not know what violin is My teacher say I would like it I like music Bibi's singing be like sweet honey My singing like sour goat milk

I miss school again I miss 7 days because Mama and animals need water I carry in yellow plastic container called jerry can It say Made In USA on bottom I want to learn about your water Headmaster say bad bacteria swims in my water and make us sick I think Papa is sick from it.

Your Turn—Neyah

PS I am quiet girl Many say to me to talk I think I will talk when purpose comes

Neyah desperately wanted to go to school to learn how to make water safe to drink. But Mama and the goats needed water. Before leaving to fetch, she checked in on Papa. Fear twisted her gut at the sight of him.

Am I carrying disease to our family in my jerry can? Am I the reason Papa is sick?

"Water is life." Bibi's voice brought her back to her task.

Bibi and Mr. Sahli were right. Everyone needs water to live, and not everyone died from it. Neyah held onto this thought as she followed the prickly fencing out of her village. Built to keep wild animals out, the tightly stacked fence of thorns worked well. Neyah wondered what might be built to keep disease out.

Neyah took one last glance at her family compound before turning down the fetching path. She watched Mama smear a mixture of mud and cow dung into the sticks on their family huts. Before the short rainy season came, she and her brothers would need to gather stiff stalks left over from the maize harvest to replace the rounded thatched roofs.

Neyah's finger grazed a thorny spike on the fence. "Ouch!"

She picked a cornhusk from the ground, wrapped the bleeding finger, and started walking. Her deep sigh rippled across the ravines and waterholes of East Africa.

As she walked, Neyah's shoulders felt tight. She tried to relax, but every movement or sound sent a warning to her brain. An orange-chested superb starling sat on the swaying acacia branches. The pretty trill song reminded Neyah of Bibi, who liked to imitate the starling's sound. Smiling, she picked up her pace and thought about school.

Neyah missed the excitement of arriving at school as the sun spilled over the horizon and students rambled in, dusty from the journey. She pictured Bosco lying outside the school on his belly doing last-minute homework. It got too dark for him to finish last evening. With no electricity and darkness falling by 7:00 pm at the equator, completing homework before dark offered a challenge.

A wild hare scampered across the trail and ran into a burrow as Mr. Sahli's newest word popped into her head.

Injustice (*noun*) an unfair act; wrong.

The day before, Neyah counted the students in school. Fourteen girls. Sixty-eight boys.

"Those numbers feel like an injustice," Neyah whispered.

NEYAH DIDN'T SEE Malaika at the waterhole. Perhaps she refused to fetch after yesterday's science lesson. Or did she return to learn Mr. Sahli's great water secret?

When it came to her turn, Neyah didn't immediately drink. Thirst sat on her lips, on her tongue. The back of her throat longed for the cool, wet taste.

Neyah dipped and poured and worried. Would parasites worm their way into her skin scrapes today? Mosquitoes and flies swarmed around her head as her eyes darted about. Bird droppings splattered the mud, and a cow peed in the water. A woman with a bloody elbow washed her wound while two others scrubbed laundry. A toddler plucked white fur from the brown water. Neyah experienced this a hundred times before, but today, she knew something different. This water hole crawled with invisible bad wigglies.

"Finished?" The voice of the girl behind her startled Neyah.

"Almost."

She didn't want to, but her dry tongue begged for it. Neyah bent forward and closed her eyes. Using her cupped hands, she swallowed a long drink before rising and stepping from the muck.

Neyah wanted to cry or pound something out of frustration as she walked along the twisting trail to home, but it required too much energy. Her head worked in tandem with her nimble feet to steady this new load of knowledge. Step by step she formed a purpose that became clearer as she moved. Without clean water, nothing else mattered. Her thoughts wrote paragraphs of facts and convincing arguments that surely would attract the attention of someone who cared.

The dreamer from Letsokoane had found her purpose.

8

A BOLD MOVE

Bibi greeted Neyah with a hug once she set her water can down. "Your papa is waiting for his fresh drink of water."

He lay on his cot inside the dimly sunlit hut. Upon entering, Neyah gagged at the putrid smell that met her. *This is what dying smells like,* she thought.

Streaming through the hut's only opening, the golden light painted a streak across Papa's face. A layer of animal skins covered him to his neck. *How can he be cold in this heat?*

"Papa, here is your drink." Knowing what the water contained, her words tasted filthy.

Papa struggled to lift his head. Barely a whisper squeaked out. "Neyah."

Tears welled in her eyes. One week her handsome Papa worked his fields and herded cattle. The next, his broken body barely spoke. Neyah forced a smile and held out the cup. She tangled with her worry. Somewhere in her mind she could hear a wicked voice. *Here is your drink. It is laced with nasty things that will make you worse.*

Papa's hands shook. He finally managed to grip the cup and drink.

Imagining slippery worms sliding down his throat, Neyah swallowed away a gag.

Papa managed a stiff smile. "School tomorrow?" Papa knew how much she loved learning.

Neyah didn't trust her voice. She smiled and nodded, even though she doubted she'd be in school anytime soon. She stared at Papa's gray face beaded with sweat. Under his eyes, dark circles made him look far older than his 38 years. Four days of a high temperature, dehydration from diarrhea, and now the shakes were taking a toll.

The village nurse had prepared herbs for him earlier. Nothing appeared to be working. She wondered if his illness affected his thinking. Why else would he be talking of trading her for cattle?

"Mama said to give you some of this fruit from the baobab tree. It will bring your fever down and help your stomach."

Neyah prayed the baobab would help. She refused to accept the possibility of Papa dying.

Neyah glanced around the hut while Papa sucked on the fruit. Papa's weathered sandals made from discarded rubber tires sat on the dirt floor. Mama's only colorful dress lay on a shelf carved from a tree branch. The twins' sleeping mats sat stored where Neyah placed them each morning after breakfast.

Turning her eyes back to Papa, she said, "Papa, I will be right back."

Neyah ran and pulled a rag from the hemp line running between two acacia trees. She glanced toward the open fire where Mama crouched and stirred corn flour into the water to make more ugali. Most families used a separate hut for inside cooking, but Mama had not found time to build one yet.

Mama does not see me. She won't miss a small amount of water. She wants me to be a doctor who cares.

Neyah poured a smidgen of the precious water from her

jerry can onto the cloth to dampen it and hurried back to Papa. As Neyah ran the material over his fevered face and neck, she prayed the family prayer.

"We rest in the knowledge of the powerful One.

"Help, heal, and give hope to our neighbors, our family, and our nation.

"May we live in peace, in good health, and in happiness."

Wishful thinking sometimes played tricks, but Neyah was sure Papa's face relaxed. "Rest, Papa."

He tried smiling. "When Paul comes home, ask him to come and tell me another story."

"I will, Papa. I love you."

Neyah knew how Papa loved Paul's stories of castles and kings and treasures.

She held vigil over Papa until he fell asleep. Once outside, Neyah glared at the jerry can full of bad bacteria. She wanted to dump it out.

It was all ironic—another Mr. Sahli word.

Ironic (*adjective*) using words to show a meaning opposite of its true meaning.

The definition didn't sink in when she wrote the word in her journal. Now she understood it. We can't survive without water. We can't survive with it. Ironic. *More like stupid*, she thought. *I will add that one to my journal.*

Stupid (adjective) foolish idea.

Neyah clenched her hands into fists. She needed something to do. Running to the fire ring, Neyah begged her mother for chores. A questioning crease formed in Mama's forehead. "What would I do without you, child?"

Neyah shook the dusty mats and hung clothes on bushes to dry. The southern wind kicked up dust and left her thirsty. Neyah didn't stop. No way was she taking a drink. Her mind racing, she busied her hands and forced herself to recite boring historical facts.

Kenya is located on the equator.

Kenya is named after Mt. Kenya, the tallest mountain in Kenya.

Sixty-eight languages are spoken. Swahili and English are the main ones.

The Indian Ocean is on one side of Kenya. Lake Victoria is on the other.

Scooping up chicken dung, she spelled journal words.

Injustice i-n-j-u-s-t-i-c-e

Ironic i-r-o-n-i-c

Stupid s-t-u-p-i-d

Hunger gnawed at Neyah's stomach. When Mama handed her a bowl of ugali, she gulped the first bites.

"Thank you, Mama." Rarely did a midday meal get prepared as the fetched water only lasted for one or two meals a day. As she watched Mama and Bibi sipping tea, her stomach tightened. Bad things crawled in their water, according to Mr. Sahli. Pretending to drink hers, she played with the thick ugali between her fingers, kneading it into spoon-sized little bowls.

If I went to school today, Neyah thought, *maybe I would learn how to get rid of the bad things making Papa sick.*

At age twelve, Neyah was only in the standard three lessons. Even though Bosco and Paul were younger, they were ahead of her in school, which drove her crazy. Last night she prepared the right words to convince Mama she shouldn't miss school today. But now, when the sun sprayed heat on the morning, her courage to speak evaporated along with the morning dew.

She inhaled deeply and blew out.

"What are you sighing about?" Mama sounded annoyed.

Picking at her dirty fingernails, Neyah managed to ask. "Why must I do all the fetching?"

"Neyah, speak up. Half the time, I cannot hear you."

Neyah inhaled and tried again. "Can my brothers fetch?"

It was Mama's turn to sigh. "We have been over this. It is not the way. Fetching water is a job for girls and done with honor. Maybe someday you will have another sister to help you fetch. For now, do not bother talking if this nonsense is all you wish to say. Now bring Papa his meal."

No longer hungry, Neyah threw her ugali balls into the bushes. She thought of tossing her tea too, but it contained a few drops of precious milk. Maybe milk would be good for Papa.

Her mouth grew powdery dry as she watched him drink it.

"How is Paul? His cough?" Papa asked.

"Better." The lie came out easily. Neyah knew the bond between Papa and Paul. It wouldn't make Papa feel better to tell him Paul coughed his lungs to pieces in school yesterday.

9

WATER IS LIFE

Waiting outside Papa's hut, Bibi sat in her faded red dress that hid her bony arms. Her weathered skin mirrored many who wandered too long under the scorching Sahara sun.

"My favorite granddaughter!" Bibi gushed. The toothless smile lit up her wrinkled face as she gestured to the bush. Bibi needed to use the toilet, and Neyah's steady feet to get her there.

Hooking her arm around her grandmother, Neyah chuckled and began walking. "Bibi, since we lost little Lulu, I am your *only* granddaughter."

Bibi stopped and placed her free hand on Neyah's cheek, massaging it with her thumb. Her dark eyes sparkled. "Lulu was my favorite too. Just like your other two baby sisters we lost. And do not forget your cousin, Nilsa!" Her contagious smile appeared again, topped with her famous giggle. "Bibi can have more than one favorite!"

Neyah couldn't help herself and laughed too. When she and Bibi talked, Neyah felt happier. Bibi's "hakuna matata" attitude easily rubbed off on her. But Neyah feared her life story would read like Bibi and Mama's life, where fetching water dominated her time. She hoped her purpose together with Team Neyah and Abby could change that.

Bibi and Neyah reached the outdoor toilet, merely a hole in the ground behind their family compound. Neyah reached down and removed the dry grass covering the hole, breathing through her mouth to avoid the stench. Bibi needed support as she squatted. When she finished, Neyah pulled Bibi back to a stand and covered the hole again with grass. Together they made it to the sitting stump where Bibi picked up a tattered sleeping mat in need of repair.

"Thank goodness the village mice enjoy nibbling on these mats, or I might have nothing to do," giggled Bibi.

Mama laughed. "There is no such thing as nothing to do here, Bibi. See you two later. I will be in the field for the rest of the day." Mama's hoe rested over her right shoulder as she called to Neyah. "Two more fetchings for you today, sweet girl."

Neyah watched Mama until she was out of sight. Then she trained her eyes on the jerry can, staring at it as she mentally battled a notion to defy Mama's wishes. Her feet led her behind her hut. Her hands dug under a tattered vinyl tarp until she felt the handle of the wooden bucket. As her strong fingers drew the bucket out and she tugged at the sturdy rope lying inside it, her brain warned her to be careful, to take her time, and make two trips to the open well—before Mama returned.

Bibi heard the rustle of the tarp and prayed as Neyah left for the open well. "Water is life."

10

BUSTED

Two treks to the forbidden well took no time at all. Mama still toiled in the field, so Neyah decided to go to the well once more. Since it was school uniform washing day, the extra water would be needed.

Following the third trip, Neyah took a moment to rest on Bibi's stool. The laughter of her brothers and other village boys returning from school drifted toward her. Kato and Hassan led the group. As soon as she spotted Bosco, she leaped from the stool. Mr. Sahli's secret to making dirty water safer to drink sat in Bosco's science notes.

"Jambo, Neyah!" called Bosco. As fast as a hyena sniffs a dead carcass, his eyes found the wet bucket and rope lying behind Neyah. Their eyes locked.

Heat climbed up Neyah's face. She hustled to the back of the hut and stuffed the bucket and rope back under the tarp. She had gone to the well against Mama's orders, and now Bosco knew it. She growled under her breath and circled back to Bosco. With her chin held high, she thrust her hand out.

Bosco gave her a long steely glare before finally pulling her homework folder from his backpack. His glare turned to an impish grin as he threw the folder to Paul for a game of keep away. Neyah often played along with this game, but she wasn't interested today. Back and forth it flew until Paul's laughter changed to a cough.

Bosco shook his head at his sister. "I dislike homework, and you cannot get enough. Mama makes me go to school every day, and I wish I could herd all day. You want to go every day, but you must fetch!" His hearty laugh made Neyah want to punch him.

"Yes, Bosco the Great. It is ironic, yes?"

Surprised to hear his sister's voice, Bosco stopped laughing, hoping to hear more from her.

Rescuing her folder from a pile of fresh cow dung, Neyah wiped it on a rock and sped to her hut. Sinking to her mat, she flipped through her homework. New words, math problems. Nothing on the secret of how to make water safe to drink. Bosco said he'd save his science notes for her. But he brought her nothing except a folder stinking of cow manure. Furious, she stamped her bare feet on the packed dirt floor before running to where he sat.

"Where is it?" Neyah demanded.

"Where is what?" He claimed innocence.

"Your science notes!" Her voice wavered in anger.

"We did not have science."

Not believing it, Neyah fumed. "What did Mr. Sahli teach today about water?"

"Nothing."

"No science lesson?"

"No." Bosco bit his lip to keep from smiling.

"Why not? He said he would tell wh—"

"He is gone."

"You are lying!"

Bosco threw up his hands. "He is not our teacher anymore."

Neyah froze. "What-what do you mean?"

Wearing the most serious face he could muster, Bosco said, "Mr. Sahli left."

11

THE WATER SECRET

"Kato, is Mr. Sahli back yet?" Neyah asked the minute she saw him running into the compound. The competitive athlete of the family, Kato often won the "race" home from school.

"Yes." Kato sprawled on the ground to catch his breath.

"Finally," sighed Neyah as her other brothers came into view. For twelve days, a substitute teacher filled in at Saramba Primary School while Mr. Sahli stayed in Morocco with his ill mother. The substitute teacher knew nothing about keeping bad things out of water and didn't teach science.

Wasting no time, Neyah ran to Bosco and stuck out her hand.

"You got another pen pal letter." He tossed the folder at her and ran to milk the cows.

Bosco was right. Her folder held Abby's letter, but no science notes or water secrets. Neyah couldn't believe it and marched to where the cows grazed. She took advantage of milking time to pull information from Bosco. No way could he run off and leave in the middle of milking Bela.

Bosco felt a sense of satisfaction seeing Neyah rush toward him. He pretended not to notice her and focused on relieving Bela of her full bag of milk. Once he began hand-milking a cow and the warm liquid flowed, he needed to direct it into the bucket or precious drops of milk sprayed to the ground.

"You forgot my science notes!"

Hearing how upset Neyah was, Bosco felt a tinge of regret for tricking her into talking.

"I did not forget."

"What did Mr. Sahli teach you about making water safe?"

Bosco smiled with his two big front teeth shining. He figured the longer he waited, the more Neyah would talk.

He is not going to tell me. Neyah stomped the ground. *I could pinch his big ears for being such an annoying tease.*

Neyah growled. "Bosco!"

"Boil it," Bosco finally blurted.

"Boilit? What is that? Was boilit the new word today?"

Bosco's entire body toppled forward in laughter, burying his head into the cow's side. "Not boilit. It is two words. BOIL IT. The water must be heated and bubbling over a fire for a certain length of time."

"Why?"

Bosco kept milking. Maybe if he didn't answer, her frustration would drive her to talk more. Bela decided to ramble to a bush, requiring Bosco to ramble with her until she stopped. Bosco squatted to finish his job.

"Ahhh!" She spun and marched away.

"Wait!" Bosco spit out his words. "Mr. Sahli said the secret to safe water is to wash with it."

Neyah twisted back toward Bosco with hands on her hips.

"He said to wash everything with boiled water."

"Like what?"

"Our dishes and hands. He said to wash our hands a lot. Before we touch food and before we eat." Bosco tried to hide his smile. "And after we pee and poop." He began to laugh so loud Neyah barely understood him. "And after we milk these cows, after we hoe..."

Bosco stopped laughing. He stopped milking. The cow's milk continued to drip into the bucket on its own.

"Neyah, I am sorry, but you will have to carry water ten times a day to make sure we do all this washing! What do you think about that?"

Disappointment and fury rained from every direction as disbelief soared through her thoughts. THIS is Mr. Sahli's big plan? Wash our hands with boiled water all day?

Neyah stared at the milk bucket and wondered, *why can't we have a cow that produces water?* She stormed off.

"Hey! I asked you a question!" Bosco called after her. "What do you think about the big water secret?"

Neyah didn't know what to think. But talking to Bosco only escalated her anger. She picked up Abby's letter and began to read.

Dear Neyah,

I like writing to you! I didn't think I would because my teachers always say my writing lacks creativity and "skills." Plus, I'm a social butterfly and like to be WITH people. But you have good questions and I never knew about girls fetching water and getting traded as a wife. Is this legal? And you're not even 13! You can't get married yet, can you?!

Okay, FIRST! I've gotta figure out a way to send you some paper. Here are a couple sheets I found in a drawer. Aren't the puppies around the border cute? Do you have a pet? We have a bulldog named Bieber. He's named after Justin Bieber who is so dreamy! I begged my parents to get me tickets to his concert next month! I CANNOT WAIT!!!! All my friends are jealous.

What do you mean-tell me about water? Are you in the middle of a desert or something? At church I remember some people went to Guatemala and built a well for people there. Do you need a well? Hey! This can be Team Neyah and Abby's purpose!—to get you water closer to your house.

And Neyah! All three of your sisters died? That's horribly sad! For the first time in my life I don't know what to say. What in the world happened?

I'm at Dad's apartment-only for the weekend. I have to share a bedroom with Millie AND Andrew. The good news is there are no chores here, so I can rest. I don't know why, but I'm so tired lately. I actually fell asleep in math class. Not good!

With my bribe of licorice and half of my allowance every week, my brother and sister are doing some of my home chores. It frees me to work on step #2 for getting Dad and Mom together. I'm painting a picture of the lake where they fell in love. I'm using a big piece of plywood I found in the shed. The painting will never get done for their anniversary if I spend all my time cleaning and doing dishes! Millie and Andrew are totally on board to help as they want Dad and Mom together again as much as I do!!

You asked about my purpose (see-I said you have good questions). No one has ever asked me this before. I have no clue. I love hanging with my friends and shopping with Mom! Oh-and listening to Justin Bieber!! Those are lame purposes, though. You got me started on an "important" purpose list. So far I've got: 1. Get Mom and Dad back together again

And, ta-DAH! 2. Team Abby and Neyah work together on your water problem. Maybe your papa will forget about this wife-thing if you can help him get better water!

(Remember I said I'd talk to Mr. Simon? He and I read up on things, and I saw videos of girls like you carrying those jerry cans. Okay, now I see what you mean—backbreaking work! I asked him if we could do a class fundraiser or something to help you out. He has to "look into it.")

What do your parents do? My dad is a sports photographer (out of work) and my mom is a lawyer who makes sure companies don't pollute too much.

Your turn, Abby

*P.S. You say you don't like to talk, but talking is like thinking. If it's important enough to think, it's important enough to say. Well, not everything or you could get in trouble. What I mean is if there's something you want changed, what are you waiting for? Maybe the only way things will change is if **you** are the one who says something.*

Okay-now my head is throbbing. Who knew writing a letter could make my head feel like it's splitting in two? And I swear my room needs better lighting. I can barely see what I'm writing lately. Bye!

AFTER THE EVENING MEAL, Bosco came to Neyah. "Here is my homework folder."

Suspicious at Bosco's sudden kindness, Neyah cautiously opened the folder to perfectly printed words.

Hygiene *(noun)* things to do to keep clean and healthy.

Neyah grinned. "Your handwriting is way better than Paul's."

Bosco nodded. "Mr. Sahli said washing hands is part of hygiene."

Washing hands. It sounded too simple to Neyah.

"Bosco, do you think it works? Boiling water and washing hands?"

"Maybe."

"Mama and Papa do not boil."

Bosco shrugged. "They did not have much schooling."

12

SAY SOMETHING

Dear Abby I like puppy paper you send We only have animals that help us like chickens give eggs and cows plow fields and give milk and we have many goats for milk and trading at market Boney dogs here steal food My brothers throw rocks at sick ones No extra food for begging dogs Papa still be sick and needs toilet too much Mr. Sahli says it is water worms fault We all get stomach sickness but it makes Papa white and bony How did your village get well What color is water for you Do you boil it I think shower be good tool My friend Malaika has grandmother with shower in city Letsokoane village not desert but no well or pump so girls and mamas fetch from water hole I am only in class three lessons It is water or school and my Bibi say water is life You like questions so I ask more Did you have good fun with your papa I do not know Justin Bieber Is he friend Tell me the injustice in USA Your purpose is good to help your mama and papa My purpose is to help Papa and water sickness My problem is that courage isn't in me yet to talk much.

Now I go wash clothes and fetch more water
Your turn Your new rafiki which means friend Neyah

The day felt different from the minute Neyah woke. Even the rooster's crow at 4:30 am sounded more cheery. Her letter to Abby was done. Once her morning chores were finished, she'd be off to school to give it to Mr. Sahli.

While Mama went off to fetch water in the early morning darkness, Neyah began milking cows. The cold morning mist caused her clothes to cling to her body as she milked Bela and Bako. Neyah didn't mind. It was just her and the cows. They didn't mind if she didn't talk.

She thought about boiled water and Abby's advice: *Maybe the only way things will change is if you are the one who says something.*

Her pen pal shared a different life, new words, and ideas while Neyah spent her life hiding her words and ideas.

Maybe Abby is right, Neyah thought. *It is time I say something.*

Her brothers' voices broke through the predawn quietness. Every morning they woke up chattering. Kato and Hassan talked and laughed as they snapped firewood for Mama's cooking fire. Paul and Bosco fought over a herding stick as they chased field cows and goats from the village. Neyah noticed how much Paul's laugh sounded like Papa's. Every morning her oldest brothers turned the hunt for water and grass into a game. Like warriors heading off to battle, they yelped and prodded the cattle with their sticks.

Neyah listened to the rhythmic clanking of the cowbells as the animals left the compound. Each cow and goat wore a primitive metal bell around its neck. The bells helped the boys keep track of meandering animals in the dark. She knew Paul and Bosco's walk to find grazing land and water grew long too, especially since precious little rain had fallen since May. But once they returned, her brothers' chores ended, and off to school they went.

The milking job behind her, Neyah hand-scooped corn into a burlap bag and beat the kernels off the cob with a thick stick. Grinding the seeds into flour came next, followed by sweeping. Neyah used a broom Mama taught her to make from dried weeds. Sweeping loose rocks and dirt clods seemed a waste of time to Neyah, but Mama insisted on it.

"Someday, you will care for your own home and be the best sweeper in the village," Mama had told her.

Neyah didn't want to disappoint her mother, but she did not dream of becoming the best sweeper.

Finished with the firewood, the twins sat eating a bowl of ugali with dirty fingers. Neyah grinned at them as she washed the pots from the previous evening's meal with a splash of the remaining water.

"How do I look in my new uniform, Neyah?" asked Kato.

Envious of her brothers' uniforms, she nodded her approval at Kato. She wanted to say, "You are lucky. Papa sells a goat every year to buy you new khaki pants and shirts." But Neyah didn't see the point.

Neyah's worn red pinafore and blue blouse still fit her but held stains. Papa told her it "was not worth it" to get a girl a new uniform since she spent most school days fetching water.

As though reading her mind, Hassan spoke with a mouth full of ugali. "Maybe Mama will buy you another uniform from the market."

Neyah shrugged. The open market where villagers went to buy needed goods often sold used school uniforms.

"Maybe Mama will trade some of her sweet mandazi bread for one!" Kato cried, excited over his suggestion.

Hassan bounced up and down as Kato helped Neyah pack

school lunches. "Bosco and Paul need to get back soon, or we will be late for school."

"They will be back soon, Kato." Neyah checked backpacks. Mama and Papa could barely read or write and relied on her to oversee homework. As she rolled bed mats, cowbells sounded in the distance.

"Finally!" Hassan exclaimed. Bosco and Paul pulled at their backpacks and hurried off to school, following the twins who had already sped off.

"See you this afternoon, Neyah!" called Bosco.

"Yes."

Surprised to hear a response from Neyah, Bosco turned and waved. She watched him brush the dust off his pant legs before breaking into a run to catch up with his brothers.

"Neyah girl. I am ready for my trip."

Bibi called her toilet trek a "trip" as it seemed to be the only distance she traveled lately.

Helping Papa came next. He made it to the toilet on his own even though it exhausted him. Neyah handed him his breakfast and tea. Her hands busied themselves while her mind raced with ways to take Abby's advice. What could she do to help Papa get better? How could she get to school more often and someday be a doctor by using her voice?

"You have learned good ways to take care of a family, Neyah." Papa's raspy voice sounded appreciative.

Neyah stroked Papa's hand.

"Thank you for helping Mama and Bibi."

She nodded. "I am going to school now, Papa. Do you need anything before I go?"

He shook his head. "Papa loves his daughter." His words brought hot tears to her eyes. She knew it. Papa would never trade her for cows.

Neyah kissed him on his forehead and ran to her hut to change into her uniform. With a hunk of cornbread in her mouth and an extra sense of bravery, she headed off to school.

13

THE BOILING EFFECT

S lipping into school three hours late, Neyah glanced at her bench. A small boy named Osley sat on it. Where was Malaika? After setting her pen pal letter on the teacher's desk, she slid in beside Osley.

Saida whispered to Neyah from across the aisle. "My sister is sick."

Neyah said a silent prayer for Malaika before studying the word she had copied from Bosco's notebook.

Boil (*verb*) heating liquid until it reaches the temperature where it bubbles and turns to vapor.

Neyah needed to know how boiling water prevented sickness. Somehow, she'd gather the courage to ask. It would be the first step in her Team Neyah and Abby plan to "say something." Her heart hammered. She stared at Mr. Sahli and pictured herself raising her hand. The thought terrified her. Others did it. *Why is it so hard for me?* Neyah wondered.

For a short time, she distracted herself by staring at her teacher's shirt. Mr. Sahli wore another colorful one. Black palm trees danced in silhouette against a fiery yellowish-orange sky. The shirt fit so snug over his round belly the buttons looked ready to pop. Neyah wondered how Mr. Sahli's belly grew round in a land where famine prevailed, and protruding ribs were commonplace.

Mr. Sahli suddenly spoke. "Neyah, your stare has been plastering me to the wall. Might I assist you with something?"

Startled at the sound of her name, Neyah sat up straight and fixed her eyes on the floor. She didn't like being called upon, but knew she better say something before she lost her courage.

"What does boiling do?" Her words tumbled from her mouth as if they were escaping from a ferocious lion. An immediate rustle of body movement filled the room as students turned in astonishment to stare at her.

"Neyah, you have a great question, but you're asking my feet." Laughter could be heard from the corner where Moswen sat.

Neyah's face burned. It felt uncomfortable for her to both talk and look in someone's eyes at the same time—especially Mr. Sahli's mismatched gaze.

"Today, Neyah, you and every young scientist in this school will learn how to boil water and understand how this easy task helps you stay healthy. First, we'll filter our water."

"Why?" asked Hassan.

"Ahh! Such an important question. We filter water because it contains dirt and animal dung that carries bad bacteria."

Mr. Sahli poured the water through a thin cloth four times, rinsing the cloth following each pour.

"Look at this!" called Moswen. "The brown disappeared!"

Neyah thought about Malaika's grandmother's water. Maybe she filtered it to get the brown out.

"Now, my scientists, we shall shift to the firepit to heat this water."

"I am not drinking scalding hot water!" Nathaniel called out.

"No worries," explained Mr. Sahli. "Once it cools, you can drink it."

Mr. Sahli led the class outdoors where Paul and his friend, Wilkey, tended a fire. "Wilkey brought this water sample today. Asante, Wilkey. Let's get it boiling."

Inquisitive students formed a tight circle around the fire pit. "When your water starts boiling, this is when you begin counting to sixty. It takes sixty seconds or one minute, for the heat to kill the bad bacteria."

Counting in unison, the students stared at the bubbling liquid as though it was part of a magic show. Mr. Sahli gripped the hot bowl with an old shirt and brought the water and students back inside. He placed a few droplets of boiled water under the microscope for students to view and directed students to record observations and write a hypothesis.

Neyah took her turn to study the droplets. When she stepped back from the viewing lens, she blinked, snatched her science folder, and furiously scribbled notes:

Observation: Not as many bacteria as before

Hypothesis: Filter + boil = fewer bad bacteria. This is how Papa will get better! Boiling changes things. Saying something works. Wait until I tell Abby!

"Dear scientists," Mr. Sahli said, "you've all peered at the boiled water. Who can predict what will happen if we filter and boil our water?"

Devison's hand shot up.

Mr. Sahli checked to see if Neyah raised her hand. She was busy writing.

Devison strained and grunted until Mr. Sahli called on him.

Devison's chest puffed up as his words poured out. "We should not see any more bad bacteria."

"And?" Mr. Sahli asked.

Neyah's hand inched up. Elated, the headmaster wasted no time calling on her.

"People will not get sick," said Neyah.

Mr. Sahli smiled and hoped she would say more. "You are partly right, Neyah. Not all sickness comes from dirty water, but much of it does. We know people who have died from cholera, right?"

Everyone nodded.

"If we boil our water, diseases like cholera will decrease. This is because organisms that make us sick won't be going in our stomach," concluded Mr. Sahli, poking his belly for added emphasis.

Neyah's worry pushed her arm up again. Mr. Sahli delighted in her eagerness. "Yes, Neyah?"

Glancing at Bosco, she saw proud tears in her brother's eyes as he watched her.

"Bosco said you told the class how handwashing is the other way to prevent sickness. Hygiene, you called it. What if we do not have enough water to wash our hands?"

"When the droughts come, it may prove difficult to find enough. However, most of the time there's plenty. In school, we'll wash our hands often to keep germs from getting in our belly, and we'll practice boiling. Then everyone will know how to do it at home. Soap helps kill germs too. Who can bring some to school?"

No one raised a hand.

Neyah wasn't thinking about soap. She thought of Abby and injustice and the next step of her plan to change things. Her mouth blurted a crazy thing.

"Most of the boys come here every day. Only a handful of girls make it."

Silence and a bit of discomfort filled every crack in the room.

Neyah twisted her hands as she continued soft and steady. "How many more days of school will girls miss if we must fetch enough water for this boiling and handwashing?" Her voice broke off.

Talking without waiting to be called on became contagious. Shala, a girl who liked to talk, took over where Neyah left off.

"Mr. Sahli, here at school, you teach about taking turns. When it comes to fetching in our village, it is just the girls."

"Even here," said Cheiru. "Valencia does the fetching."

Shala and Cheiru gave Neyah a shot of courage. She sucked in some air and flooded the room with her greatest fear.

"I am the only girl left in my family. I already miss most days of school. If it is up to me to fetch more water to boil and wash hands...to keep my family from getting sick and Papa from dying..."

Even though Neyah's voice fell to a whisper, every ear heard her clear as clean water. "If I do all this, you will never see me in school again."

14

BABY LULU

Maybe she'd said too much. Or not enough. Either way, Neyah needed to leave. She bolted from her school bench and out the door. She ran stumbling and crying down the steep path before her brothers even packed their backpacks. Her shaky legs pleaded with her to rest. A twisted tree root caught Neyah's bare foot and belly-flopped her onto the unforgiving ground. Sucking in warm gulps of air and licking dust from a bloody lip, she let her head drop on the rocky path for a few seconds.

Neyah then crawled to a tree and leaned against its massive trunk. Her ankle pulsed. The thick afternoon heat zapped what remained of her energy. Neyah longed to curl up and sleep but didn't want a monkey to come poking. Exhaustion crawled into her limbs and found a path to her head.

Behind closed eyelids, Neyah's mind wandered to another who slept curled up in a ball. Lulu was asleep that tragic day—her knees tucked up under her belly and hands fisted near her plump cheeks. Neyah recalled Mama calling to her.

"Neyah, help me get little Lulu in my back sack. Time to go to the well."

When Neyah picked her sister up and stuffed her into the colorful cloth funnel, Lulu snorted softly.

"Grab both water cans," said Mama. "And our rope and bucket too."

Neyah had tied the jerry cans around her waist and followed Mama out of the village, fingering the frayed rope as she walked.

Getting to the open well had taken no more time than an evening meal. Neyah sleepily smiled, remembering this. The short trip meant she attended school more often back then. Some days they made six or seven trips for water. She and Mama sang church songs along the trail, or made-up silly ones with Lulu's name in it. As they made their way to the well that day, Neyah begged Mama, "Tell me another story about when you grew up in a Pokot village." Mama obliged as they plodded on in the midday heat.

When they arrived at the open well that measured over forty meters deep, Neyah thirsted for a drink. More than a dozen women waited in line. One heaved her rope hand over hand, while another watched for the bucket as it surfaced from the dark, cool ground. The woman groaned under the weight. She leaned back as she struggled to keep her dirty sandaled feet anchored in a dugout hole. Her scarred hands pulled until, finally, her bucket made of an old rubber inner tube appeared. Her helper reached for the makeshift bucket and brought it to the ground, being cautious not to spill. The dark liquid carried a dead animal scent, but it was water.

Neyah remembered resting near the well, head tipped back, caught up in the clouds adorning the distant mountain range like a fluffy crown. A reassuring breeze cooled her. *This slice of life could keep me anchored to Kenya forever*, she recalled thinking.

Opening her eyes, Neyah took a nostalgic look at the well. The village elders claimed a camel herder built it years ago. Large stones stacked around the opening helped to prevent people and animals from falling in. Neyah stared at the logs circling the stones. Years of rope pulling created an artful grooved pattern in the wood, documenting the backbreaking work of hoisting heavy water from the deepness.

"It is our turn," Mama called. "We can finish before Lulu wakes."

Neyah hopped up and placed a stone in the bucket as a weight. She tied the rope around the bucket handle and lowered it into the well. Mama wedged a foot on the side of one of the rocks lining the well to anchor her body. She held a loose grasp on the end of the rope until she felt the weight of the water.

"Pull, Mama!"

Mama firmed her grip and carefully began to pull, groaning and grunting.

As Mama's callused hands pulled hand over hand, the rope fell in a heap behind her. Neyah watched Mama's strained face as she bent back with sheer determination in the day's sweltering heat. Her stained teeth clenched to counter the effort of pulling a vessel of water with a rock in it. Sweat beads glistened on Mama's upper lip. Neyah felt a mixed swell of pride and sadness at her mother's strength.

Neyah readied herself, knowing the valuable water would soon be within her reach. She braced herself against the worn wood.

With one last "Uuuuh!" her mother pulled. Neyah grabbed the bucket and maneuvered it to the ground. Together they poured it into her jerry can.

"Well done," Mama said between heavy breaths. "Two more."

Little Lulu awoke and cooed as Neyah lowered the bucket again. The second pull always felt tougher for Mama. She focused on her task and braced her feet again knowing water was her family's lifeline. Pull. If she wasn't using it to scrub dishes or children or clothes, she was cooking or carrying it. Here it comes. Pull!

Neyah reached into the well as far as she dared to grab the slippery container. As her fingertips wrapped around the wet handle, a dull crack echoed inside the cavernous walls. The frayed rope had snapped where it had been tied to the handle. The bucket swayed before descending into the dark and sent out a loud whack as it struck the water. The sudden release of the bucket forced Neyah's belly forward into the stone barrier and lifted her feet off the ground.

"Neyah!" Mama's scream brought the other women running. Mama's arms flew upward and wide as the loose rope snapped back, smacking her chin. The sudden release flung Mama onto her back with a sickening thud, crushing Lulu against the hard ground.

It took Neyah a few seconds to register the disaster. Once her feet found the ground, she scrambled to Mama and rolled Lulu over. The baby's head hung at an odd angle, and blood gushed from it. Pulling her sister from the back sack, Neyah sucked in air as she attempted to right the tiny head.

Blood dripped from the back of Mama's head. Once she regained a sense of what happened she snatched her baby and moaned like a wounded animal. "Nooo!" She tore her scarf off and wiped blood from the gaping hole in Lulu's head before tying it tight around her head. Lulu's neck twisted in a way necks shouldn't twist, causing Neyah's stomach to lurch.

Neyah didn't remember how long they stayed at the well. Two women accompanied them home. Neyah knew Lulu was gone even though Mama kept repeating, "Lulu will come back to me. She needs a rest. Lulu will come back to me."

"Neyah! Neyah!" Paul shook her awake and out of the nightmare of reliving Lulu's death. Her four brothers stared down at her.

Bosco helped her to her feet. "Time to go home."

15

THE COST OF COURAGE

"Mama! Mama! Kato and I passed into standard two classes!" Hassan yelled the good news as he flew into the compound after the final day of school.

"Ah, I am proud of you both! What about your brothers and sister?"

Bosco jumped high and pumped the air. "We all passed, even Neyah!" he teased.

Mama smiled at Neyah, "She is on her way to becoming our village doctor! And since the school year is over, it will be good to have you all here to help for a month while Papa rests."

Like most Kenya schools, Saramba Primary School ended the school year in November. Mr. Sahli did home visits during this time, bringing donated supplies of paper, pencils, and books to families. His first visit included sweet honey candies he brought from Morocco.

"Kato!" Mr. Sahli threw his head back laughing as he rested on Bibi's tree stump. "That's your fourth candy. How about you save some for another day!"

Kato shook his head with a grin and took another lick.

The headmaster took an envelope from his backpack. "And a special delivery from Minnesota to you, Miss Neyah."

"Asante, Mr. Sahli."

Mr. Sahli left with a slice of Mama's sweet bread in his mouth. "See you on my next visit!"

Neyah's teacher ambled past her family huts. Before he left their compound, he stopped and peered into her parent's hut where Papa lay so ill. Neyah expected to see a sympathetic look on her teacher's face. Instead, she saw a scowl. Had Mr. Sahli heard about Papa's plan to trade her for cows?

With a deep sigh, Neyah plopped down on Bibi's stump and read Abby's letter.

Dear Neyah,

It's a happy day when Mr. Simon gives me another letter from you! I feel bad about your problems, though. Every time I use water now, I think—wow, Neyah needs to walk so far to get some of this. Maybe this is a dumb question but can you move closer to the water or pipe it to you?

I'll try to answer your questions. First, I have a question for you! You have all those brothers—don't they help get water? You asked about injustice. I think you doing all the fetching and missing school while your brothers get to go is an injustice. Maybe you need to say something about this. It doesn't seem fair, but Mr. Simon says not all cultures do things the same way. I'm learning.

And sure, there's injustice in America. Some people are bullied or not given a chance to do things because of money or how they look or the way they act. People speak up so it can change and get better. Maybe if you explain and ask for help, things can improve.

As far as wells—I really don't know anything. Cedar Grove has a water tower I can see from our house. Mom says the water flows from the tower through pipes under the ground. When we turn a handle, the water comes out, hot or cold, depending which way we turn the faucet. No boiling required!

According to Mom, no one gets sick from the water here because all the bad stuff gets treated with chemicals. I guess there are laws about it. Which reminds me. This is why there are laws. To keep injustice from happening. Does your village have laws on clean water? Or about selling girls?

You might be in third-grade lessons but you sound as smart as any twelve-year-old I know. I'm sorry you miss school. Actually, I wouldn't mind missing school some days to sleep. Mrs. Standberg is my math teacher and acts like math is the only class we have. I'm talking MOUNTAINS of homework! I'm having trouble keeping up. She actually (did you notice how _actually_ is my favorite word?!), yes, she actually threw my test away because I laid my head down (hey I was tired!) She thought I was looking at Connor Schmidt's answers, which I'd never do because Connor is math-challenged, never does homework, and will flunk.

If I missed school, I'd miss art class, and you know I love art!

Hey! I added to my purpose list:

1. Keep trying to get parents together (my painting for them is almost done!)

2. Get going on Team Abby and Neyah project! (I hope you don't mind if I tell my friends about your water issue)

3. Stop being so tired!

Your pen pal from Minnesota, Abby.

P.S. We had a blast with Dad—he took us to the zoo and we ate junk food but I was so tired afterwards! I miss Dad lots. He lost his job and got depressed over it. Mom says he needs to see a counselor and get a job. Dad says he'll never find work again *after getting fired. So they argue over it. I don't care if he works. I want him home!*

Here's a picture of Justin Bieber the famous singer! I told you he was dreamy.

Now remember-say something!

P.P.S. Mr. Simon says it might be December when you get this letter so Merry Christmas! Do you celebrate Christmas? I'd like a new head that doesn't hurt for Christmas. Ugh!

Your turn!!

Three meters from where Neyah sat reading, Liza nibbled contentedly on Bosco's uniform sleeve.

"Neyah, please bring the laundry in before that goat eats our clothes! It is getting dark and those clothes are more than dry."

Startled by Mama's voice, Neyah jumped up and stuffed Abby's letter in her pocket.

The short rainy season had finally arrived, providing crops much-needed moisture. It also meant the clothes Mama scrubbed and spread across the bushes to dry often got a second wash from the afternoon rains.

As Neyah jerked the clothes off the bushes, Mama's skirt caught on the prickly thorns and made a ripping sound.

"Neyah, be careful," Bibi called out, "or we will not have any clothes left!" Although Bibi's vision was poor, her hearing remained sharp.

Neyah gritted her teeth and scratched her arm. "Yes, Bibi. I wish I had your patience. But my arms are so itchy tonight. I cannot stand it!"

"Ah child, hakuna matata. Think of all the years ahead to learn patience. Let me feel those arms."

Bibi rubbed her aging hands gently over Neyah's bumpy

rash. "No wonder you are scratching and pulling clothes off those thorns like a crazy girl!"

"My skin feels like fire ants are crawling under it, Bibi. Mr. Sahli said dirty water sometimes causes a rash."

Bibi closed her eyes and gave Neyah's words some thought. "Finish the laundry before Liza snatches it again. I will find my special rub."

When Neyah heard Bibi's shuffling feet return, she reached for her grandmother's hands. "Bibi! The moon is so bright tonight. I wish you could still see it."

"Child, my memory sees it perfectly. But let me say this. Are you going to ask for that moon, or just stare at it?"

Rubbing her itchy skin with the shirt she'd rescued from Liza, Neyah giggled. "What am I going to do with a moon, Bibi?"

Bibi whispered, "Nothing. What I mean is, sometimes you must ask for what you need."

"All right," Neyah giggled with exasperation, "I will ask! Can you PLEASE put your rub on my arms right now?"

"That is not exactly what I meant but come here. I will take care of those itchy arms. Then we can eat!" chuckled Bibi.

Bosco and Paul helped Papa and Bibi to the family's only bench. Everyone else sat on cow skins. As usual, ugali made up the evening meal.

When Mama dished it up, Hassan pleaded, "Mama, can you add some root vegetables, like cassava, to our ugali next time?"

Bosco agreed. "Yes, and I miss your sukuma wiki."

"I do too," sighed Mama. "After my bout with typhoid during the planting season, our tiny garden did not last long. Unless you know how to turn weeds magically into collard greens, we will not have vegetables for a while."

"We do not have fish anymore either," Kato whined.

"Field work keeps me from the market," replied Mama.

"I will go!" offered Paul. "School is done until January. I have time!"

"And what will you trade for the fish?" asked Bosco. "We have nothing to spare."

A mischievous smile resembling Papa's crept across Paul's face. "I will trade the twins! One fish for Kato and one fish for Hassan!" He laughed at his own joke, but the laughing set off his cough.

Bosco jumped up. "Neyah has an announcement before we eat."

Neyah pressed her lips together and fired a pinched glare at him.

Mama set the last bowl of ugali in front of Kato. "What is it, Neyah?"

Staring into her bowl, Neyah didn't know if she could do what Abby and her own head encouraged her to do. For weeks she planned to mention the hand washing but always lost her courage.

"Our food is getting cold, Neyah."

She swallowed and squeaked out her words. "Mr. Sahli told us we need to wash our hands...before we eat."

Her eyes scanned the table. Mama's forehead wrinkled. Her brothers were suddenly fascinated with the hands in their lap.

Neyah wanted to add that Mr. Sahli said to wash after using the toilet and handling the cattle too, and if they boiled water, Papa might get better. But she couldn't get any more words out.

Papa looked at Neyah with vacant eyes. "Speak up girl when you tell us something." He sounded tired.

Even though she knew everyone heard her the first time, she obeyed. "We need to wash our hands before we eat."

"Why?" Papa's voice wavered.

Neyah cast Paul a pleading look. She knew Papa might listen to him.

After an awkward silence, Paul mumbled into his lap. "To wash the germs off our hands, so we do not eat them and get sick."

Mama sighed. She grabbed at Kato's small hands and flipped them over. "Do you see anything on these hands? These things you call-what? Germs? No? Now eat."

Never one to rely on outside help or follow educated advice, Mama depended only on herself and insisted on doing things the way they'd been done for generations. Much like Papa.

Mama threw her hands in the air. "Sometimes I wonder why we send you to school. This outside nonsense about—what is the word? Germs? What are they teaching you, anyway?"

Everyone began eating except Neyah. She went over to the water pot and washed her hands. Her brothers exchanged glances, unsure if they should join her.

THE NEXT EVENING, Neyah tried again after the family settled in for dinner. "I boiled water. Mr. Sahli says boiled water kills germs on our hands. We all need to wash our hands with boiled water before we eat. Otherwise, we could all get sick like Papa."

No one moved except Neyah. After washing her hands, she returned to her eating spot on the ground.

Bosco's beaming smile gave her courage.

With closed eyes, Papa sat hunched forward on his bench. His clothing hung like loose elephant skin on his frail frame. He didn't appear to have even heard her.

Neyah squared her shoulders. "I will not eat until we all wash our hands." It came out as a timid plea rather than a demand.

The hungry boys scrambled to their feet.

Papa's eyes opened. He put his arm up as a sign for the boys to sit. His trembling hand motioned Neyah to him. She knelt in front of Papa with her hands on his lap. His eyes watered and yellow matter crusted into the corners.

Looking into her father's bloodshot eyes, Neyah waited for him to speak. But no words came. The back of his hand to her face struck like a lightning bolt, delivered with more power than she thought Papa had left in him.

Mama and Bibi gasped. Kato and Hassan whimpered into Mama's lap. Bosco's face froze in shock.

The slap caused Neyah's head to twist to the right and sent her reeling to the ground, knocking two porridge bowls over as she attempted to catch herself. Her hands landed on the rocky surface among the broken clay bowls. Blood trickled over her fingers.

Bosco rushed to help Neyah, but Papa ordered him away.

As Bibi rocked back and forth and mumbled prayers in Swahili, Neyah took only seconds to gather herself and wobble to a stand. Her temples throbbed and her face burned, but her heart hurt the worst as it shattered into pieces. Shocked and confused, she turned toward Papa.

With eyes closed and head cast downward, it appeared as if Papa hadn't moved. Did Papa actually hit her? For trying to help?

"I am doing this for you, Papa," she whimpered.

"Go to your hut." Papa's cold voice wavered, barely recognizable. It sent a raw shiver through Neyah's already shaken body. "Bosco, send your teacher to me the next time he visits."

Neyah examined the face of each family member before walking away. Only one met her eyes. Bosco's quivering lips shook the tears from his round eyes and sent them dripping into his bowl of ugali.

Neyah collapsed onto the mat Bibi wove from the strong fibers of the sisal plant. Digging her bloody fingers across its rough surface, she recalled the advice of her wise grandmother as well as her new American friend, and Mr. Sahli. *They all told me to say what is on my mind. But if this was the result, why say anything? Papa never lifted a hand to me before. Kind and gentle Papa—who cried for days over Lulu—struck me. The bad water must be destroying his brain too.*

Mental exhaustion and sleep found Neyah long after her tears and bloody hands dried.

16

GIFTS ABOUND

Watching the afternoon drizzle sweep over the corn and beans, Mama mumbled a prayer of gratitude for the rain. She took cover under a large bush along with Paul and their field hoes.

"I love the rain, Mama," said Paul.

Mama nodded, grateful for Paul's cheery outlook and improved health over the last week. Her husband used to be cheery too. Like a thief, his poor health stole it from him.

"Paul, this may be one of the last rains for months. The heat will drink it up faster than the cattle."

"Mama! Mama!" The cries interrupted their conversation and alarmed Mama. Running through the rain, Kato and Hasan laughed and squatted near her. Bursting with good news, Kato yelled, "Mr. Sahli is here with a big bag of gifts, Mama! It is almost Christmas!"

"He is? We better get back home then!" squealed Mama. Giggling and splashing through puddles, all four ran to where Bosco, Bibi, and Neyah huddled under a tarp with Mr. Sahli.

"Merry Christmas everyone!" called Mr. Sahli. "I come bearing gifts from our generous mission friends!"

Mr. Sahli laughed as the boys bounced and pulled at his arms.

"Good timing! The rain has stopped!" screeched Kato as he and Hassan pushed the tarp aside.

"How are you today, Neyah?" inquired Mr. Sahli. Dull eyes were the only response he received.

"Well, then. Who is ready for your gifts?" shouted Mr. Sahli.

"We are!" the boys cried.

Mama watched her sons' excitement as Mr. Sahli pulled the first item from his bag.

"Please give Papa Haji this fine first aid kit and new sandals."

Mama smiled. "He needs both. Asante sana, Mr. Sahli."

"For you, Mama Sara, a token for five pounds of fish from the market, two cooking pots, and...a new dress!"

"NEW? Is it new, Mr. Sahli?" Mama's eyes filled.

"Yes, Mama Sara. So new the smell of dye is still in the fabric."

"This is the first..." Mama's voice cracked as she held the patterned dress against her body. "This is the only new dress I have had. Asante! Asante!"

"I'll tell the mission you are grateful."

The teacher touched Bibi's hand and laid a small colorful burlap bag on her lap. "And for your family's most special person, here's something extra special."

Bibi giggled like a young girl and felt her way into the bag. Immediately identifying its contents, she beamed with delight. "Asante! And just in time! My bead supply is running low."

Handing a large cotton bag to Bosco, Mr. Sahli's jovial face turned somber. "Boys, I'm sorry. This is all they sent for the four of you."

The boys slumped in obvious disappointment. Bosco

dropped the bag on the ground, and everyone stared at it. Curious, Hassan gave it a slight kick, causing the gift to roll out.

"Aiiiiiii! A soccer ball!" The boys' enthusiasm rang so loud that the goats scattered.

Paul grasped the ball and inspected it. "It is a *real* one!"

"And brand new, just like Mama's dress!" laughed Bosco, as he snatched it from Paul and gave it a kick toward the twins.

Kato cautiously picked it up, handling it like he would a newborn goat. He stroked its shiny leather-like surface before his giddy voice spilled into the air. "It *is* a real one! Clean...and smoother than a baby calf's skin."

Neyah eyed the old soccer ball next to her hut. Bosco made it last year by wrapping a worn hemp rope around old rags and paper scraps from school.

Mr. Sahli's merriment showed in his face as the boys passed the ball back and forth down the village road. "That's the last you'll see of them for a while!"

Mr. Sahli turned his attention to Neyah.

"Neyah, you get to open your gift in peace and quiet."

For several seconds she sat like a stone, staring off into nothingness.

"Neyah," Mama said. "It is your turn."

Neyah blinked, then accepted the gift Mr. Sahli handed to her.

He watched her as she slowly opened her box that held writing supplies, a book, and a new smock-style dress. She stroked them one by one as if they were some strange find.

"Neyah, this book is about a family who travels around the world. You'll have to tell me all about it after you read it."

Neyah simply stared at the book. Mr. Sahli knew her family seldom received new things. He expected an enthusiastic response from Neyah but got nothing.

"My, it's good to see you all," said Mr. Sahli. "Before long

I'll see the children back in school. I hope for a Christmas miracle for Papa Haji's health. And Neyah, I hope the dress fits."

Her blank stare sent a shiver down Mr. Sahli's back. Standing, he shook the stiffness from his stubby legs. "Ah! The rain stopped. I must walk to one more family today to bring joy."

"Wait," Neyah muttered and ran into her hut.

Mama touched Mr. Sahli's arm. "My husband wishes to speak with you."

Neyah stepped out of her hut and, without a word, handed Mr. Sahli her letter to mail to Abby. As she headed to the field she thought about the letter she wrote. It felt good to get her feelings out of her head and onto paper.

Dear Abby I am sorry I not write for too long I have sad time with hurt inside my heart Papa is worse I see him shake and the fever is bad The worst part is he is angry for me boiling water and washing hands to keep germs off I not allowed to feed him or eat with family My belly hurts Maybe I have water sickness too

Do you have best friend to tell troubles Mine be Malaika She is beautiful friend and smart and wears colorful skirt from city grandmother You would like so much her long hair of cornrows She is not afraid of bugs live in it She sings and laughs on path when we fetch She asks me my purpose I tell you my purpose I have three I use my voice and writing to bring water closer I help papa be healthy and love me again and I pass class 8 exams someday so I go to secondary school and study to be doctor.

Your turn

Your friend Neyah

PS Short rainy season watered our scorched fields good

You ask about boys fetching It is a job for girls and women Yes Christmas time is near Sometime we eat meat with ugali to celebrate I send greetings across the world for good Christmas tidings to Abby and family

Here is picture I drew of me I am not good artist like you

17

THE DRY SEASON

January and the dry season arrived, and with it the start of a new school year.

"Mama, we are home!" called Bosco, as he and Paul set their backpacks down.

"Ah! Good to see you boys home early. Change out of those uniforms and see what grass you can find for the livestock."

Mama shook her head in disgust. "Our short rainy season did not give us what we prayed for, and now here we are in the dry season."

"Do not worry, Mama. We will find something for the animals." Paul smiled with assurance.

Mama bit her quivering lip. "Paul, everything about you reminds me of Papa's good nature before he got sick."

Grinning, Paul said, "I will tell Papa one of his favorite stories before we head out, Mama."

Wiping a tear from her cheek, Mama replied, "Please do, kind son."

Noticing Neyah and Bibi returning from the toilet, Bosco handed Neyah a folder. "The Great Bosco brings you another America letter!"

"Asante."

As soon as Neyah finished spreading chicken manure on the bean field, she found a shady spot near the edge of their family compound to read Abby's letter.

Dear second-best friend,

We've only been pen pals for a little while, but I tell you things I only tell my best friend, Jada. She's kind of quiet like you and likes to tell jokes. I think you'd like her. That reminds me—yesterday (January 14) was my 13th birthday, so I had 13 friends (including you!) for a sleepover. Thankfully our blizzard didn't cancel it! I only invited 12 friends because you are my 13th friend! I put the picture you drew of yourself on my wall and told my friends about you. We sat up half the night thinking of ways for you to get to school and have water closer. I wish you'd been here! After my friends left, I slept for 14 hours. Mom finally woke me because she thought I was sick. To be honest, I am. My head is swimming, and it's hard to eat. Maybe too much birthday cake.

I GOT MY CELL PHONE!!! I'd love to call you, but I should learn Swahili first! And you'd need a phone...

When is your birthday? Do you have special birthday traditions?

What's this about your papa? He should be happy you're helping. At least your parents are together. I'm still working on mine! I told Dad he should pretend he just met Mom and ask her for a date. He liked the idea so he asked her to go skiing together! She said yes!

I see the doctor Tuesday after school because I have monster headaches and sometimes my vision is blurry. Mom thinks I need glasses. Nooo! I'll look nerdy in glasses! Do you think Isaac Allen will ever look at me again? I have a crush on him, and I KNOW he likes me. Well actually, I'm hoping.

Let's see what else is going on... Oh yes, until I get better, my horse-riding lessons are on hold. It's fine, because all this snow means the lessons are inside, and it's pretty boring riding around in circles inside the arena. I miss Jazzy!

Write soon! Your friend, Abby Larson

P.S. Here's a picture of Jada.

I bet you want to see what I added to my purpose list. You're the reason I even have one so thank you! (And, hey! I like your list)

1. Get Mom and Dad together -slow progress ☺

2. Finish painting Mom and Dad's anniversary present- almost done!

3. Use my art to help people, including you!

4. Feel better so I can ride Jazzy again!

Your turn!

Within weeks, Neyah's job of dipping water changed into a more serious one of digging for it. After a short bout of dysentery, Malaika joined Neyah at the water hole, or what remained of it. For a week they knelt and dug in the mud until water trickled up from the dry earth. Today they didn't even try. Instead, they watched five women dig nearly six meters down to pull up sandy sludge. Malaika bit her lip. Neyah's chest tightened.

"I will never do that," Malaika said with authority. "Last year this hole caved in on some diggers." She shook her head. "Look at those thirsty cows. They are going to fall in if they get any closer."

Neyah's eyes burned as she trekked home with a dry jerry can. She examined the smoldering hillside. Lack of rain turned acres of dry vegetation into a torched wasteland.

Neyah rarely spoke to anyone since the day Papa struck her. Today, she had no choice.

"Mama, the water hole is gone."

Mama stared at Neyah, "Are the animals drinking there?"

Neyah shook her head.

"Did you try digging? It takes a while. Eventually, the water seeps through."

Neyah nodded.

"Child! Speak!"

Neyah heard the annoyance and tension in her mother's voice. She thrust both of her hands forward for Mama to see. Her broken nails polished with hardened mud resembled animal claws. The skin on her hands and arms appeared raw and infected.

"Yes, Mama. I have been digging for a week. First, I got sludge. Today, nothing."

The dry season from mid-December through February crawled like a giant sloth across western Kenya. Some called it the hunger season when some animals and people died from lack of water, or starvation, or both.

Mama wrapped her thin arms around Neyah's neck as hot tears poured from Neyah's eyes. "I am sorry my dear daughter. I do not mean to be angry," whispered Mama. "My nose and eyes know what is happening. The land is burning. The village gardens and fields are scorched. Our maize is suffering. We will need to trade a goat or milk for maize soon."

Mama stepped back and wrung her hands before beginning to grind maize.

People died of water-borne diseases all year, but during the dry season when water sources disappeared, many more perished. It affected small children and babies the worst for they couldn't bear the strained mixture of stifling heat, malnutrition, and less water.

"We are not in control of the weather." Mama pounded the maize vigorously. "When the rainy season returns, you will walk to the waterhole. For now, you must fetch from the dam, starting tomorrow."

"But the cliff ⸺"

"There is no choice, Neyah. We need water."

"I could walk to the well."

"NO!"

It came like an explosion. Mama threw down the rock she used for grinding. Neyah jumped back.

"To honor your sister, we will never go to that evil place again." Neyah heard this time after time and here it came again.

Mama angrily beat the chaff from her dress. "I must talk to Uncle Aman. Finish grinding the maize."

Neyah kicked the grinding stone and watched Mama leave. She wondered about honoring a dead sister by not drawing water from the closest source. What about honoring a sister who is still alive? The one who longs to go to school and become a doctor.

If Mama knew how many times she hiked to the open well against her wishes, she'd be furious.

Bibi overheard Neyah's argument with Mama. Her hands crawled across her beadwork in rhythm with her swaying body. The necklace Bibi worked on resembled a sunburst with multiple shades of yellow and orange. Although her eyesight was poor, Bibi's years of beading experience and her sensitive fingertips now served as her eyes.

"The river is not much further than the watering hole, child. You can still go to school one afternoon a week."

"Bibi, one afternoon a week? I will never become a doctor on a few hours of learning!"

"Neyah, listen to you! It is heavenly to hear you using your sweet voice again!"

Neyah didn't care to hear about her sweet voice. "Bibi, the cliff to the river is steep, and the trail is dangerous! Bandits beat two Saramba school girls. I would rather go to the well and fall in than get beaten."

"You are talking out of your head, dear child. Water is life. You will never become a doctor or anything else if you do not have water. Go early to draw river water. The drunken bandits will still be asleep. There is no danger in the early morning."

"What is the purpose of fetching this water if Papa strikes me for washing with it?"

"Neyah, your father—he is not well. He is angry at his sickness and took it out on you."

Kicking at the ground, she asked the question she feared most. "Bibi, is Papa dying?"

"No one knows who is dying or when. Only the Great One knows this, child. What I do know is your father refuses to consider he is sick from drinking water. Our people always believed if sickness comes, it is bad spirits testing the soul, tempting to wear it down."

"What if Papa is wrong?"

"Wrong?"

"What if he is sick from our water, and the answer is to boil it and wash more often?"

"I believe your good father would be the first to admit he is wrong."

Now who is talking out of one's head? Neyah thought.

Bibi shuffled a few steps and took Neyah's small hands in her wrinkled ones. "During my time, girls could not wait to fetch and felt proud to do it. I fetched six or seven times a day and never attended school at your age."

Neyah's eyes filled. "Then how did you get this wise, Bibi? And why are you always happy?"

"First of all, wisdom is not taught in schools. Only knowledge. And, things change. As a girl, I did not know anything beyond fetching water. But you have learned many possibilities of what you can do for yourself and others. The question is, what will you do with it? Hold everything in and never talk? Be angry and miserable? Or happy and useful? What will you do with this lesson you learned on washing and boiling?" Bibi returned to her beading.

"One more thing," Bibi said. "I am happy because I want to be happy."

INSIDE HIS HUT, Papa's breathing sounded irregular, yet his stomach lurched, and fingers ached as he drew the frayed blanket to his chin. But like his mother, his ears still worked. His head refused to listen to Neyah's voice. She disobeyed him. He wouldn't have it. And yet, his heart strained to overhear the conversation between his strong-willed daughter and his wise mother.

18

FETCHING AT THE RIVER

"Malaika said she will walk to the river with me!" Neyah shared her good news with Mama who swept around the chickens pecking at the maize crumbs.

"You will go with your cousin, Nilsa."

Not Nilsa! Neyah's shoulders sagged.

Mama shooed the chickens out of her way.

"I made a deal with Uncle Aman. You walk four days a week with Nilsa since she is too young to go alone. Uncle Aman hired a herder with two donkeys to fetch the other days. Each donkey carries four pots. Two will be for us."

Neyah's mouth fell open as she dropped the mats she'd been shaking.

"Mama?" Tears filled her eyes. "You mean?"

Mama's face nearly burst with the news. "You can go to school two days a week!"

Neyah squealed. "Two days!" She squeezed tight around Mama's neck as Bibi clapped from her perch on the stump.

"Mama, you asked for help? Thank you! I love you!"

WATCHING Neyah and Nilsa leave for the dam, Mama considered her family's dilemma. She felt Neyah's growing discontent over missing school, and yet their need for water grew. Water had ruled Mama's entire life. She longed for something more for her daughter, including a sister.

Heavy with the knowledge that water could be causing her husband's illness, Mama peered in at him. Might he die from the water? She stifled a sob and prayed for her husband's health and Neyah's safe return. Mama knew one thing for sure; her family and animals needed water. Without it, they all would perish.

Mama picked up her broom. Using quick, short strokes she whisked away small stones and a pesky chicken looking for a second breakfast. "Abilene, if I did not know you were a chicken, I would take you for a begging dog." She laughed to herself as she threw Abilene a few kernels of corn.

"Enough talking to a chicken," sighed Mama. "I have field work to do before the sun melts me."

MAMA STOOPED and entered the hut where Papa lay. Resting her right hand on his, she felt the fever in his fingers. "Haji, I am going to do some tilling now. Bibi is just outside. She will check on you. What can I do for you before I leave?"

Hearing no response, she brushed her lips across his knuckles and made her way to the field.

THE SUN FLIRTED with the horizon as Nilsa and Neyah stepped on the path. Soon enough, the temperature would rise, but the morning served the girls a cool sendoff and held the aroma of honey. Superb starlings with their iridescent blue backs and orange breasts whistled through the crimson flowers of the flame trees overhead.

The path to the Turkwel River ran around gentle knolls before quickly turning into a rocky, slippery nightmare over the river gorge. Bibi was right. The distance to the river might be similar to the water hole trek; however, the rough cliff terrain and word of frequent attacks made for a nerve-wracking hike.

"I wish Papa would let me fetch water alone," Nilsa whined.

"No one goes alone on this path. Your papa wants you safe."

"Are you talking about bandits? What do they want from me? My dried berries?"

"Maybe. Or water." Neyah didn't know how much her Uncle told Nilsa about bandits. She didn't want to scare her with stories of beatings.

No one went barefoot on the trek to the river. Neyah wore her thin rubber sandals with a hole starting to work through the left heel. Mama had repaired the strap of the right one with a band of goat hide.

"Papa said to be careful on the hill."

"You mean the cliff?" asked Neyah.

"No, the hill to the river," insisted Nilsa.

"It is steep and slippery. It is a cliff."

She didn't want to waste time convincing her stubborn cousin why "cliff" better described the drop-off to the river. Neyah recalled stories of women and girls who died falling down the steep, rocky cliff. Broken limbs, cracked skulls, ugly gashes. She wouldn't be one of them. She had dreams to chase.

A distant rumble in the sky interrupted their conversation. Neyah shielded her eyes from the blinding African sun. An airplane. The dream of flying in one of those silver birds brightened her young face. Maybe a plane could fly her to

Abby's next birthday sleepover—whatever that was. Or to Malaika's grandmother to view her see-through water. Or to a school where more than a hundred books about the moon and science and being a doctor sat waiting for her.

Nilsa showed no interest in singing or sharing dreams the way Malaika did. While Nilsa chatted about chores and wild animals, Neyah watched for snakes and scratched her rashy skin.

"Papa wants to know what is wrong with you."

Neyah frowned.

"You know," Nilsa said, "why you do not talk."

Irritated to know her Uncle Aman talked about her, Neyah replied, "I talk...when I have something to say."

The girls concentrated on their feet. Roots and loose rocks caused occasional stumbles. Thorny bushes poked at bare ankles.

Near a knoll known as the Three Ancient Pots, the girls rested. Staring at the "pots" and challenging her imagination, Neyah could visualize three roughly-shaped clay pots from the three tall stones perched on the small hill. Formed in a perfect semi-circle and standing proud like fancy artwork on display, the "pots" held a legend. It was said that great descendants placed them at this spot by the earth's first animals, then gifted them to all animals so they would never thirst. In reality, the "pots" harbored no water. Neyah knew this for a fact as she once climbed the knoll to investigate.

Nilsa and Neyah continued along two wide bends to the left.

"See that tree all by itself?" whispered Nilsa in a poetic trance. "I want to climb it!"

Neyah gazed at the lone distant tree. Although it seemed eerily out of place among the scrappy bush landscape, she felt its meaty low branches beckoning them closer.

"You will get plenty of climbing when we get to the cliff. I mean, the hill," replied Neyah.

Nilsa gave her cousin a pat and continued along the path.

Heeding the advice of both her father and Neyah, Nilsa descended the "hill" with caution. She occasionally slipped and slid a few meters on her bottom. "Good thing we have sandals."

Neyah hung onto rocks as she stretched down over steep embankments. Focusing on every step, she barely noticed hyenas yipping in the distance, or her scraped hands.

After nearly two hours and very few words from Nilsa, the pair heard the roaring river in the gorge and knew they were close. They exchanged a look of relief.

"You are right," sighed Nilsa.

Neyah turned to Nilsa and tilted her head quizzically.

"This is not a hill!" Nilsa said with teeth partially clenched.

Neyah laughed and hugged her cousin.

The girls finally reached the base of the cliff. With plenty of shoreline for those who dared the trip to the gorge, no one needed to wait in line to draw water. The cousins scampered to the river's edge and cupped their hands for a long, noisy drink. Thirst and exhaustion overruled Neyah's reluctance to drink from the river.

On the other side, herdsmen kept watch for hungry crocodiles while their cattle lumbered into the river. Thirsty camels and goats jockeyed for a drinking spot. Several women and a few men made the trip with donkeys. Each donkey wore crude worn saddlebags that held water containers.

Nilsa peered longingly toward them. "I wish I had a donkey."

"Your papa has two," said Neyah.

Nilsa nodded. "He needs them in the field."

Neyah noticed monkey excrement on nearby rocks and glanced around. The striking black-and-white colobus monkeys sometimes scampered down from Mt. Elgon for a drink and, perhaps, an adventure.

"Nilsa!" Neyah pointed upward where a row of long bushy colobus tails hung from overhead branches.

Cranking her neck, Nilsa smiled at the cloud-like tails flowing in rhythm with the breeze. "Do they ever come down?"

"Not while we are here. Do you remember Mr. Sahli showing a picture of their babies? They are pure white."

"No. Maybe I stayed home taking care of Mama that day," Nilsa said.

Neyah bit her lip. Nilsa's mother died last year of typhoid. *If she had boiled her drinking water, maybe she would be alive,* thought Neyah.

Both girls filled their water cans next to a trio of women doing laundry. One bathed with her clothes on, rubbing smooth stones over her arms and legs.

The cousins settled back under the shade. Neyah opened her brown cloth sack and found her dried cornbread. She ate and hummed while Nilsa played a game of "toss the banana peel" in the fig tree. Once it caught a branch, she pulled down a handful of the fresh figs and shared them with Neyah.

"Neyah, look! Rock hydraxes on the cliff."

The furry rodent-shaped animals sat still as statues, sunbathing in the late morning heat. Mr. Sahli once said the hydrax were distant relatives of the elephant, which Neyah found difficult to believe. Suddenly, one whistled. Then both rotated their tailless gray bodies and scooted off, causing the girls to giggle.

Neyah leaned back and admired the blue sky. Her eyes grew heavy. A nap sounded perfect, but a commotion downstream halted her plan.

Two young tribe boys screamed! Crocodiles were after their goats as they drank on the muddy riverbank. The boys threw rocks at the crocs, which only served to anger them. As the goats sunk into greasy mud, the stealthy reptiles took advantage of the situation.

"Oh no! The goats are stuck!" Nilsa cried.

One crocodile grabbed at a goat's leg, dragging the pathetic thing into the water. As the goat screamed for its life, one boy held onto the goat's tail and slid dangerously close to the crocodile's mouth.

The girls held their breath. Neyah thought about her brothers herding goats to find water and shivered.

The second boy extended his herding staff into the water and dragged the first to safety. Meanwhile, the other croc snatched a goat in its mouth. Both crocodiles clamped the goats in their jaws and rolled them until they drowned. The boys commandeered their herd up the hill and, in exhaustion, collapsed amidst the animals and wept. The loss of two healthy goats wouldn't be welcome news to their family.

"Nilsa, we need to go." Shielding her eyes with scraped hands, Neyah studied the terrifying cliff. The uphill climb appeared formidable, especially with water weight. *But crocodiles do not climb bluffs and I will be back in school tomorrow,* Neyah told herself.

"I need one last drink," Nilsa said. After a few swallows from the river, the girls began their strained ascent against gravity. Neyah's palms grew sweaty. Heat gathered around her ankles. Her foot failed to clear a jutting rock causing her to collapse to her knees. The jerry can twisted sideways, but the cap held. Her knees burned from the fall, and her back ached.

Nilsa carried a smaller container and seldom lost her balance as they climbed.

Between breaths, Neyah said, "You are made for this, Nilsa."

"I am short. Tall people like you tip over."

Neyah chuckled.

By the time the girls reached flat land, their damp dresses stuck to them.

"Set your water down and rest, Nilsa."

Without a word, Nilsa collapsed to the ground. The day burned feverishly hot. Neyah wiped her wet face with her dress.

"How is your papa?" Nilsa asked once she got her breath back.

"Weak."

"He will love a cold drink of water from you."

Neyah didn't reply. No use telling Nilsa that Papa refused to see her.

It took an hour to return home, more than enough time for Neyah to decide how to make things right with Papa.

Maybe I should tell him I am sorry and that I will not wash my hands or boil water or talk about it anymore. Then we will be back to where we were. Papa and daughter.

When she arrived home, Neyah rushed to Mama.

"I am back. How is Papa? I want to bring him some water. I need to tell him something."

"He will not allow you to talk to him," said Mama.

INSIDE THE HUT, Papa covered his ears to avoid her voice. Or, at least, he intended to.

A tug-o-war inside Papa's head made his head throb. Back and forth his thoughts fell. Tradition pulled him to one side, expecting him to do what was expected of fathers who had a daughter. Raise them up to be obedient. Formal schooling was not necessary for the plans he had for her. It was water fetching, hut building, cooking, and having babies that were important.

Those skills would lead to a nice offer from a cattle owner who wanted another wife.

But the other pull came from a deeper place. It came from inside his very soul. It didn't just tug. It yanked and dragged his emotions round and round until his stomach churned. Neyah was his only daughter. He had lost his other three to disease and rotten luck. Could he bear to let her go and have her despise him for selling her off?

He muttered to himself. "What choice do I have but to trade her?"

To be a man in his village where tradition is honored, it was not only an expected thing to do; it was often necessary for survival.

"I have a family to feed," Papa whispered.

19

FILLING THE HOLE IN A HEART

I want to say birthday greetings to you Abby What dreams do you have for thirteenth year of your life March be my birthday Mama does not know what date Every day we give thanks for birth and life not just one day

I weave pictures you sent into my grass roof so you and Jada and Justin Bieber all look at me. Your friend Jada she has skin color like me but much more hair What sleepover mean We learn English words in school but not sleepover It is dry season I fetch by walking long way to river on slippery cliff The good part is I go to school more days

PS Is your head better I fell with water one day and cut my head Mama scolded me because the water spilled out Your Isaac must like you for big heart and not for big glasses A boy his name Devison looks at me too much in my school I do not like it I still work on all my purposes, most important one is helping Papa He not want to see me though I gave him water and he threw it on ground.

Your words help fill hole in my heart left from Papa
Your turn
Neyah

The shuffle of Mr. Sahli's sandals stopped beside her bench. "During the outdoor break, I wish to speak to you, Neyah."

Her teacher's voice sounded serious. Noting his dusty sandals from the corner of her eye, she nodded. Mr. Sahli's feet didn't move. Realizing he expected more, she said, "Yes, sir. And, here is a letter for Abby."

Mr. Sahli grinned. "I will see it gets translated." He and his feet shuffled on.

Neyah waited for her teacher on the bench outside while Moswen, Paul, and a new boy practiced boiling water. Others sat in the shade and drank water that students had boiled the day before.

Mr. Sahli sat beside Neyah.

"I got you in trouble with your father." Mr. Sahli wore a smile ninety-nine percent of the time. This moment was part of the one percent.

"Yes, sir. I mean, no, sir. I got myself in trouble."

"I taught you handwashing and boiling, and you did what good learners do."

This time she stared at her own feet.

"Your father struck you."

Her fingernails dug into the bench. "Who told you?"

"Bosco."

Of course. The Great Bosco. Neyah pressed her lips together. She felt like screaming.

Mr. Sahli felt her anger. "Neyah."

She wanted to be done with this talk.

"Please look at me."

Kicking the powdery dirt with her bare feet, Neyah finally allowed her round dark eyes to meet the one looking at her.

"I am your teacher. You follow my rules here. Papa Haji is your father. His rules are the ones to follow at home."

Neyah's stomach felt like someone wound it tight as a spring. She closed her eyes. When she opened them, heavy tears slid out.

"Then why am I here?" Her voice a squeaky whisper, she continued. "You tell us to go home and apply what we learn. You told me to use my words and not leave them on paper. So, I did. Papa is sick. He might..."

She couldn't say it. *Little Lulu gone. Maybe Papa is next.*

The gentle teacher placed a hand on Neyah's shoulder.

"Neyah, I talked to him. You showed bravery to speak up and show your family ways to prevent illness. I told him."

Neyah's jaw dropped. "You talked to Papa?"

"He needs time. These hygiene practices are not something he learned. It is not easy for a father to learn something from his child that he wished he had known. Neyah, do not give up. Your voice matters."

Neyah wanted to tell her teacher she tried to make things better with Papa, that Papa was still too stubborn to see her. But Mr. Sahli had already walked to the boiling group.

Malaika watched Neyah mop her tear-stained face from a few meters away. As soon as their teacher left Neyah's side, she rushed in with a cup of water.

"Is Mr. Sahli mad about something?" A few minutes of silence and sharing the water cup passed. Malaika waited for a response.

Neyah sniffed. "No, he is never mad."

Malaika hopped up. "Play catch with me!"

It's one of the things Neyah loved about Malaika. She didn't pry. She had a knack for chasing Neyah's brooding away simply by being there. The girls ran and threw a handmade ball of rags back and forth and shrieked when the boys tried to snatch it away. They giggled and sang. Neyah didn't even care who heard her monkey voice.

After school, the two friends strolled home together with Malaika's sister, Saida, close behind. "I do not know if I passed my math test," Malaika said.

"I bet you did fine."

"I would sure like to test into the next grade!" exclaimed Malaika.

Hoping for the same, Neyah considered what she needed to accomplish before medical school. First, she needed to complete primary grades, then sit for required exams, and with luck, advance to secondary school.

Several meters ahead of them, Neyah's brothers kicked their new soccer ball back and forth. "Here it comes!" Paul called out as he kicked it to Neyah.

She returned it with a strong kick.

"Good one!" shouted Paul.

Neyah swallowed a smile as she watched her brothers. She was proud of them but envied them too, for she knew their chance of advancing beyond primary school far exceeded hers.

Malaika's excited voice interrupted Neyah's thoughts. "I almost forgot! In a few days, I start walking to the river because our donkey carrier raised his price. Mama wants me to walk with you."

Neyah jumped up and down and hugged Malaika. "I have missed you on the trail. Will you tell me all about your visit to your Bibi?"

Malaika's eyes squinted in amusement. "Of course! See you at sunrise in three days." Malaika waved as she and her sister turned toward the ravine and home.

NEYAH HUMMED as she scooped corn flour into a burlap storage bag.

"You are in good spirits these days, my daughter."

"Yes. I love going to school two days every week."

"Mmm." Mama cooed as she rocked with the rhythm of her grinding stone. "Talk to me about school. What lesson have you studied lately?"

Neyah gave her a puzzling glance. Mama seldom showed interest in her lessons. "We are reading about Lake Victoria. Did you know it is the biggest lake in Africa, Mama?"

"Is that so? I have heard of it. Tell me more."

Setting her bag down and gazing dreamily toward the plains, Neyah spoke. "Mama, lakes are like huge water holes. They do not ever dry up. And Lake Victoria is a freshwater lake, and you know what else? It borders Kenya! I think it would be great to live by Lake Victoria!"

Neyah ran to Mama and took her by the shoulders. "Mama! Do you want to see it? Promise to go with me someday!"

Mama stopped grinding and tried not to look shocked at all the chatter from Neyah. Laughing, she returned to grinding. "Why not! You and I could jump into that lake and have a good bath."

"Yes! And we can take a boat and cross it to see who lives on the other side!"

"Maybe some cousins we do not know or wild animals who will want to eat us!" giggled Mama.

Sitting in her usual spot, Bibi worked on her beading and listened to her granddaughter bubble with conversation.

"Think what we could do with our time, Mama, if we had a huge lake right next to us?"

Mama's smile faded as if someone had snuck in and erased it.

Neyah changed the subject and helped Mama tie off the flour sack.

"Guess what, Mama! Malaika is soon going to walk with me to the river."

"Ahh! No wonder you are in high spirits! Remember there will be three of you. Keep your distance so if one slips, you do not all go tumbling."

"We will," Neyah smiled. "Did you know Malaika's grandmother has a pipe that comes right into her house and when she turns a handle, water comes running out?"

"Nonsense!"

"Mama, Malaika saw it. And her city water is a different color than ours! And guess what else?"

Mama and Bibi both giggled to hear Neyah talk so enthusiastically.

"Malaika told me the water runs into a big bowl she sits in to bathe."

Mama placed her hands on her hips. "I believe things I see, and I have never seen that yet. Hand me more corn."

"Let me see it for you, Mama. Malaika asked me to go to her Bibi's. I can see her pipes and bathing bowl and bring you water in a gourd."

Mama wrinkled up her forehead as she picked up a broom and began sweeping up the corn husks. "If you can bring back a week of water in your gourd, yes. Since that is not possible, I need you here to fetch water, not be off wasting time in the city gawking at miracle water."

Relaxing her shoulders, Mama smiled at the excitement in her daughter's eyes. "Neyah, I cannot remember when I have heard you talk this much!"

Pointing to the empty jerry can, Mama continued. "And I hate to break the mood, but you need to go to the dam alone today. Nilsa has chores and Bibi and Papa need me here."

The moment of dreaming and hoping had passed. "Yes, Mama," mumbled Neyah as she took over the sweeping to give Mama time to water the cattle. "I wish you did not have to work so hard."

Mama waved her arm in response as she picked up a bucket.

PAPA WAS sleepy but had heard every word of the cheerful conversation between Mama and Neyah from his hut. His daughter's energy and interests made him wonder how he might take advantage of it. Mama wanted her to be a doctor. But she could bring a handsome bride price, for sure. If he waited until she was a doctor to offer Neyah as a bride, might she be considered too old to be a second wife?

In his head, Papa listed reasons his cousin's neighbor, Silas, or any number of other men might need a wife like Neyah. She was a smart, strong girl who worked hard and quickly. Unlike most young girls, she didn't say much. Perhaps this would be an attractive trait to many men.

What would Neyah be like as a mother? It was obvious that her care for her brothers came naturally. It would be a loss to them to see their sister go.

For a moment, Papa had a frightening thought. He sucked in a breath. *What if I die? If Neyah becomes someone else's property, someone else's wife, who will help my wife, my mother, my four sons?*

Papa's head throbbed. It didn't block out the humming he could hear from Bibi and Neyah just beyond his hut.

20

MAMA MAKES A DECISION

B osco watched Mama pace in the family compound.
"I knew better than to let Neyah walk alone on that trail," Mama said.

Mama scolding herself wasn't going to help find Neyah.

"I will check the trail again," insisted Mama.

"Mama! You have gone at least ten times already."

Bibi sat wringing her hands and mumbling prayers.

"Bosco," Mama urged, "hurry and get your cousin, Kanono. He can help you find your sister." Her strained voice struggled to maintain control.

"Yes, Mama."

But Bosco didn't need Kanono. He knew Neyah wasn't on the river path. He had checked behind the huts; the missing well bucket told him exactly where his sister was. Bosco set off at a run with the worst on his mind. Neyah should've been back hours ago if she'd fetched at the open well. Mama would go crazy if something happened to Neyah, especially at the same place where Lulu died.

Two women sat weaving baskets near the well when Bosco arrived breathing heavy. Neither had seen Neyah. He peered into the dark pit. His stomach lurched at the thought of her falling in.

"Dry for two weeks," one of the women mumbled.

Bosco vacantly looked around. His chest tightened. This is where Lulu died.

Bosco shook his head to clear his thinking. Did Neyah go to the river after finding this well dry? If so, Mama was right. Neyah would be home by now. But she wasn't. Did she fall on the cliff? Get kidnapped?

Hurrying toward home like a madman, Bosco tripped on loose rock. Wincing at the pain in his twisted ankle, he took a minute to sit and massage it and think about Neyah having to fetch water on these uneven, dangerous paths. He pounded his fist against his thigh and sputtered his thoughts aloud. "I should be helping her fetch!"

As Bosco rubbed his ankle, he heard a familiar gurgling sound. He cautiously stood to test the strength of his injured ankle before limping around a circle of bushes. The gurgling sound came from his snoring sister sound asleep against a boulder.

"Neyah! Wake up. WAKE UP!" Shaking her, he shouted in exasperation. "What are you doing? Mama is worried sick about you!"

Neyah sat up startled and confused.

"Bosco," Neyah moaned. "I-I-I feel so tired for some reason."

"I do not care. We need to get home and somehow hide those buckets from Mama. Come on! And start thinking of an excuse why you have no water."

NEYAH TOLD Mama most of the truth. "I am sorry Mama. I did not feel good and fell asleep on the side of the trail."

Too distraught over Papa and relieved to see Neyah, Mama only sighed. "I am happy you are safe. As for water, we will ask Uncle Aman for some."

Papa no longer felt strong enough to sit on the bench for meals. His sunken eyes filled with yellowish matter and his dry mahogany skin sagged on a thinning frame. With increasing trips to the toilet, Papa needed both Bosco and Mama to assist him.

When the traveling doctor finally arrived, he turned his sympathetic eyes to Mama. "It is cholera."

Mama showed no sign of surprise.

"This causes diarrhea," the doctor explained. "Give him these salt pills four times a day. Feed him bananas. Keep your children away."

"Then he will get better?"

Neyah listened outside the hut, crushed to hear Mama wailing.

"I cannot promise anything. He is extremely dehydrated and needed medical attention sooner."

Mama's grief grew to rage. "Sooner! Who could come and give my beloved husband help sooner? Letsokoane has no clinic, no doctor. There is one doctor for 300,000 people in this region. It is like...like feeding an elephant herd with one peanut."

The doctor's words and Mama's outburst hit Neyah like a fist to her middle. She longed for Papa to hold her and tell her everything will be fine. But he still refused to see her.

Neyah inched closer to his hut and strained to see some evidence of her father through the entrance. Was there anything left of him? Bones, flesh, or even love for her?

Bibi motioned Neyah over. She laid her head on her grandmother's lap and began to sob. Her mind squeezed out questions. "Bibi, how will we survive if Papa dies? Who will work the crops and handle the cattle?"

"No need to worry about something that has not happened."

Bibi's comments didn't help. Mama was already taking over much of Papa's work. Neyah could see the toll it was taking on her. Mama couldn't do it alone forever. Neyah knew what would happen. She'd be forced to drop out of school. She knew children who quit school when a parent died. How would she ever become a doctor without school?

Another sickening possibility swept through her. "Bibi, if Papa becomes desperate for crops and food, will he sell me?"

Bibi's hands stopped pulling beads onto her wire and sat still for a moment before shaking her head. Neyah read doubt in Bibi's hesitation. Other girls her age stopped going to school because they got married off to someone twice their age in exchange for cattle. She knew of two girls who were second wives to married men. Some fathers even sold daughters to pay for their sons' school expenses.

Recalling Mr. Sahli's advice, Neyah took her grandmother's hands in hers. "I will not give up, Bibi."

After the doctor left, Neyah scraped corn kernels off the cob and mixed them with beans Mama picked. As she worked, she wondered if Papa would get better, or if she could escape being sold as a wife.

"Mama, this is the first nyoyo you have cooked in months. I thought beans were only for trading."

"The nyoyo is for Papa."

Neyah gripped the bowl and locked eyes with Mama. "Why?"

Before Mama could look away, Neyah saw the sadness filling her mother's eyes.

Neyah felt a rush of weakness race through her body. *Is Papa dying? Is Mama giving him one last good meal?*

Neyah set her clay bowl down and began pouring water from her jerry can. She strained water several times through a thin towel.

Mama's forehead furrowed. "What are you doing?"

She held up the towel for Mama to see. "Filtering dirt out." Between each pour, Neyah rinsed the dirt from the towel.

Mama watched in silence with hands on her hips.

Next Neyah boiled the filtered water for tea. As she counted to sixty, she saw Mama open her mouth to say something. Neyah braced herself.

Silence burned between mother and daughter.

Finally, Mama spoke. Her voice sounded surprisingly calm. "Let me know when Papa's nyoyo and tea are ready. I will bring it to him."

Neyah released a choked sigh. "Yes, Mama. Yes. Asante."

Neyah boiled water morning and night. Mama used it for Papa's food and tea. Neyah felt more hopeful about Papa's condition knowing Mama was on her side. And yet, each time Mama emerged from Papa's hut, Neyah held her breath, expecting the worst.

By day, Neyah's stomach felt like a twisted branch; by night, she found herself in the arms of a nightmare, tumbling down cliffs into muddy water only to pick her shriveled Papa out of the mud with a stick. Neyah fought her fears and exhaustion through a vigilant effort of boiling and requiring her family to wash hands often.

After two days of boiling, Mama stared into an empty jerry can. The chickens huddled around her feet hoping for a drink.

"When you boil water, Neyah, much disappears. And all this hand washing! Either you fetch more water, or we cut back somewhere."

Sounding like an adult instead of a ten-year-old, Bosco spoke up. "How can we cut back? The milking cows will fall over if they do not have water. They need water to produce milk, and we need their milk. I will help fetch water."

Neyah's eyes sparkled with emotion. She wanted to hug her brother.

Mama studied her daughter with sad eyes. When she shook her head at Bosco, the sparkle in Neyah's eyes turned dark with fear. The moment she'd dreaded was here. She felt it coming like a dust storm you can't outrun. *This is when Mama tells me I need to quit school.* Her knees went limp.

Lifting her eyes skyward, as though looking for guidance, Mama spoke. "You will only boil water for Papa, and..."

Neyah held her breath.

"...Uncle Aman will take another donkey to the river for us."

Bosco threw his hands in the air. "How will we pay for another donkey?"

"We will not have to. Papa helped Uncle Aman put his crop in when he lost his wife. He remembers."

Relieved, Neyah squeezed her mother's arms. "Asante, Mama! Asante!"

Neyah couldn't help but wonder if Mama's heart and eyes were finally opening to the possibilities of things unseen.

Maybe Letsokoane housed more than one dreamer.

21

ABBY'S NEWS

Neyah settled onto her mat and reread the letter Bosco brought home. Life was far different in Abby's world and yet it seemed challenges arose no matter where one lived.

Dear Neyah,

What's new in Kenya? How is your father?

Here's what's new in Minnesota-I persuaded my Dad to take me to see Jazzy today. That horse loves carrots! And the Justin Bieber concert-it literally rocked! Mom and Jada went, too. We ended up leaving before it ended because the music made my head feel like it was going to explode. ☹

The other new thing is bad. I have a tumor. In my BRAIN of all places. The doctor says I need to take medicine that makes me puke, but he claims it will get rid of the tumor and my headache. At least I don't need glasses. And you're right. Isaac should care about my heart more than my face! Thank you for reminding me of the important things.

Mom says lights off, but I want to tell you two more things! First, I finished my parents' painting of the lake and was sneaky about inviting Dad over so we could give it to them together. Andrew helped me lean it against the shed. Mom happy cried when she saw it, and Dad hugged her! When she was all done crying, Mom said, "I suppose we should have a picnic by this 'lake' like we did 18 years ago!" And they would have, except it's freezing cold here, so they had their picnic in our house. I even saw them kiss! Success!

Second-regarding your water problem. Mr. Simon and I came up with an idea to teach kids in my school about water problems in other parts of the world and discuss what we can do to help. I'm FULL of ideas, he says. This stupid tumor better not stop me from my great ideas!!

For your journal: <u>Sleepover</u>-when your friends come and stay overnight with you. But not much sleep happens! Ha! Probably the name should be changed!

Sorry, this part is messy. My hand is a little shaky lately, and I'm writing with the light from my phone so Mom doesn't get mad!

Your turn!

YOUR rafiki ☺Abby

P.S. Remember when I told you Andrew was a pain? Not so much anymore! I bet your brothers help you too. Here's to great brothers!

Malaika's skirt flapped like a welcome flag as Neyah and her cousin neared the cutoff.

"Jambo, Nilsa!" Malaika shouted from 100 meters away. "Jambo, Neyah!"

Her best friend's greeting and beautiful skirt breathed fresh energy into Neyah's trip.

"She is too loud," whispered Nilsa.

Neyah giggled. "Yes. Maybe you can remind her to be quiet."

Nilsa ran ahead. "Neyah says to tell you to be quiet."

Malaika gave her a guilty smile. "Sorry, you are right."

Nilsa reached to touch Malaika's skirt. "This is the prettiest skirt."

"Thank you! It is a new one from my grandmother."

Neyah touched the skirt. "What kind of flowers are these?"

"Poinsettias. Bibi knows red is my favorite color."

Neyah grinned. Seeing Malaika's new clothes felt almost as good as having them herself.

Treading briskly along the path, Malaika talked about her visit to her grandmother's city. "The markets are exploding with juicy fruit samples, fish of every size, and children riding shiny bicycles with flowers flowing from baskets."

"Did you take a bath in the big water pot?"

Malaika giggled. "You mean the tub?"

The English word *tub* sounded funny to the girls' ears, and soon all three laughed uncontrollably, momentarily forgetting about the need to be quiet.

Their conversation came to a halt when they reached the cliff. The three girls focused on each rock, each potential hazard. Malaika hadn't made this trip for nearly a year.

"My legs feel shaky. I need four legs like those donkeys."

Somewhere between a squeal and a grunt came the unmistaken sound of a warthog. The girls made every attempt to back away from the hideous growling snort but climbing backward on steep, rocky terrain proved risky.

The ribs of the mud-caked pig showed. His eyes reflected weariness and hunger. However, his tusks spoke another language.

"Give him some food." Nilsa sounded desperate.

"No!" whispered Neyah. "He will only want more. Follow me."

Neyah led them through bristly bushes and away from the

warthog. Malaika watched to ensure the beast didn't follow. His loud grunts faded away as they descended.

Relieved, the girls reached the river and dipped their hands into the swift-moving water for a drink.

Malaika spread her cornbread out on her skirt. "I forgot how hard this walk is."

"Wait until you have to lug the water back up," sighed Nilsa. "I wish there were no hills in Africa, only flat land like on the Serengeti."

"Nilsa, you would never survive walking those plains. If a lion did not eat you alive, the hippos would. Or the cheetahs or the..."

"I get your point!" laughed Nilsa. "But some of those animals hang out around here too. This is why we all wear these whistles around our neck!"

Neyah's family didn't own a whistle. She wondered if a whistle would actually scare a wild beast away.

"Your skirt is like a flower garden, Malaika," said Nilsa. "Where do those pintos flowers grow?"

"Not pintos!" Malaika giggled. "They are poinsettias!"

"Sorry! Poinsettias."

"Hmm...not sure where they grow. But someday I will grow them and set them on Bibi's piano when I play it."

The young girls flooded their water cans and started their climb, leaving a few meters of separation between them. Neyah led the way with Nilsa behind her, followed by Malaika. With water containers strapped to their backs with hemp rope, their arms were free for balance and to catch themselves if necessary. Every ounce of energy was centered on delivering their precious commodity to home. The sounds of heavy breathing, occasional grunts, and crunching rock beneath their purposeful steps eventually brought them up out of the riverbed onto flat land, only to be met by another challenge.

"Vaaaaaah!"

The unexpected noise caused the girls to gasp in unison.

A bandit!

A short troll-looking man with open blisters on the right side of his face staggered before them.

Neyah froze. The man glared at her as his body leaned forward on a willowy cane. She noticed how loose his ragged clothing hung. He wore a ripped scarf of filth around his neck.

"Vaaaaaah!" A fit of coughing followed his second guttural command causing him to sway.

"Is he going to hurt us?" Nilsa whimpered.

Shaking her head, Neyah's heart pounded. Based on his condition, she doubted this feeble man was capable of attacking them, but still...

As Malaika began to ask if he needed help, the man croaked a frightening demand.

"Giveittome." It came out as one word.

Neyah instinctively reached behind her to protect her jerry can. *He wanted their water!* Her eyes darted around to see if he was alone.

Malaika muttered a soft but stern command. "Do not do it."

Neyah found her voice. "Our families need this water. My father is sick and needs it or he will die."

"UH." The man grunted. He coughed some more and spit into the rocks.

"Giveittome!" His second demand grew angry, and he began hobbling toward them.

"Nilsa, get behind me." Malaika scooted past Nilsa and made it to Neyah's side before the man got to her.

"You look thirsty," Malaika spoke tenderly. "We will share. Open your flask."

He suspiciously eyed Malaika. He shook his head back and forth in protest.

"We have water," Malaika explained. "For you."

The little man slowing began to open his dirty flask made of goatskin. Neyah helped Malaika get her jerry can off her back. The frail man held his flask while Malaika tipped her can and carefully filled his worn vessel.

This man is no bandit, thought Neyah. She noted his raspy breathing. It sounded painful. And he really stunk. His body looked old and sick and thirsty.

The girls watched in silence as he guzzled the water. After he finished, his heavy breathing relaxed some.

"More?"

"UH."

Malaika took it as a yes. She filled his flask again.

Touched by Malaika's kindness, Neyah surveyed the man. He wore sandals too big for his feet. Flies crawled on his open hand sores. Neyah knew this man would never be able to carry their forty-pound water can.

"We come this way often." Malaika gently spoke to him as if he were an old friend. "Watch for us. We will give you a drink."

His vacant stare made it difficult to read. Matter dripped from one eye.

Neyah and Nilsa helped Malaika strap her water can back on.

"Save some of your water for later now," Malaika advised.

Taking note of his location, Neyah walked around the man and never looked back.

Nilsa whimpered most of the way home. When they reached Malaika's path, Neyah held Nilsa by the shoulders. "Nilsa, you are done crying. You do not want your papa to worry. That little man is not dangerous. He just needed our help."

"But he scared me. I am like that. I get scared."

Neyah hugged her cousin. "We are almost home."

She hugged Malaika too and whispered, "You are brave. I am glad we are all together today."

"Me too."

"See you in school tomorrow."

"Yes," replied Malaika. "We have our math test! I stink at math."

Neyah laughed. "But you are brave!"

2 2

PAPA'S PLAN

Maybe the pills from the doctor helped. Or the water Neyah boiled for his tea. Perhaps Bibi's prayers cured him. In less than two weeks, Papa's fever dropped, and his eyes began to clear. Although he still appeared paper-thin and weak, Papa's appetite grew. With assistance, he made it onto the bench for dinners.

However, Neyah hadn't been invited back to family dinners. She watched from her hut as her brothers danced around the meal mat to celebrate Papa's improved health.

Hassan exclaimed, "Papa! We can finally sit on your lap again." The twins jockeyed for a spot on his bony legs.

"Maybe you two should sit beside me until my legs grow back."

The twin boys giggled. "Legs cannot grow back, Papa!" squealed Hassan.

"No, but if your sister keeps boiling bad things from my tea water, I may have strong legs again in no time!"

Neyah could not believe her ears.

Papa knew she boiled water? Did Mama tell him? Or maybe that big mouth Bosco said something.

Neyah shrunk into her hut, confused. Papa sounded pleased, even happy about the boiled water. She listened anxiously. Her entire family was eating and laughing and celebrating—without her.

Leaving her dinner behind, Neyah slipped behind her family compound and breathed in the evening air. The crescent moon peeking through the root-like branches of the baobab momentarily lifted her spirits. Bibi's advice to ask for the moon lingered on her mind like dust on her feet.

With the lively chirp of crickets surrounding her, Neyah pressed her weight against the tree and sunk to the ground. Holding her head in her hands, she allowed the relief of Papa's recovery and grief from his abandonment wash over her. Tears sprung first, then sobs wracked her body.

"The doctor stopped by again yesterday."

Startled by Papa's voice, Neyah sucked in air.

"Mr. Sahli came too."

Neyah froze. Mr. Sahli came to see her father again?

She braced herself for Papa's scolding–or worse.

"They said you were right. Boil water. Wash hands." He sounded calm.

Neyah's shoulders relaxed. *Maybe it was like Mr. Sahli said. Papa needed time.*

She wiped her drippy nose on her sleeve and lifted her head enough to see Papa's feet.

"Hassan told me," Papa said. "He said you have boiled water for some time. For me."

Little Hassan told Papa?

"And Mama told me something I never thought I would hear from her. She said we must try believing in things we cannot see, like germs on our hands and in our water. According to Mr. Sahli, the nasty little bugs are too tiny to see."

As Papa touched Neyah's head, she flinched.

"Stand up."

Neyah hesitated but finally did as he said. She lifted her tear-stained face to Papa.

"I thought for sure I would be gone by now. Although I am not completely healed yet, I believe there might be something to this water boiling."

Quivering with emotion, Papa spoke his daughter's name aloud for the first time in months. "Neyah."

This is it, thought Neyah. *Papa's love: my moon, the thing I need. I will ask for it!*

She fell into Papa's arms. "Oh Papa, I am glad you are better. I have been afraid. Hold me. Please hold me."

Her embrace nearly knocked his feeble body over. As Neyah steadied Papa, his emaciated hands grasped both sides of her head. He tightened his grip and gave her a shake. At first, she thought a seizure gripped him. But his words erased all doubt.

Papa's stern voice spit out his words, "It may not be right to strike my child, but it is *never* right to disobey your papa. There will be consequences."

Neyah stumbled to her hut in shock and collapsed onto her mat. She curled her trembling body into a ball. *Why would Papa say such an awful thing to me?*

"What happened, my child?" Bibi sensed awfulness.

Neyah choked on her answer. "I did what you said. I asked for the moon."

HOPING NEYAH WAS ASLEEP, Bibi lay on her mat listening to Papa argue with Mama.

"It is time to buy another pair of field cows, Sara."

"Nonsense, Haji. I do the fieldwork and can barely handle

the ones we have."

Papa grew louder. "I am stronger and can run one, and you, the other. More goats for our herd will help too."

"Help?" Mama didn't hide her frustration. "It is the dry season. Where will we find water and grass for more cattle? Your head is still sick. You talk crazy."

"There is water out there."

"Yes. But who has to find it? Who has to carry it? If Neyah goes, who is left to help me fetch?"

Ignoring her question and logic, Papa continued. "I know a man, a good man. Silas." Papa sounded winded. "He has cattle I need. He wants another wife. It will be a good trade."

"Haji, you would trade your only daughter for animals you are too sick to care for?"

"Sara, you know how this works. Your own Papa traded you for a team of cows."

"At fifteen, not twelve years. And Neyah is not me. She is not like other girls who do what has always been done."

"She will turn thirteen in a few weeks. It is time she learns. I made the arrangements. She and her selfish dreams will be gone in six months."

If Bibi's legs and eyes worked, she would have gone to her son and reminded him what crushed dreams would do to the soul.

If Neyah wasn't so shocked at the words she was hearing, she might have cried herself to sleep.

23

RUN OR STAY

Dear Abby,

I wish to share two things 1 Papa is better 2 Papa is not my papa anymore because a Papa be kind Mine no longer kind You lucky your papa be kind and not make plan to trade you for cows and goats A man will come and take me for wife At first I want to run but now I know my purpose is to stay and persuade Do you know the word persuade

I have new questions What is your tumor Is it a worm crawling in brain You find good doctor I am happy you get medicine to wash tumor out We have no hospital or clinic or doctors in Letsokoane I see your heart full of love for your Mama and Papa Soon your papa he come home I know this for you My Bibi tell me to ask for moon if I need something Asking did not work for me but maybe for you it work to ask your Mama and Papa to be family again What be your good idea for my water problem I am thinking of one also Your turn.

Your Friend Neyah

PS Why does your telephone have light

Neyah loved clean pages. They reminded her of a new day, a new beginning. A chance to start over. She sat on her school bench and wrote neatly on her next clean journal page.

Persuade (*verb*) cause someone to do something through reasoning or argument.

She whispered it. "Persuade."

Devison cast a questioning glance her way.

Neyah repeated it and sketched a girl standing in front of a crowd. Over the girl's head, she wrote: *Say something.*

Energy ran through Neyah, startling her. She dropped her pencil and stared at her hands. Strong. Focused. Undeniable. Touching her lips with her fingertips and sliding one hand to her neck, she whispered to herself, "Say something."

Trembling with excitement, Neyah leaned toward Devison. "I am not running."

Devison scrunched his forehead as if asking, "What in the world are you talking about?"

"I will speak and boil water every chance I get! And find a way to get clean water to our village!"

Speechless, Devison could only stare at Neyah. She had never spoke directly to him before.

Neyah clutched the edge of her bench with curled fingers. Initially, she felt an urge to escape when she heard Papa's plan to trade her for cattle. She knew running served no purpose, and where would she run? Staring at the other girls writing in their journals, she saw another reason to stay. Running wouldn't help any of them. She'd stay and say something for all girls who fetched.

Devison handed her a piece of paper he'd written on. *WHY?*

She flipped the paper over. When he got it back, he smiled at what she'd written. *So I can change the world the way I know you will.*

Neyah knew her quest for clean water held a huge risk. Papa's life might be saved, but what about saving his love for her? If she disobeyed him again, would he sell her immediately? If she became a man's property, where would her dream of becoming a doctor go? And who would bring clean water to Letsokoane?

Mr. Sahli's booming voice interrupted her dilemma.

"A persuasive essay is a writing used to convince the reader about a certain issue you hold an opinion on. Today we hear from Moswen."

Moswen hopped up and strode to the front of the room carrying his paper. His poor reading skills challenged his confident attitude as he struggled to read his own words. "I am... writing to...writing to p-persuade our good teacher for...NO... MORE HOMEWORK!" Moswen snuck a glance at Mr. Sahli to gauge his reaction. Seeing nothing, he continued reading through to the end.

Everyone clapped including Mr. Sahli. "Good job finishing your assignment, Moswen. However, I still plan to give homework."

"Aww, Mr. Sahli, why did I write this if you will not take my suggestion?"

"Moswen, perhaps you did not persuade me about the value of no homework."

Moswen groaned.

"Students, you're writing persuasive essays because stating what you believe carries power. To persuade or convince others to believe the way you do is an important life tool to bring justice. But your reasoning must not be selfish or mean, or show you are lazy. When you're searching for someone to join you in a cause to benefit others, a person is more likely to be open, and help you take action, if they're convinced it's going to improve lives."

Mr. Sahli looked toward Neyah. Her heart began to race.

He is going to ask me to read mine.

"Devison, you're next."

Neyah exhaled. The thought of talking in front of the class made her stomach churn and her mouth feel like dry cornmeal. She desperately wanted to overcome this fear but, for now, she'd rather do anything else—even fetch water.

Devison snuck a glance at Neyah as he sprang from his bench. "Yes sir, Mr. Sahli."

Neyah started to sweat. *Why on earth does he keep looking at me?*

With perfect posture, Devi positioned himself at the front of the room.

Neyah was sure Devi's essay would be boring. His favorite friend, it seemed, was the hydrogen atom.

"Go ahead, Devison," urged Mr. Sahli.

"My persuasive speech is about..."

Devi's eyes roamed the ceiling before settling on the floor.

Neyah didn't expect Devi's hesitation. *He looks the way I feel when I am forced to talk*, Neyah thought.

He started again. "I would like to persuade Malaika to be my girlfriend."

What? Neyah's jaw dropped open. She turned to Malaika who looked as though she'd just witnessed her own death.

Neyah snuck a peek at Mr. Sahli. His expression twisted halfway between a grin and shock. Neyah pretty much knew what Mr. Sahli was thinking. The Devison everyone knew might try to persuade him to get more history books or persuade the world to research the causes of some rare disease. Not persuade someone to be his girlfriend!

Devison glanced at Malaika and twisted his hands together. "She is smart, and I think I would be a good boyfriend because I am smart too." He gave a shrug and returned to his bench.

Neyah couldn't believe it. *That's it?*

Moswen started it. An explosive, choking laugh. Contagious as cholera itself, laughter and snorts spread to everyone, except Malaika. Mr. Sahli smothered a smile.

Malaika's eyebrows arched, as she covered her face with her hands. Then her arm shot up.

Mr. Sahli tried to quiet the chaos. "Class, we have a comment. Malaika?"

The room faded to silence. To everyone's surprise, Malaika smiled at Devison. "Devi, you were not exactly persuasive, but maybe I would like to be your girlfriend. Someday."

It took a few seconds. Nathaniel started with a slow and quiet rhythmic applause; others joined in until the whole room thundered.

Devison blew out a long breath. "One more thing." He jumped back up. "I first picked Neyah because she has big plans like me, but she is shy and seldom talks. You know me. I need a girlfriend who talks."

Why did I come to school today? Neyah hid her face in her arms.

"I think it's time for our morning tea and exercise break," Mr. Sahli announced. "Your math tests are corrected, and we'll go over them when we return."

24

ALMOST A PERFECT DAY

"I cannot believe I passed! I passed my math test!" Malaika shrieked into the early morning wind with as quiet a voice as she could muster.

She and Neyah ambled along the dark, dusty path to the river without Nilsa, who stayed home with a sick stomach.

"Malaika, you are smarter than you think. If you studied, you would outsmart your 'someday' boyfriend."

Malaika giggled at Neyah's teasing. "Studying is boring. I would rather make things with my hands instead of my head. That is why I cook and weave, and someday I will play the piano!"

"My pen pal plays the violin," Neyah said.

"A violin? I have seen one of those in a concert Bibi took me to. What else does Abby do?"

"She likes to draw and ride horses and talk. And there is a tumor in her head. Do you know what that is?"

"No."

"It makes her sick. Her head hurts, and she has trouble seeing."

"That sounds bad."

In the dim, predawn African light, Neyah motioned to the lone tree. "I wonder what makes that tree grow better than anything else out here?"

"Maybe someone is feeding it," giggled Malaika, "which reminds me." Pulling a folded banana leaf from her front pocket, she unrolled a thin piece of bread. "Hungry?"

"Always!"

"I fried this flatbread using maize and bananas."

"Where did you get bananas?"

"Mama gets them from the market. She wants to grow a big grove of banana trees, but the land here is too dry."

Neyah loved testing Malaika's cooking experiments. This one felt gritty and tasted sweet. "Mmm...not bad. Maybe if I ate another chunk, I can tell if it is any good."

Malaika coughed as she adjusted her neck scarf. "You can test it again at the river. We need to get out of this dust storm!"

Once the dusty gale fell behind them, the two friends softly sang the Do Re Me song Mr. Sahli taught them in English.

"Malaika, why do you always wear your new skirt to fetch? It will get ruined."

"You sound like Mama! Bibi told me if I do not wear it now, I will grow out of it without enjoying it."

"You could save it for something special."

"Like what?" Malaika asked. "Bibi says every day is special, so I am wearing it!"

"Your Bibi needs to talk to my Bibi. Mine is always telling me to be patient. But I do not want to wait and watch my life run by."

"That is right," said Malaika. "You and me—we are not waiting for anything. We are going to do things now!" She shook hands with her friend.

"Neyah, do you want to wear my poinsettia skirt to school tomorrow?"

"Yes! But I need to ask Mama. She insists I wear my uniform."

Malaika's generous offer created a giddiness in Neyah's step. Even if Mama didn't agree to let her wear it, she could at least try it on!

The girls continued to sing as the sun spilled over the horizon to announce a new day.

As they passed the area where they'd met the thirsty man, Neyah looked around.

Malaika turned to Neyah with a knowing look. "We have not seen that little man lately."

Neyah nodded. "I wonder if anyone is helping him find water and food. Papa would be dead if we did not help him." She sighed. "Of course, it seems the part I loved about him died anyway."

Malaika stopped and touched her friend's arm. Her own father died of malaria. It upset her to learn of Neyah's Papa's threats. "I am not letting your papa sell you. And, guess what? You would make a terrible wife, anyway."

Neyah laughed. "I think you are right!"

After a silent but grueling climb down to the river's edge, the two friends rested. The crowd at the river swelled larger than usual. Downstream, elephants from the reserve cooled off as they drank. Donkeys, long-legged birds, and cattle lined the opposite bank.

Malaika handed Neyah another corner of her maize-banana bread.

"Why did you mix maize and bananas?"

"I saw monkeys do it."

"What?" Neyah giggled.

Malaika giggled back. "I saw the Sykes monkeys around our huts dip our banana peels into the spilled maize."

"What else do you add that monkeys eat?" teased Neyah.

"Bugs and beetles. Leaves. Bark."

Both girls laughed and took turns naming things.

"Science experiments."

"Poinsettias."

"Devil!"

Giggling, Neyah dug into her pocket. "Do you want to read my new letter from Abby?"

"Sure!"

Dear Neyah,

I forgot to say thank you for drawing a picture of yourself. I pinned it to my bulletin board.

A tumor is a nasty blob that grows and mine is pressing against my brain and optic nerve causing my eye problems and headaches. The medicine affects my stomach and food tastes terrible. And major bummer-we can't go to Hawaii because of my treatments. The worst part-my hair fell out! At first I cried, but then I looked at your picture and a cool thing happened-I realized I look a little more like you-except I'm completely bald!

And fantastic news! Purpose #1 accomplished! Dad moved back home after his "anniversary picnic" with mom. He and Mom look SO happy! I think it was my painting that clinched the deal . And your advice to ASK FOR THE MOON! I asked them what the most important thing was, and that got them thinking! Dad said our family is a team, and we all needed each other. He's SO right. He's doing some free-lance photography jobs now. It's awesome to have my Dad back!! I especially like it when he rubs my bare head and reads my homework to me. So thank you SO much for that ask for the moon tip!

Speaking of Dads, there's no way your papa stopped loving someone like you. I bet he's thinking it's hard to see you grow up. You keep on boiling that water. It's probably what saved him!

I'll always be your second-best rafiki!

Abby.

P.S. Are you getting braver to talk to people? Practice in front of a mirror! Someday you'll be a great speaker with super ideas, and everyone will want you to run for president!

P.P.S. And again, WHAT!? No doctors and stuff! I am a DIY kid, and I'm starting with this bucket I found in our basement. I painted it bright yellow! Mr. Simon and I talked to the student council about sponsoring a fundraiser. We got more buckets, painted them, and set them all over my school and even at businesses to raise awareness for communities like yours. The next time I write, I bet they'll be overflowing with donations-maybe someday it can be used for a well beside your house! Oh! And I drew a picture of you and me holding a bucket of water on all the buckets!

Your turn!

As Malaika read, Neyah ambled along the river's edge. She couldn't remember such a fine afternoon. Spending time with her best friend helped.

Malaika returned the letter to Neyah. "A tumor sounds bad. But it sounds like she is a generous friend."

Neyah nodded. "Abby is like you. Nothing stands in her way. In fact, I bet she would wear a new skirt to fetch water too!"

Malaika giggled. "With her yellow bucket! And it sounds like she has plenty of them!"

In a rare sullen moment, Malaika pointed across the water. "See all these animals, Neyah? If this river dries up, where will they go to drink? And where will we get water to fill our yellow buckets?"

"Malaika, I do not know how to get rid of the dry season, but if we could bring a well and pipes to our villages, we will not need to come to this river anymore! Write to your Bibi and ask her how to get pipes and a well. You and Abby and I are going to figure this out!"

Malaika smothered her with a hug, causing the two of them to topple into the tall grass. "I knew you would find your purpose Neyah Jabari!"

After taking a drink and filling their jerry cans, the girls began the steep ascent up the rocky terrain. Their callused feet held tight to their sandals as their eyes surveyed the path to avoid a dangerous fall. Bending forward to compensate for water weight, they crawled upward, grabbing onto rocks jutting from the cliff.

Malaika collapsed once she reached the flats. Between heavy breathing, she exclaimed. "We made it!"

After a short break, they trudged on under the merciless sun. Neyah squinted as her eyes swept the area where they met the little man before. She saw thorny bushes, rocks of all sizes, and two yellow masked weavers, but no thirsty man.

Pain shot through Neyah's foot. "Ah-oow!" She grimaced as she fell forward. The weight of the water thrust Neyah's container over her head causing the rope to snap. The jerry can skidded and came to a stop two meters away.

"Neyah!" Malaika slipped her weight off her back and dashed to her side. "Are you okay?"

Neyah cradled her right foot in both hands and rocked back and forth, gritting her teeth. A two-inch thorn pierced Neyah's thin-soled sandal and stuck in her heel.

"I need to pay better attention! I hate these thorny bushes. Pull it out!"

"It will bleed. Hold on."

Neyah squeezed her eyes shut as Malaika yanked.

Neyah yelped and tore her sandal off. Malaika began wrapping her scarf around Neyah's bloody foot.

"No, don't ruin your scarf."

Malaika shrugged and slipped Neyah's sandal over the scarf. "Your foot is more important than my scarf."

Neyah lifted her eyes to her friend. The sun's glare framed Malaika's face like a halo and caused her dark hair to glisten. As usual Malaika's hair lay parted and sectioned off like a perfectly planted cornfield. Each section held chunky plaits of braided hair. Her longer braids were drawn to the nape of her neck and cascaded down her back.

"Your name suits you, Malaika. You are an angel. Asante rafiki."

"Karibu."

"I took my eyes off the path to look over th—."

Malaika turned to see what startled Neyah.

The little man stood several meters away. This time he looked worse. Once again, he wore dusty torn clothes and oversized sandals. Even from a distance, the girls could see dried goo caked in his eyes. His pained, pinched face reflected his bent stance.

Malaika motioned him over, but he didn't or couldn't move. She carried her water to him. His flask was missing, so Malaika used the cover of her jerry can to give him several drinks. His left arm, hanging limp at his side, appeared small and deformed.

"What is your name?" Malaika didn't expect a reply and didn't receive one. After a few moments of silence, she stated, "We will call you Aden. That was my brother's name." Her nostalgic tone relaxed the worry on Aden's face.

Neyah remembered little Aden. Malaika's brother died from a hyena attack before his second birthday.

Malaika dug out the last hunk of her bread. "I made this for you." Aden grunted and snatched it with his good hand. He shoved it whole into his mouth and chewed noisily.

Neyah noticed his upper teeth were gone. She made a mental note to bring Aden some of Mama's soft bread next time.

After he picked crumbs from his beard and licked dirty fingers, he pointed beyond them and mumbled. "Bandits."

Alarmed, both girls jerked around, surveying for danger. Did they hear him right? When they glanced back, Aden was lumbering off.

25

BANDITS!

"Where is Aden going?"

"Maybe home," answered Neyah as she adjusted the repaired rope holding her water. "We need to get going."

Back on the trail, Malaika led the way. "How does your foot feel?"

"Fine. I can take your scarf off now."

"Leave it. I don't need it."

Neyah focused on the path. "I did not pay attention."

"Just an accident. Besides everybody steps on a thorn someti —hey, HEY!" Malaika's screams pulled Neyah's eyes upward.

Bandits! Aden was right. Neyah raced toward her friend as fast as a forty-pound load of water would allow.

A tall man pulled the tail of Malaika's hair.

"Ahhh! Leave me alone! What are you doing?"

"What is this?" The man's gruff voice sounded angry as he yanked Malaika toward him, winding her braids around his fingers. "You need to cover your head."

"Let her go!" Neyah's eyes darted around for something to strike him.

"Who lets you out without your head covered?" His words

were slurred like those of the village men when they drank bushberry wine.

"We do not need to cover our heads!" yelled Neyah.

"Liar!" shouted the tall man.

"Wait!" cried Neyah, "my friend—she has a headscarf!"

As Malaika struggled to break free, Neyah bent and hurriedly unwrapped the bloody scarf from her foot and held it for the men to see.

Neyah's words tumbled from her mouth. "I stepped on a thorn. She gave me her scarf to protect my foot." She reached forward. "She can cover her head now."

"G-g-get back!" The man staggered, pulling Malaika's head with him. "I am afraid we will have to teach your friend a lesson." He jerked Malaika back so roughly she nearly fell. The short man drew his rusty machete.

Malaika screamed. Neyah felt a weakness in her lower body. The forty pounds of water felt twice as heavy.

"No. Please." Neyah's voice shrank.

The tall bandit stretched the ends of Malaika's hair high and with one swift swing, the short man slashed off a clump of her braids. The tip of the machete nicked Malaika's neck sending blood trickling onto her blouse.

"Malaika!"

In one motion, Neyah slipped the water container off her back, swung it around to get an even grip on both sides, and lifted it as high as her arms would take it. The yellow jerry can crashed down on the tall man's head with a force strong enough to kill, knocking Malaika's chopped hair from his hand. He stumbled sideways and hit the rocky ground with a sickening thud. Neyah went for the machete, but the other bandit grabbed it first. His whiskered face inches from hers, she gagged at the strong stench of his breath.

"You just made a big mistake, little girl." He drew his

machete back and heaved it into the middle of Neyah's jerry can. Her water gushed out onto the injured man, mixing with strands of Malaika's shiny hair.

Now free, Malaika worked fast to pull the water off her back. She swung it high and with an angry grunt, slammed it into the short man's face. He fell backward into the thorny bushes.

"Malaika, are you all right?" Neyah's voice shook.

Malaika didn't answer. Loose strands of her chopped hair framed her small face in a frightening way. Hoisting her jerry can onto her shoulder, she gave an order. "Go!"

Neyah snatched the machete.

A hundred meters later, they heard footsteps and angry voices.

"Malaika, drop the water! We must run!"

"No! My family is out of water. And *we* have the knife."

The girls quickened their pace. Running for your life carrying a machete proved as difficult as running with a sloshy pack of water. Neyah's eyes darted back and forth searching for somewhere to hide, but the scarce vegetation offered no options. Within minutes the bandits caught up and demanded the machete.

"Leave us alone!" screamed Neyah, hoping someone nearby heard.

"Give us that knife and we will leave."

"They are lying. Do not do it," Malaika muttered as she wiped blood from her neck.

The men separated and closed in on each side of the girls. Malaika yanked the water can off her back once again and positioned it in front of her chest as a shield. Neyah grasped the machete with sweaty hands and thrust it toward the short man. He jumped back. She used Papa's machete to cut grain, never as a weapon. With shaky arms, she jabbed the blade forward again, this time catching his shoulder. The bandit yelped and covered his wound.

"You will pay for that!" Red splotches leaked through his dusty shirt.

Suddenly both men charged. The tall man snatched Malaika's water can and tossed it aside. The cover popped and water gushed onto the dust.

"NO!" Malaika attempted to retrieve it. Strong hands caught her shoulders and tossed her to the ground.

"Ahhh!" Malaika's screams shifted Neyah's attention to her friend, giving the short bandit time to slap the machete from her. He wrenched Neyah's arm, twisting it across her back and wrapping his other arm tight around her jaw. Neyah sank her teeth into his forearm. Pain from the bite temporarily loosened his grip on her chin, but he still held her other arm.

"My family needs that water!" yelled Malaika.

The tall bandit growled and straddled Malaika's small body. "Here is your stinkin' water." He picked up the water can and dumped the remaining water on Malaika's face leaving her sputtering. Grabbing both sides of her skirt, he yanked it off. Using her arms to brace herself, Malaika managed to lift both her legs and kick the man in the nose.

Holding his nose, the bandit moaned and cursed loud enough to let the entire kingdom know how he felt. Blood streamed through his fingers and dripped onto Malaika. She rolled away, but the man caught her ankle. His filthy, blood-streaked face growled into Malaika's eyes.

"Jeremias, kick that machete over here!"

Dread filled every part of Neyah's being.

"What do you want?" Neyah demanded. "Food! Water? We can get it for you. Goats too. Please, anything! Let her go."

"I will let her go when I am done with her."

Malaika flipped over and tried crawling away, but the short

bandit got a tight grip on her legs as he handed over the machete.

The tall man grabbed Malaika's hand and with one mighty whack, he cut it off.

Two shots rang out amidst the girls' screams and both men collapsed. Aden stood expressionless in the bushes, gripping a sawed-off shotgun.

Neyah saw her body bolt toward her friend before she even moved.

Malaika reached for her severed hand in a chilling scream. "My hand!"

Neyah picked up Malaika's scarf and wrapped it tight around the bloody stump. Neyah tasted a sickening bitterness in her mouth. She yelled to Aden for help, but he was gone.

From nowhere, three women, on their way back from the river, appeared.

"We heard screaming!"

One woman made an arm sling for Malaika from her shawl while Neyah knelt and sobbed over her friend. She held Malaika's remaining hand and stroked her head, never losing eye contact with her dear friend. She knew she should say something comforting to her, but the words wouldn't come.

Rocking back and forth, Neyah finally whispered. "We will get you home. We will."

Malaika's color paled and her body shook. Neyah pleaded with Malaika to open her fist. She finally gave in, and the bloody hand tumbled out.

"Water...my family needs it..." Malaika clenched her teeth.

"I will bring them water." Neyah gulped back tears. She couldn't believe it. A good day gone bad, very bad.

One woman twisted leaves and bark from a nearby sickle bush. Snapping them into pieces, she sprinkled them into Malaika's open bloody wound. "This will help kill the pain."

Malaika arched her back as spasms of pain shot through her body. "My skirt." Her words sounded pathetically desperate and pained.

Neyah yanked the poinsettia skirt from under the tall bandit and laid it in Malaika's lap. The terrified girl cradled it like a baby in the crook of her injured arm.

As Neyah strapped Malaika's empty jerry can on her own back, she noticed a vulture pecking at Malaika's severed hand. The famous, piano-playing hand.

Stopping only twice to give her a drink, the women and Neyah carried Malaika home.

As they entered Malaika's village, her sister, Saida, sat grinding maize. Seeing Malaika's limp body, Saida rushed to the field to find her mother and brothers.

"I will find Aluna!" cried a woman.

Aluna, the village nurse, wasn't a trained nurse but knew basic first aid. She came running and applied numbing herbs and a tourniquet to the raw wound while Malaika's mother sobbed and held her good hand.

Malaika lay frighteningly still while Neyah stood frozen in fear.

"Find someone to construct a carrying cot for her," ordered Aluna. "Get a donkey. Now!"

While neighbors hastily built the cot from sturdy branches and goatskins, Aluna tipped Malaika's head up and managed to get her to swallow some medicine. "This will help you sleep."

From somewhere an uncle and a donkey appeared. In a whirlwind of food, water, and first aid supplies, the uncle guided Malaika and the donkey out of the village toward the mission hospital, a day's walking trip away.

Shaken and sobbing, Neyah ran home.

26

MR. SAHLI UNDERSTANDS

Dear Abby,

I like to learn new words, but not bad words like tumor If it hurts my new friend I do not like it You have big heart to fill yellow buckets for strangers I will be filling my bucket with prayers for tumor to leave your head

Bandits is the bad word here They found us on the path when we carried water home Bandits take our precious water and cut Malaika hand and beautiful hair It be so awful I cannot tell you rest I see Malaika no longer I cry and cry and cannot stop

What is DIY Tell me good news from your Minnesota My angels and prayers fly across ocean to Abby I yearn for your letters much like I yearn for Malaika and Papa and for big rain for thirsty fields.

Your turn Your friend Neyah

PS I knew your papa would come back if you asked for the moon

Mirror is new word I have not heard of And the yellow bucket you drew on your letter needs cover or water will spill

Neyah couldn't keep her eyes off the empty spot on the school bench where Malaika usually sat. It looked hauntingly empty. *Was Malaika dead?*

Mr. Sahli spoke. "Stagnant water doesn't move, and that's when mosquitos that carry disease increase in number."

Mr. Sahli held a malaria net. "This is why you must use one of these every night. Now, I know we all get a little lazy about this, so I'm reminding you. Your nets protect you from the serious disease of malaria. By the way, these aren't fishing nets! Don't let me hear you're using them to fish."

Moswen and Nathaniel exchanged mischievous looks.

"Some of you may not own enough nets for your family or they may have holes. Raise your hand if you need a new one."

Everyone in the room put their hand up except Neyah. She stared off. Other voices buzzed in her ear. Aden had tried warning them: "Bandits." A drunken voice threatened: "You just made a big mistake, little girl."

Neyah rubbed her sweaty palms together. She heard Malaika's voice repeating the same things over and over in her head. "My skirt. My hand. My skirt."

Neyah touched the skirt of her school uniform and stared at her own hands folded in her lap. Tears spilled onto them.

Maybe if I had not struck the bandit with my water can...

Students hustled outside for an exercise break, but Neyah remained. With eyes closed, she relived the terrifying attack on Malaika.

Quivering from the memory, Neyah opened her eyes and gazed out the school window. A game of "escape the lion" floated in from the playground. Students laughed and roared as they formed a circle around the blindfolded "lions" and attempted to steal the lions' treasure, or in this case, cloth bags filled with corn.

A gentle hand on her shoulder made her jump.

"Neyah, when do you wish to read your persuasive writing?" asked Mr. Sahli.

"It is not done."

"Do you need help with it?"

Blankly staring into her lap, Neyah pondered his question.

Her whispered voice cracked. "I know what I want to say." In truth, she wondered whether words made a difference anymore.

"Good. We look forward to hearing it."

From the corner of her eye, Neyah saw Mr. Sahli still standing near her. Like a raging river overflowing its banks, Neyah couldn't hold back any longer. Her body collapsed forward allowing the flood to consume her. Mr. Sahli knelt close, with a hand on her shoulder. Neyah cried until there was no crying left in her, her teacher crying with her.

27

BIBI'S BALM

Neyah sat alone among the chickens and tried not to think about why she was not allowed to accompany Papa and the rest of her family to the church service. "Tell her she must stay and sweep," Papa had told Mama before they left.

Neyah locked her eyes on two words in her journal as she rolled a kernel of corn in her left palm. Mr. Sahli's social studies unit on balancing resources in the world included fascinating words.

Self-reliant (*adjective*) relying on oneself; not needing help from others.

Humanitarian agency (*noun*) an organization that works to save lives, alleviate suffering and maintain human dignity.

A sudden thumping caused Neyah to catch her breath. She twisted around. Nothing. Probably an animal or someone beating mats together: things she'd heard a hundred times. Exhaling, Neyah tried to relax.

Ever since Malaika's attack, Neyah felt jumpy. A numbness set into her body. Everything good appeared dim. The evening stars. The taste of Mama's bread. Even Bibi's songs. While Mama walked to the river in her place, Neyah went through the motions of home chores. Worry for Mama's safety tore like a cattle stampede through her veins. But mostly, she was scared for her own safety.

Another sound. Neyah's heart raced. Alone in the family compound, she gripped her journal. Was that a cough? Paul? She stretched her neck and saw the familiar faces of her family returning from the village.

Neyah's pulse slowed, and she ducked inside her hut. Papa didn't want to see her and wouldn't be happy to see her sitting outside. Neyah wondered how long Papa intended this shunning to go on.

Watching from her hut entrance, Neyah saw Bosco skipping into the family compound. "Mama, no one chased us out of worship from not bathing!" he called.

Mama laughed. "Maybe the Good Lord does not mind a little stink."

"All He cares about is forgiveness and love," smiled Bibi.

Paul's bleating goat welcomed them. Picking up the newborn kid and wrapping it around his neck, he announced, "Mama, we are taking the goats into the valley on the other side of the village. The pastor said there is grass there."

"Take this tea for your cough and mandazi for your belly. It will be a long day. Do you have a name for your new friend?"

Paul grinned. "Yancy." The tiny goat lifted its head and bleated loudly as if to say she loved her name.

Giggling from inside her hut, Neyah watched Mama shoo Bosco and Paul away.

Mama entered Neyah's hut and squatted in front of her. "Your friend has blood poisoning Neyah, not many survive it."

Neyah shuddered.

Mama took her daughter's hands in hers. "Maybe Malaika will."

Neyah closed her eyes with a silent prayer of thanks. Her friend was still alive.

EVENING MEANT it was time to prepare a meal. Papa was resting inside his hut, so Neyah was allowed to be out of hers.

Mama put her hands on her hips and looked at her twin boys. "Where is my firewood?"

Kato and Hassan raced off. Their jumpy bodies made Neyah smile.

Hassan gathered branches while Kato swung the ax. Small for their age as twins sometimes are, it didn't slow them down. They loaded wood bundles twice their height on their backs and carried them to the fire ring of grey stones.

Mama fanned the smoky ring with a goatskin. "Just in time!" she declared.

If Mama's fire went completely cold, she would have to borrow a hot coal from a neighbor. Neyah knew Mama considered it a disgrace to let her fire go cold. Every night before turning in, Mama tucked her last burning coals under the ashes so it could be rekindled in the morning.

"Kato stabbed something for your dinner, Neyah!" Hassan waved his bush knife in front of her face. On the tip hung a limp African bullfrog. Fat. And quite dead.

Neyah couldn't help but smile. "Nice work, Kato. I love frog porridge. What about you, Kato? Did you bring me something?"

He skipped over and sat in Neyah's lap. "Yes, I did!" He clapped and sang a silly song he made up about fetching firewood and frogs. Hassan and Kato took turns creating new verses.

Bibi heard the entertainment and hobbled from the hut. After Neyah guided her to the bench, her wrinkled hands clapped in time until the boys ran out of song ideas and hurried away dribbling the soccer ball they'd received for Christmas.

Bibi held Neyah's hand. "Tell me what this moment is for."

"What do you mean, Bibi?" Familiar with Bibi's questions designed to get her to talk, Neyah waited.

Bibi's arms made a circle motion. "Look closer, listen sweet child."

Neyah looked at the azure sky over the hilly ridge and fields begging for rain. Monkeys screeched in the distance. Colorful birds sang their optimistic tune. Nothing seemed special or different to her.

"Neyah, this moment will never come again. The silly games of your brothers, you and me together. This is it, the moment we get to bless the world with our gift."

Neyah had no idea what Bibi meant.

"Yesterday is gone. What happened is done. Tomorrow we get another chance if we are lucky. Today is the gift. What will you do with this amazing gift to make it count? What will you do, child?"

Neyah knew what she would like to do, but it wouldn't get done today. Laying her head in Bibi's small lap, she slept with the weight of exhaustion as her blanket.

PAPA LOOKED AWAY from his daughter. Or at least he planned to. Her wispy body looked frail lying in Bibi's lap. One strong African gust could snatch her away.

Mama had told him the horror of the bandit attack and what

happened to Malaika's hand. It stunned him to hear how his young daughter fought to defend her friend. How had Neyah managed to slam a forty-pound can of water against her attacker? He shuddered to think what would have happened to her if the stranger hadn't been there to shoot the bandits.

If he felt this way about Neyah, could he give her up? Papa wondered. Was there another way? Could he maintain some honor among other village families if he didn't trade his daughter? How could a poor farmer like himself afford not to trade Neyah when he had the chance? Offering her as a wife would nearly double his cattle herd. He likely wouldn't have this chance again since she was his only daughter. The answer was getting clearer as he worked his way through the choices. He had no choice. Neyah would be traded.

28

NEYAH HATCHES A PLAN

Neyah insisted she'd never return to the river.

Bibi tried soothing her. "Whether you sit home or fetch, you will never forget what happened to sweet Malaika."

"But Bibi, it is March! The big rains-where are they?"

"They come when they come. Maybe in honor of your thirteenth birthday."

She did walk for water again. But behind a team of Uncle Aman's donkeys. She and Nilsa accompanied him on the longer route. Neyah knew they didn't need her. She felt sure Mama planned it in hopes she'd get over her fear of bandits.

Bandits usually didn't bother men, but this fact gave Neyah little comfort. Silent and on edge while Nilsa and Uncle Aman talked, Neyah stayed on high alert. She found it impossible to not think about the last fetch.

Bibi is right, she thought. *Malaika is always on my mind.*

As she followed the donkeys' tails, Neyah considered her persuasive essay. After weeks of putting it off, Neyah felt a sudden urgency to write it. Papa's threats to sell her, and Malaika's words to do something, stirred in her. "You and me— we aren't waiting. We are going to do things now!"

Whispering her promise to the wind, "Malaika, I will do this for you, my rafiki, and all girls who fetch...before Papa sends me away."

Uncle Aman called to Neyah, "Doing all right back there?"

"Yes, I am writing a letter in my head."

That is it! she thought. *The essay will be a letter. I will ask for the moon. It will be like writing to a new pen pal—hopefully one who knows how to dig a well.*

Dear Humanitarian Agency. We need water. Please help.

What else needed to be said? Words and questions swirled in her thirsty head. *Where is the humanitarian agency? Why do they care?*

Neyah felt sure if someone sent her such a letter, she'd advise the person to move to a place with more water. Hadn't Abby thought the same?

But where would her family go? No one she knew ever moved away except Malaika's grandmother. And why did she move? Neyah would ask Malaika the next time she—then she remembered. She wouldn't be asking Malaika anything anymore.

"The donkeys need a break," said Uncle Aman.

While Nilsa wrote in the dirt with a stick, Neyah peered out over the rocky terrain to the distant mountains. The sun played peek-a-boo with the clouds and mountain slopes, creating moving patterns in the deep valley below.

Gentleness rolled through Neyah's thoughts. *During all the trips to fetch water, I stare at a path and never see the wonder of this place. Beautiful Kenya is my home—it just needs more water.*

"Neyah. Neyah!" called Uncle Aman.

"Yes?"

"What are you dreaming about?"

"It is...pretty here."

"Sure is. Now, are you coming, or daydreaming on that rock all day?"

Taking one last look across the valley brushed with small promises of green, Neyah shouted joyfully, "Coming!"

As she ran to catch up, Bibi's words revolved in her head. "Yesterday is gone... Tomorrow is a chance...*today* is the gift."

29

TRIUMPH AND TRAGEDY

S undays used to be a joyous family day. Now they bothered Neyah. Everyone attended worship service except Papa and her. Papa had suffered a setback and needed rest. He napped in his hut; Neyah sat in hers. Flies buzzed about her in the bright sunlight illuminating the inside, but she didn't notice. It baffled her how boiling water and washing hands turned Papa into her enemy. She wanted nothing more than to go to him, but the decision didn't stand with her.

She picked up the letter Abby's mother sent and read it for the third time.

Dear Neyah,

This is Abby's mother. She's sitting here on her bed telling me what to write while her dad holds her.

Hi Neyah. It's Abby. First of all, happy March birthday!!! You're thirteen too. This letter is your present! I'm SO sorry I haven't written. My handwriting is a mess since I can barely see. The chemo shrunk the tumor, but now there's more. Ugh! Never mind that. I have a surprise!

Our student council sponsored the Every Drop Counts campaign (MY idea!). I brought my yellow bucket to school and my sleepover friends made DO IT FOR NEYAH posters, with a copy of the picture you drew of yourself on them. They plastered them around school and town encouraging donations. ☺

My bucket alone has $228.32 so far. If your village finds someone to dig a well, this money can hopefully help with the cost. Dad says wells cost a lot, so I'll keep bugging people to break their piggy banks over this. Andrew says I'm good at bugging people! But come on! Everyone should have clean water.

I also talked Mr. Simon into asking the principal to let us have a talent show to raise more awareness and money for your well. She said YES! I bet we raise thousands!

I'm sending you and your brave friend Malaika big hugs! It made me cry to hear about her hand. Where are the police?!

Your other rafiki, Abby

Your turn to write!

P.S. Your letters are one of the most special things I look forward to. I did not know some kids have to do what you do to get water and miss school. You gave me something to work on, so I don't sit around having a pity party for myself. Thank you Neyah. You are saving me!

P.P.S. DIY means Do It Yourself. Like I mean NOW! Start talking to your teacher and everyone you see about needing a well. DO NOT WAIT another day.

Chewing her bottom lip, Neyah set the letter down. Her mind raced in many directions. Abby was so sick she couldn't even write anymore, and yet she found the energy to help her.

Glancing at the letter again, she saw the words: DO NOT WAIT. Malaika said it. Now Abby.

Neyah's attention shifted and fixated on Malaika's skirt. She reached and stroked it as gently as she would a new baby chick. Folded nice and neat, the poinsettia flowers stood in stark contrast to her faded clothing.

Neyah thought back to six days ago when Mama had brought her the skirt.

"Malaika's uncle came by while you were in school. Malaika wanted you to have this."

As Mama handed her the skirt, Neyah noticed it was stitched back together. The faded red stain near the waistband caused her lips to quiver. Tears clouded her vision changing the colorful flowers into floating blotches of blood.

Mama barely heard Neyah's strangled whimper as she collapsed to the ground. "They are giving her clothes away?"

Mama gathered Neyah in her arms and rocked her like a baby.

"Malaika is asking for you."

Neyah sprang back and clamped onto her mother's arms. "Malaika is alive?"

"We heard nothing until today. Malaika is alive but still weak. She is a fighter."

"Oh thank goodness! I must see her. Can I go? Please, Mama. I need to."

"They brought her home from the hospital yesterday. I will ask Papa if you and Bosco can go see her."

Neyah's eyes nearly popped from her head. "You are asking Papa? Thank you, Mama!"

NEYAH GENTLY TOUCHED Malaika's skirt one more time before she ducked out of her hut. She sat tending the fire coals as her family returned from church. Her brothers' laughter spilled into the compound as she watched Papa painfully crawl from his hut wearing his woven Sunday hat. She used to love seeing him in it. Today she thought he looked like a thin old man in an oversized hat.

"Are you ready to see Malaika?" Bosco shouted.

Neyah hopped up in excitement. "Today?" She looked toward Papa, but his eyes turned away.

Mama handed her a burlap bag. "Yes, today. Please give Malaika our love and give her family this fresh flatbread."

Neyah touched Mama's cheek and whispered. "Papa said yes?"

Disappointment flooded Mama's face. "No. But I said yes. Now go!"

As Bosco and Neyah started walking to Malaika's village, Papa's weak voice stopped them.

"You are lucky to have a family." His words sounded stone cold.

Bosco and Neyah stopped to listen.

Papa continued. "You know about my brothers and sister. And my own Papa."

A few years earlier, Bibi had told Bosco and Neyah the awful story. Neyah prayed she'd never hear it again.

"At five years old." Papa struggled with his words. "I woke in a pool of blood with parts of my family scattered around."

The urge to run to him swept through Neyah.

"Bibi and I only had each other and our grief to live on. We wandered with a few cows for days and lived in a refugee camp for over twelve years. With no school, I went crazy with boredom."

Neyah wondered why Papa chose this time to share his tragic story.

"I have spent half my life thinking, 'Why did they not hurt

Aman and me?' We lay right there. Your Bibi would have gone insane if they killed us too. Thankfully, she went outside to feed the baby when the murderers came."

Baby? Bibi never mentioned a baby.

"Bibi stopped feeding the baby. The poor thing starved to death." Papa choked on his last words. "They stole most of my family from me."

Neyah wanted to remind him he had a new family, that he would lose this one too if he forced his choices on them. But Papa had crawled back into his hut.

AT THE EDGE of Malaika's village, Neyah stopped. "Bosco, maybe this is a bad idea."

"You make no sense. Mama said Malaika asked to see you!"

"I made the bandits mad. What if she thinks it is my fault her hand got sliced off?"

"Stop worrying about yourself. Come on. We are almost there."

Malaika sat on a low cot inside her family's thatched hut. Sunlight streamed through the window opening offering Neyah a clear view of her friend. She could see Malaika was thinner.

Bosco nudged Neyah. She took a breath and walked in.

Malaika smiled and sang out. "Jambo Neyah! Jambo Bosco!" She reached with her good hand and drew Neyah to her.

Malaika's warm gesture brought relief as Neyah settled in beside her. She tried to keep her eyes off Malaika's injured arm but wasn't successful.

"Malaika, your thumb," Neyah cried in surprise, "You still have it!"

"Yes, those guys were a terrible shot."

Neyah shivered at the memory. "How...is it?"

Malaika rubbed her cast that extended to her elbow. "The doctor says I am healing. A few more weeks, and I will be back carrying water with you before you know it."

Neyah shook her head. She wondered how Malaika could ever think about fetching again? And how does one carry water with one hand?

"How is school?"

Neyah liked hearing Malaika's questions again and smiled. "Oh, you know..."

"No, I do not. Tell me!"

"We do your favorite things. Math and math tests and math homework."

Malaika giggled. "I hear you are fetching water with your Uncle Aman and his donkeys."

Neyah held Malaika's hand in hers. Anguish swept through her. "I am sorry, Malaika." Hot tears spilled onto her dress.

"For what? It was not your fault. Those guys were bad."

"Your hand is gone. You...you wanted to be a famous piano player." She took deep, shaky breaths between words and slapped her tears away.

Malaika squeezed Neyah's hand. "I am still alive, and who knows? Maybe I can be the first one-handed piano player!"

Neyah wrapped her arms around Malaika's neck and stroked her friend's hair.

"They are rotten at cutting hair too," muttered Malaika.

Neyah released an explosive mixture of laughter and sobbing. Finally, she raised her head. "And they ruined your new skirt."

"No, it still looks great!" Malaika insisted. "Did my uncle get it to you?"

Neyah nodded with fresh tears filling her eyes, "But it is yours. From your Bibi! You can still wear it."

"I will. But I want you to wear it...to give you confidence when you read your persuasive essay!"

"I could use confidence. And thank your grandmother for me. By the way, why did she leave this village in the first place and move to the city?"

Malaika turned sullen. "A crocodile took her legs off on her tenth birthday and she nearly bled to death. Her Papa died the next year, and her Mama went crazy, so my grandmother was taken to an orphanage in the city."

"Malaika, I did not know..."

"That is the past." Malaika's perky voice returned. "My grandmother thinks the crocodile changed her life for the better somehow. And her hands still work! She plays piano, and she sewed the poinsettia skirt for me!"

Neyah sat trying to absorb this news. "But your family lives here instead of the city."

Malaika giggled and pointed outside. "Papa met Mama in that cornfield. He came here from the city to teach farmers about irrigation and fell in love with Mama. Mama promised to marry him only if he moved to her village."

Bosco tapped Neyah on the shoulder, "We need to get back."

Giving Malaika a gentle hug, Neyah sighed. "I am relieved you are all right."

"Me too. Thank you for coming. Good luck reading your essay."

Neyah's eyes dipped down.

"Neyah! You have not written it yet? Let me help. I—."

"No. I—I know what I want to say."

"Good! And you will wear my skirt! And this new scarf Bibi made." Malaika threw the orange scarf at Neyah with her good hand. It landed on Neyah's head.

"BIBI WANTS YOU, NEYAH!" Kato yelled as she and Bosco returned from Malaika's village.

"Must be toilet time," Bosco smiled.

"Sit down sweet granddaughter, and no, I do not need the toilet. Yet."

Neyah laughed.

Bibi held Neyah's hands in hers before she spoke. "Your father said some things to you before you visited your dear friend Malaika. Now it is my turn."

"You are a child and see as a child. One day, if you have a child, you will see it as a mother. You will want to hold your child's hand forever, and you will want to hold it tight so you do not lose the bond that ties you."

Bibi took a deep breath and let it out slowly. "Sometimes as a parent, we hold on so tight, we end up getting the opposite effect. We squeeze so hard that our children cannot breathe. The young hands pull away, and they never come home. I believe this is what your papa is afraid of."

Does she think I will run away?

"Your father is confused. He lost much at the hands of bad people. He still does not know what to think of it and why he was spared."

Neyah's hands twisted the scarf Malaika had given her.

"Your papa also lost three daughters, and fears losing control over the only one he has left. He sees his neighbors selling their daughters off in exchange for cattle or grain. It eats him up to think he might be expected to do the same."

Neyah wondered if Bibi knew Papa already had a plan to do just that.

"Do you know how much he wants you to get schooling? He

sees how smart you are. How fetching water is not what you are willing to do much longer. But he also sees your schooling taking you away from him, from this family, this village. Never to be seen by his eyes again."

"Bibi. What are you asking me to do?"

"I am not asking you to do anything, child. I am simply telling you why your papa squeezes so tight."

AFTER EVENING CHORES Neyah sat and wrote.

Dear Abby,

I search for right words to say thank you for getting money in yellow bucket for my village I wish to do something for your tumor but I not a doctor yet

I find my purpose to say something You and Malaika tell me don't wait I wait long enough Time to do something I will write letter to persuade humanitarian agency to build clean water well in Letsokoane The well be big need for girls to have time to learn and for people to stop dying of dirty water You and Malaika be my courage when it come time to read this letter in school

Maybe Papa not trade me or maybe he will I not worry about me I keep eye on purpose to make change to help I sorry you be sick Your heart take over for your eyes You meet success of having your Mama and Papa back I pray you meet success to get health back

My good news—Malaika be home She lost one hand but she not lost strong love for life I see her today and cry and laugh together

Your turn

Rafiki yako Your friend Neyah

PS I ask my teacher what be a talent show and chemo

Talent show fun but chemo not fun Here be picture of my yellow jerry can It not have money in it but I send it with much love and healing flowing from it for my USA friend

30

A BREAKTHROUGH

Standing near the tattered multiplication table, Mr. Sahli waited for the crowded classroom to settle, happy to see faces he hadn't seen for a while. Three and four students scrunched together on the benches. Others sat along the walls. The extra bodies caused the room to feel warmer than usual. Using the back of his hand, the young teacher wiped the sweat from his brow.

"Today we hear the last persuasive essay. Be mindful of listening as Neyah's voice, although quiet, is as important as someone with a booming one like mine." He smiled wide and ambled to the back of the room.

For the first time in her life, Neyah could not wait to talk. It felt strange not to be nervous. She rubbed her thumbs back and forth over the flowers on Malaika's skirt. Mama agreed to let her wear it today. Massaging the raised stitching of the poinsettia print one last time, she got to her feet. Rather than look at the waiting faces of other students, she focused on the cracks in the blackboard and took a step forward.

As Neyah walked stiffly to the front of the room clutching her essay, she pictured Abby and Bibi's proud smiles urging her on. She felt Malaika's confident hand clutching hers. Standing before her classmates, Neyah lifted the paper and glanced at the first line. Rolling her shoulders, she turned her eyes upward.

Hassan and Kato sat in the front row sharing a bench with two other squirmy boys. Her twin brothers' dark eyes smiled curiously at Neyah. Sitting further back, Bosco gave her a thumbs up. He was the only one who had seen her essay. Neyah had asked him for help with punctuation and grammar. Devi stared dreamily at her in great anticipation. Everyone, except Moswen who looked bored as usual, waited anxiously as if the president of Kenya had come to speak. Even the breeze settled in to listen to the quiet girl.

Neyah's heart began to hammer in her chest. The nerves were back. Her eyes dropped to her feet. She folded her paper in half and stood in total silence.

Mr. Sahli closed his eyes in disappointment.

Folding the paper a second time, Neyah dropped it. A gasp from Devison caused Moswen to stop doodling. Without moving his head, he rolled his eyes up to see what Neyah was doing.

She took a step forward and placed a foot on the words she'd written. Lifting her head high, she recited her letter from memory.

Dear Humanitarian Agency,

I have a slow-moving dream. Actually two. The first one is to stay alive. My second dream is to give the girls and women of my village a chance for something more than fetching water. My dreams are tethered to you. I need your help to bring clean water.

You ask, why Letsokoane? People and dreams are dying here. Babies, children, papas, and mamas. Most of our time goes to fetching filthy water and getting sick from it.

Do you drink water from a hole that animals use for a toilet? I do. Do you walk six hours a day to get it? I do. Do leeches and bad bacteria swim in your water cup? They do in mine. Did your baby sister get crushed to death at your open well? Mine did. Does your stomach whine from dirty water? Mine does. Do your children miss school? And do they watch dreams fly away because their Mama needs water to cook? I do. Did your best friend get her hand chopped off by bandits on the trek home from fetching? Mine did.

I started fetching water at age five. It is a job for girls so I miss school and fall behind. If I do not fetch, our animals and maybe my family will die. If I fetch, my dream dies. These are not good choices.

I write to persuade you to come and dig for clean water in my village because fetching and sickness are stealing our time, our learning, and our life.

I thought my purpose was to be a doctor but no more. A doctor only fixes sickness. My new purpose is to bring good water so there IS no sickness. To bring change so there is a future. To not wait. To say something. To do something.

No one can live without water. And I cannot live without a dream. Can you?

Neyah Jabari, 13 years old, Letsokoane, Kenya

The students clapped as they did after each persuasive speech. But the applause for Neyah lasted longer than usual. Three brothers, who recently lost their mother to malaria, wiped their eyes. Others reached out and patted Neyah on the shoulder as she returned to her desk. Mr. Sahli fought the cloud in his eyes.

Neyah's fingers found the raised flowers on the skirt again and rubbed them until her breathing returned to normal.

196 | MARY BLECKWEHL

"We will take—." Mr. Sahli's voice broke. He cleared his throat and tried again. "We will take our morning break."

Students scattered to the sunny outdoors. Many took advantage of the break to find a bathroom bush to squat under.

As Shala went out the door, she grabbed Neyah's arm. "Your speech was perfect. It is what I have wanted to say for a long time."

Cheiru ran toward the girls and wrapped her arms around them. "We can celebrate with a game of tag!"

Neyah giggled. "Okay, okay! but I have to give something to Mr. Sahli first."

Returning to the dark schoolroom from the bright sunlight, Neyah's eyes took a few seconds to adjust. Standing in the doorway gave her the time she needed to gather her courage and thoughts. Mr. Sahli sat alone on the edge of one of the student benches. This was her chance to do something with her words.

ALONE IN THE CLASSROOM, Mr. Sahli felt light-headed and sat on a student bench. He listened to the student laughter float in through the open doorway. It was music to his ears to hear them happy and carefree, if only for a few minutes a day.

But the words Neyah Jabari had written and read aloud told the rest of the story, the real story of life in Letsokoane. The reality of it bit into the headmaster's soul. He slipped from the bench and sank to his knees, then fell forward sobbing.

Neyah's words circled in his head. "I have a slow-moving dream... The first one is to stay alive... People and dreams are dying here."

"I haven't done enough," Mr. Sahli whispered between gasps. "What else can I possibly do?"

As the headmaster of Saramba, Omar Sahli served as the

principal, teacher, and custodian all wrapped into one. A school the size of Saramba would usually employ two teachers, but attracting teachers to poor rural areas proved challenging. He spent each day fighting despair and lack of resources and death. Just yesterday two more students died, no doubt from illness tied to contaminated water.

As Mr. Sahli sobbed, he considered his calling. *This is where I should be. Where the most needy can be inspired to reach beyond survival.*

Drying his tears, the headmaster lifted his head to find Neyah staring at him.

"I AM READY TO MAIL IT."

Neyah's presence and confident voice brought the Headmaster to his feet. He cleared his throat. "Your pen pal letter?" His throat felt tight.

"Yes." She handed it to him. "And this one too."

A puzzled expression formed on Mr. Sahli's face. "You want to mail your essay to someone?"

"Yes. Letsokoane needs a well. Now."

"Neyah, you can't just—"

"Yes, I can." Her volume surprised herself as well as her teacher. "The whole village is sick. Papa nearly died and is still a skeleton. Paul coughs all day. Amel and Fatima died. And think of all the girls who *never* get to school because they fetch or do chores while their Mama gets water."

Neyah stopped yelling and looked downward.

"Sorry, sir."

Mr. Sahli laughed his hearty laugh. "Don't be sorry. Neyah, we are finally hearing your voice. Sometimes it's fine to be loud.

You are saying something important. But you need one more thing. Neyah, you need to—"

"I know. I need to do something."

Neyah stepped closer to Mr. Sahli. She swallowed hard. "I need your help." Her voice wavered, but she didn't stop.

"Devi says some villages have drilled deep wells right next to them. Then no one misses school or gets sick from water." Neyah stopped to catch her breath. "Mr. Sahli, we need one of those."

Her teacher's mouth dropped open. He stared into Neyah's eyes. They no longer shied away. They were bold and determined. These eyes held purpose.

Mr. Sahli chuckled warmly and folded his hands across his round belly. "Neyah. I didn't mean that kind of 'do something.' I mean that everyone needs to practice good hygiene. Boiling, handwashing and—"

"It is not enough."

Her interruption surprised him.

"We need a well."

"Neyah—."

"Clean water."

"We can't suddenly start digging a well."

"Why not?"

Mr. Sahli gritted his teeth. Through the window, he saw students enjoying their morning break. Two of them jumped a rope made from twisted tree bark. Another dashed to get a drink from the boiled water container. Neema and Tulani sat on the ground scratching their legs. They had the shakes today and shouldn't be in school.

Rubbing the back of his dark patch of bristly hair, the patient teacher settled onto a creaky student bench and sighed. Neyah's eyes followed him. Mr. Sahli tried to make this school a place to learn, but it lacked latrines and electricity. Small holes popped up everywhere-evidence of critters or burglars. He stared at the cracked blackboard. Math problems, spelling words, and assignments crowded it.

What was the use of teaching these kids to read and write if their future was only about water fetching and sick babies?

Mr. Sahli looked at Neyah who continued to stare at him. He saw a girl desperately searching for something so far out there. So out of reach for anyone, let alone a wisp of a child. He gnawed his lower lip. After another deep sigh, he spoke.

"I tried it." The sound of failure flooded the room.

"You tried digging a well?"

His teeth showed easily in his smile. "I ache to get a well here! I wrote and called and begged for a deep well for two years."

"Who did you ask?"

"There are many people who fund projects like this."

"Humanitarian agencies?"

Mr. Sahli smiled at the term she used with confidence.

"Yes."

"They said no?"

Mr. Sahli's silence gave her the answer.

"*I* will ask them," said Neyah.

"Neyah, don't bother."

Neyah's glare gobbled his words up.

"Okay." Mr. Sahli threw his hands upward. "I don't want to get your hopes up, but I heard about an opportunity. It's a long shot."

Neyah smiled. "I am used to long." She thought of her long walks, long waits, so why not a long shot? Whatever it is, it might be her only chance to save her village and her dream. Then maybe she could catch up in her school lessons and make her Papa proud again.

Neyah ran to the used paper pile and pulled out a wrinkled

half-sheet. Rummaging through several pencils before finding one with lead, she sat with the dull stubby pencil in hand and peered at Mr. Sahli. "What is it?"

"Wells cost a lot of money," Mr. Sahli tried to keep rejection out of his voice.

Neyah listened.

"Big equipment is required."

Her eyes didn't leave his.

"What I am saying, Neyah, is this. There are organizations around the world that help communities like ours dig wells. People give money to the organization and the organization decides where to use the money. They get government approval, then find local business partners with the right equipment. What I'm saying is—it could take *years* to even get one to notice us. If another village or region needs a well more than we do, they will dig there first."

"I need their names."

"I do not have them."

Neyah ignored his response. "Addresses too."

Mr. Sahli sighed. "I—I can get a list but—"

"Get me envelopes and postage."

"Sure."

"And paper."

Mr. Sahli wiggled in his seat. "Yes, I've got paper too. But Neyah, the list is endless. A couple of hundred organizations. Maybe more."

"Good." She smiled. "I will need a lot of paper."

Mr. Sahli leaned in and touched Neyah's arm gently.

"There's a lot to this. Hydrogeologists survey. Government paperwork. And they search for people willing to do what they say."

"Like what?"

"They need to know your village will maintain the well."

"Maintain?" Neyah felt her head drowning in new information.

"Maintain means take care of it, raise funds to pay for repairs. Someone in the village needs to be willing to learn how to fix it when something breaks."

"I will find someone to maintain it," Neyah assured him.

"And good hygiene and sanitation practices must be in place."

Neyah nodded. "Like boiling and hand washing."

"Yes, but also building latrines to replace open toilets."

"What are you saying?" asked Neyah.

"I'm saying, don't get your hopes up. If you write to a hundred places, they might all say no."

Neyah smiled with new confidence. "One might say yes."

Neyah waited for Mr. Sahli's belly laugh. She just got another sigh.

31

UNSTOPPABLE

E xcitement over Malaika returning to school ruled the day.
During the exercise break, classmates clumped around
her to view what remained of her hand. Malaika wiggled her
thumb and demonstrated other skills she could accomplish with
only one finger.

"Since I am right-handed, I am lucky the bandit whacked
my left hand."

Neyah smiled as she took in the conversation. She knew
Malaika had a cheery outlook on life. But how could she
consider herself lucky?

Carrying a small stack of envelopes, Mr. Sahli strolled
across the dirt playground to Malaika's circle of listeners.

Hoping she got a response from one of the organizations she
wrote to, Neyah's heart raced.

"Pen pal letters are here!"

Her heart sank. How long was this "long shot" going to take?

"Here is yours, Neyah. You and Abby must have lots to
discuss!"

As she opened Abby's letter, she smiled at Mr. Sahli's
words. No one ever told her she talked a lot. However, she

certainly had plenty of people prodding her to talk. Bosco and Bibi, Abby and Malaika, Devi, and of course, Mr. Sahli.

Dear Neyah,

This is Abby's mother again. I'm here with her in the hospital. She's very ill and begged me to write you. Her body is weak, and she can only see light now, but her spirit is as strong as ever.

Abby's father and I want you to know you've given her a life-changing gift of inspiration. You shared experiences that sparked an idea, and more than that, your words and needs changed her heart. She spent thirteen years thinking mainly of herself. Suddenly Abby's cooking up ways to help someone else —someone she's never even met: you! and your community. And it is giving her a reason to keep fighting for her life.

Abby told you about the Yellow Bucket talent show. She talked the doctor into letting her out of the hospital to play her violin. I have to admit, I wasn't in favor of it. I didn't think she was strong enough, but she sat in front of nearly 1,000 kids and teachers and played her favorite piece, Clair de Lune, with the drawing of your yellow water can pinned to her shirt. After playing she sat in her wheelchair and shared your dream with the teachers and kids—your dream to get a well—and what it will do to change girls' futures and save lives in your village. Neyah, your dream is now Abby's dream. It has given purpose to her days.

I almost forgot—Abby wants you to know her "sleepover" friends made up a water can dance for the talent show and wore shirts that said Fill the Yellow Bucket for Neyah and her village!

Abby is one of the most persuasive people I know. A more accurate word to describe her is pushy, *but guess what! Her* pushy personality raised over $2,000! And this is on top of the $5,500 raised in our community so far.

The problem is we don't know how to get the money to your community. Is there a water department person? Abby's dad says it probably isn't enough for a well, but it's a start.

We read the persuasive essay you sent to Abby. Your voice is strong and important. Abby says, "You go, girl!" She also says you'll get a well if you continue to express what is needed and get others on your team. So use that voice you were given, Neyah! Gather your own "sleepover" friends. The Abby and Neyah yellow bucket team may get that well!

If you have time to write, Abby would love to hear from you. And PLEASE be careful as you walk for water. Abby sends her love and hugs.

Take care,

Annette Larson

Abby says to tell you about her next purpose—to meet you and get a drink from your well!

Abby is very ill. The words sounded...ironic. Abby drinks clean water, but she still gets sick.

Mr. Sahli came over and sat down on a rusty pail beside Neyah.

"It's fun to get these letters, huh?"

Neyah stared into space. "What does inspiration mean?"

"Inspiration means something gets you excited to act."

Confusion settled into Neyah's thoughts. Did she inspire a sick girl to help her village? She wondered if she was being selfish to want a well.

Mr. Sahli intruded on her thoughts. "I've done some research on the kind of well your village needs, Neyah. It's called a bore-hole and costs $10,000-$15,000 plus costs for getting large equipment in. And, the roads and bridges on the way to your village are in bad shape."

"Neyah?"

She turned and stared with blank eyes at Mr. Sahli.

"Did you hear what I said? The cost of a well may—."

Neyah interrupted. "I heard. $15,000. And more for equipment."

Neyah thought about the amount Abby's school raised. It wasn't enough. And, after reading about Abby's condition, a well didn't seem as important.

Mr. Sahli kept talking as Neyah gazed toward the mountains. "These organizations fund the neediest projects. Do you know what this means?"

Neyah stood and shuffled toward the school entrance.

"Where are you going? Neyah, I am trying to explain! There are things expected of those who get a well."

Words were swimming in her head. *Abby is sick. People here are sick.* She felt sick.

Omar Sahli didn't anger easily, but he didn't stand for a student to walk away while he talked to her. He marched after her and into the school where she sat.

"These people who decide where to dig a well expect people to practice good hygiene and—."

"I know sir—maintain it. You told me."

"Neyah, what I'm saying is, a well doesn't just bring water to a village, it brings change, and some people don't like change!"

His words confused her. *Some people don't like change.* Is that what this was all about? Keeping things the same? No well, no water, no purpose?

Neyah twisted her hands behind her back. Maybe this big crazy dream of hers was just that: crazy. But if Abby can be sick and still hopeful, and raise money for her village, then she, Neyah Jabari, had no intention of giving up either.

Looking into Mr. Sahli's one good eye, she calmly spoke. "Look out at the sky. Three weeks into the rainy season and not a drop of rain. It means more fetching, more missed school, and more lost dreams. If one of these organizations builds my village a well, I will talk to every family myself. I will teach them what you taught us. I will help them see this change is worth it if they want their children to survive."

She opened her word journal and added a word.

Inspiration (*noun*) something happens that gets me excited to act. Abby, Mr. Sahli, Malaika.

Watching her write, Mr. Sahli couldn't hide his enormous smile. Another amazing word floated into his head. Unstoppable.

32

SILENCE KILLS

Dear Abby

I look at your picture I am sad You are sick and your hair fell out It will grow back though I wish to tell you something No one ever done such nice thing for me as you You are sick and still think of my village and big water problem I say this to my USA friend You not stop helping even when you sick so I not stop my talk until well is built and it gives clean water here When it flows you come and taste By then you be healthy and brother Paul will stop the cough No one says it but I know he keep getting worse

I have something more to tell you I be quiet all 13 of my years You show me my words matter I need to talk for purpose of injustice and make change I be quiet no more Maybe I not become doctor You be inspiration to turn me into writer or speaker for justice I dream to meet you someday Abby You and me We be dream partners and fill yellow buckets of kindness all over our world

I read your letters to Malaika We wish you to wear her poinsettia skirt for good healing I will ask Mr. Sahli to mail it I be sorry your eyes can't see beautiful red flowers but

touching them feel good I now reach out to say Be brave be
well I wait for next letter for you to tell how you are healed.

    My prayers fly across ocean
    Your turn
    Neyah
    PS In loud voice I say Asante Thank you

W hen the chickens scratching for bugs in the dirt suddenly scattered, Neyah didn't notice. She sat next to Bibi and her beadwork, lost in thought. Abby was in the hospital. Somewhere across the sea, money sat in buckets donated by strangers. But what good is money if no one here knows you need a well and there's no one to dig one?

Neyah didn't see the mighty creature until a snapped twig brought her out of her trance. The lion took a step toward them. Neyah grasped Bibi's arm and froze.

"What is it, child?"

The beast took another step closer.

Neyah felt her pulse in her fingertips. The giant stared into her frightened eyes and shook his full golden mane before lifting a mammoth paw and pushing it forward.

Papa said lions never came into villages unless they were hungry. He claimed they lived in the grasslands where zebras and wildebeests kept them fed. Other than in the reserve, West Pokot County had neither.

Another step.

Neyah's heart hammered until she thought her chest might explode.

"Bibi, a lion." Neyah didn't know if her words were spoken or not.

Two more steps. The lion got into an attack position on his back haunches.

Pulling Bibi to the ground, Neyah screamed.

CRRRACK!

The sound of Papa's whip over her head sent a jolt through Neyah. She crawled, dragging Bibi with her along the hard ground as the lion spun and hurried off.

Papa rushed to his mother's side. "Bibi, are you all right?"

Shaken, Bibi mumbled, "I am fine."

He took Neyah firmly by the arm. "Neyah, you are done being a quiet girl." Papa's voice rang so loud it hurt into the middle of her ears. "Silence kills. You scream, you run, let others know you are in danger! Do you hear me?"

Neyah fell away as Papa's emaciated body staggered. She watched as his body shook. She could see how the effort of cracking the whip had zapped every ounce of his energy.

"Now, help Bibi back to her hut, and remember the jerry cans." He took deep breaths in between raspy words. "Uncle Aman just arrived and is ready to fetch water. I want to be sure that lion is gone."

Neyah's mind flashed from one thought to another as she listened to her father. *The lion. Papa. Papa talked to her.*

Papa's eyes followed Neyah as she left with Bibi. Covering his mouth in relief, he leaned over clutching his chest with his other hand.

Papa had made a pact with himself. Until his daughter honored what he asked of her, he didn't want to see or listen to her. But he had overheard her practicing the reading of her persuasive essay during chores. He wondered if she would ever get her well. If so, what then? He knew a father's role was to provide for a daughter's future, not let someone from the outside do it.

Papa's eyes turned to the whip in his shaking hand. He whispered to himself as he began to sob. "If I didn't come by when the lion showed up...what then?"

212 | MARY BLECKWEHL

"I AM HOPING this is the last trip until June," said Uncle Aman as he guided the donkeys. "Those clouds are telling me rain is near!"

Nilsa trailed along behind the donkeys, watching Neyah's bright orange scarf flap in the African breeze. "You have a new scarf."

"Malaika gave it to me. Her Bibi made it."

Neyah thought about her own Bibi and Papa's words after he chased the lion off. "You are done being a quiet girl. Silence kills." His first words to her in weeks confused her. Did he want her to say something, or not?

As they neared the river, Nilsa asked Neyah. "What happened to your new scarf?"

Neyah's hands flew to her neck and looked back. "Oh, no!"

"Maybe you will find it on the return trip," Nilsa said.

33

THE DREAM LIST

S itting on her mat with her legs folded under her, Neyah scratched her itchy arms and studied the list of organizations Mr. Sahli had given her two months ago. She crossed out the most recent one to respond. Nineteen replies and each one nothing but a form letter stating their process for considering a community "water project."

"Ahhh!"

Neyah nearly jumped out of her skin at the roaring sound. "Bosco! You are worse than lions sneaking up on zebras!"

Bosco roared his best lion roar again and laughed gleefully before snatching Neyah's list. "What is this?"

"Give that back!" Neyah bounced up and attempted to grab it.

Bosco ran from the hut shrieking with delight. "Neyah has a secret. Neyah has a secret," he taunted as Neyah chased.

He began weaving in and around the stacks of firewood and playful goats. "This looks like your boyfriend list! Hey Paul, did you know Neyah has fifty new boyfriends? Devi will be jealous. And what about Moswen? He is a perfect catch for you! He can do all the talking, and you can keep on saying nothing!" His laughter made Neyah burn with anger.

Bosco slowed enough to let Neyah get near him.

"Tell me what this is, and I will give it back!" She grabbed at the paper and missed. Bosco spun and took off.

"If you do not tell me, I might be burning it." He held the list over Mama's fire.

Neyah jumped at Bosco, knocking him over. When she yanked the paper from him, it tore in half. Neyah burrowed her knee into her brother's side until he cried out in pain.

"If you must know, this is my dream list," she yelled. "One of these groups is going to build us a well someday. If we have a well, I can go to school and Mama will not wear herself out fetching water. The water will be clear of nasty bugs that kill people. And we will not have to bury Papa!"

Bosco's eyes grew large. He had never heard his sister shout.

"Your bellyaches will disappear, and no one will get their hands cut off by crazy bandits. We will have more water than we know what to do with!"

Finally, her voice dropped to a whimper and tears dripped from her dark eyes onto Bosco's dusty shirt. "If we had built a well a long time ago, we would still have Lulu." Yanking the other half of her list from Bosco, she picked herself up.

Hearing the commotion as he returned from planting, Papa stepped forward to intervene. Mama shook her head at him and started calling out chores.

"Bosco and Paul, grind maize. Kato and Hassan, I need firewood. Neyah, you and Nilsa need to go to the river today."

Neyah's body tensed.

"One of Uncle Aman's donkeys broke a leg," Mama said. "He had to kill it."

"He has another donkey," Kato said.

"Uncle Aman needs it in the field. Neyah, you will have to go the regular route."

The regular route? With bandits and machetes?

The twins moved their eyes from Mama to Neyah and back to Mama.

"Mama," Neyah pleaded.

Mama could feel the fear brewing inside her daughter.

"Neyah, it is March, and yes, the rain is overdue. It may come by morning. We need water now. One fetch is all."

"You think the rain is coming tomorrow, Mama?" asked Paul, whose cough had returned. "I guessed tomorrow will be the first rain! If it rains, I will win the school contest!"

"I hope we are both right," smiled Mama as she waved Neyah off.

Tilting her head skyward to the fast-moving clouds, Neyah prayed the rains would hold off until she was off the cliff.

The girls weren't alone on the trail. Apparently, everyone in the village needed water. This comforted Neyah.

Walking by the site of Malaika's attack, Neyah welcomed Nilsa's conversation.

"What did you guess for the first rain, Neyah?"

"I missed school the day Mr. Sahli asked for guesses."

"Do you think it will rain next Thursday?" Nilsa asked excitedly.

Neyah giggled. "I sure hope so because it sounds like you would be the winner!"

"Yes! I want to win the rain crown this year!"

Neyah hoped the rain would come sooner than Nilsa's prediction, but she didn't want to ruin her cousin's enthusiasm.

Soon, the girls passed the lone tree. Its waving branches beckoned them closer. Neyah wanted to take a rest against its sturdy trunk but chose to stay close to the others.

The descent down the bluff proceeded without incident.

Once they climbed out of the valley with their water, Nilsa let out a huge sigh. "My legs feel like weak porridge!"

Neyah nodded. "We have not done this climb for a while."

After a short rest, the girls walked on with the other fetchers.

"The tree!" A woman's shriek brought the caravan to a stop.

Neyah held her arm over her eyes to shade them from the bright Kenya sunlight. The special tree that grew all alone had something...no...someone, slumped against it.

"Neyah!" Nilsa whispered. "Is that your scarf?"

"Do not look," a woman in the lead called out. "Keep going!"

Neyah pulled her jerry can off and let it slide to the ground. She started toward the tree.

"What are you doing?" The lead woman scolded. "Do not go over there!"

Compassion drew Neyah to the tree. She recognized the baggy clothes and oversized sandals. His torn leather flask lay on the ground. Around the little man's neck, the orange scarf she'd lost cradled his sagging head. The tails of it fluttered in the thick afternoon heat.

A mournful cry rose from somewhere deep inside Neyah.

When the wind brought a whiff of his decaying body her way, Neyah covered her nose and turned away. She picked up a stick and scratched a single word into the dry ground.

ADEN

34

FINALLY, RAIN!

For days, Mr. Sahli felt the anticipation in the air. Giddy students played rain games during breaks and giggled over silly jokes. Excitement over the school's upcoming annual rain festival and outdoor games grew as each day passed without rain. The crowning of the Saramba School Rain Queen and King was the highlight of the year, and no one wanted to miss it. The girl and boy who guessed the closest date of the first measurable rain earned the crowns and led the festival parade.

Following the morning gathering, Mr. Sahli looked to the sky. "Students, for a week, dark clouds have threatened. Still, no rain! In my bones, I feel we're close. Before we leave today, let's board windows and every hole in the walls. Your help is appreciated!"

A crease formed on Mr. Sahli's forehead as he scanned the faces of his students. He took attendance noting the unusual and eerie quietness.

"This is a small class today. Is there a pre-rain party going on that someone forgot to invite us to?"

Somber faces indicated there was no party. Moswen rose

from his bench. "Sir. Nilsa went to fetch yesterday alone. She never came home."

Mr. Sahli thought about today's lesson. He planned to give his final teaching on the cycle of rainy and dry seasons. Since civilization began, people had built their homes near water sources. He doubted students cared about that today.

Journal words and definitions filled the blackboard: drought, rainfall, and reservoir. His plan to surprise students with new pencils and prizes for the "name-the-season" game would wait.

Among the absent—Neyah and her brothers, home, mourning the loss of their cousin.

THREE DAYS later as villagers slept, the night sky over West Pokot County put on a light show. Thunder rumbled for an hour to announce the official end of the long dry season. When the Letsokoane villagers first heard the slap of raindrops on their thatched roof, they poured out of their homes and into the village center. As rain smacked the dry land, the jubilee began.

Even Papa was energized by the rain.

"I do not want to miss the celebration!" Bibi called.

"I will help you," offered Papa.

As Mama and Neyah scrambled to set out pots to collect the gift from above, Kato entertained himself by spouting water from his mouth in a perfect arc high in the air. His three brothers, totally drenched, screeched and chased each other in circles.

As the crowd swelled, each raindrop worked hard to find its way over the people and into the thirsty soil. Laughing and singing, the villagers washed their worries away and drew new life into every thirsty pore.

Papa sat with Bibi under the tarp. He watched as children

threw back their heads, drinking in the cool drops. Elders raised their arms skyward in praise for the return of the much-needed rain. The celebration went on until exhaustion chased the dripping crowd back to their huts to finish the night's sleep.

Thankful for the rain, Papa fell asleep with sadness on his mind. Something got little Nilsa, his brother's only daughter. And only days before the rain came.

Two DAYS LATER, a rusty pail of water sat outside the school entrance. Each student, splattered with mud from a slippery walk to school, washed their feet in it before entering the school.

"I'm happy you made it safely today," Mr. Sahli shouted as the rain hammered the tin roof. "This is a blessing of a day. We have rains soaking our newly planted fields and water holes and...it's finally time to learn the winners of the Rain King and Queen! But first, here are some announcements. I'm ending this first trimester a few days early due to the danger of navigating the muddy trail to get here. Crawling to school on your hands and knees is no joy."

Students tipped their heads in agreement.

"As usual," he continued, "we're running out of supplies. The chalk is gone, and pencils too. After today's lessons, take what is left of the paper and other supplies to practice your writing at home."

"Now for the *big* announcement!" Mr. Sahli yelled. His wide smile was contagious. "Some of you guessed close to the rain date, and some of you were simply great wishers!" His laughter, muted by the roof racket, hid what he was feeling.

"The winner of the Rain King crown is...Mr. Nathaniel!"

Like a rabbit chased from his hole, loud Nathaniel raced to the front of the room while everyone hooted and hollered.

"And the winner of the Rain Queen crown is...Miss Saida!"

Malaika hopped up and hugged her sister. Saida beamed and proudly took her place on the other side of Mr. Sahli. As the teacher placed the crown on Saida's head, he thought of the true winner of the Rain Queen crown: Nilsa.

WATER FETCHING LOOKED different during the heavy rainy season, which lasted until mid-May. It meant collecting rainwater in the village from scattered clay jars, pots, and bowls.

"The gourds are all full, Mama." Neyah's soaked dress stuck to her body after the last downpour.

Mama handed her a pile of goatskin bags. "Start using these to store the water."

Bibi laughed. "Neyah girl, are you happy now that fetching water is no further than the nearest pot?"

"Yes, Bibi, except school is closed."

"Ah, with the rainy season we get floods and slippery paths. Too much water is sometimes a bigger problem than lack of water."

35

MAKING AN IMPACT

Cool, dry air crept into the Rift Valley at the end of May. Field crops grew tall and strong. With the rainy season behind them and the stored water already gone, women and girls returned to the water holes to fetch.

"Malaika, you and your thumb hold your water can pretty good!" Neyah said.

Malaika smiled. "I guess I did not need those other fingers after all."

Neyah watched Malaika descend the ravine to her village. "See you tomorrow!"

Hoping her brothers brought her mail, Neyah hurried home. The April school break meant no mail, and even when school resumed in May, she'd heard nothing from the organizations she'd written to. With June only two days away, she ached to hear from more of them.

As she unloaded her water, Paul handed her a folder with shaky arms. "Here is your homework! There is a letter in there, too."

Neyah's heart raced. "Paul, this might be a yes!"

After a coughing bout, he asked, "A yes about what?"

The envelope she found in her folder looked official.

"About getting a well for Letsokoane!" she squealed as she flipped it over. Disappointment drained her excitement when she saw the USA return address in the corner with the translator's name under it. She found a cool place under the acacia tree to read Abby's letter.

Dear Neyah,

I hope this finds you safe and healthy.

This isn't a letter a mother ever wants to write. My news is such sad news. Your friend and our dear sweet Abby died on April 10th at home in our arms.

Neyah gripped the paper in disbelief. Praying she read it wrong the first time, she reread the first lines. *Abby died on April 10th*.

Nearly muted by the hungry bleating goats, Neyah's strangled cry bled through the compound. She cried on and couldn't be consoled even when Mama came running and rocked her like a baby. Neyah choked out the same words over and over. "Little Nilsa gone, and now Abby. My rafiki died."

Once Neyah's tears let up, she noticed the circle. Bibi, her brothers. Everyone except Papa. Her heart ached for his arms to console her.

Reaching across the family circle, Bosco picked Mrs. Larson's letter from the ground and cast a sympathetic eye toward Neyah. After a moment of silent communication with his sister, he read the letter aloud.

Dear Neyah,

I hope this finds you safe and healthy.

This isn't a letter a mother ever wants to write. My news is *such sad news. Your friend and our dear sweet Abby died on April 10th at home in our arms.*

Words cannot say what this means to lose our precious angel. She fought for life to the end.

Abby asked us to read your letters to her over and over. She wanted to thank you for sending Malaika's skirt. Like a blankie in her arms the last days, she found great comfort rubbing the soft flowers.

Knowing she awakened your voice delighted Abby and made her proud. Thank you for sharing the priceless gift of your voice. It gives her short life a greater purpose, even beyond the joy she brought us all.

Before her thirteenth birthday, Abby told us she changed her mind about what she wanted for a gift. For two years she begged for a cell phone. We couldn't believe our ears when she claimed she didn't need one after all! Instead, she insisted on birthday money to add to her Every Drop Counts campaign. She received over $250 that she put toward your well fund. (We still got her the cell phone ☺).

The past months changed Abby. Her illness caused her to stop and consider priorities. But we believe you are the catalyst who moved her to stop thinking so much about herself and to consider what it's like to walk in other people's shoes. She talked constantly about you walking miles every day for water. It bothered her. A picture she drew of you fetching water is still taped to the ceiling over her bed with the words "Do Something" written across it. When I asked what that was about, she said, "It's my purpose!"

Abby's "sleepover" friends brought thirteen yellow buckets to her funeral. They overflowed with donations. We asked for all funds given in her memory to go toward your well. There is no doubt this is what Abby wanted.

A week after Abby's service, kids in our neighborhood

planned a water balloon fight. Participants donated money for every balloon they tossed. I got drenched pretty good when I walked in on it! By the way, the balloons were-you guessed it-yellow!

I'm finally getting to the most amazing part. Word spread on social media and over $400,000 has poured in so far.

Abby's dad checked into groups that build wells in African communities. It seems everyone he's contacted has heard from you already! Good for you!

Speaking of Abby's dad, another wonderful thing is his return home to us, and he has a job he loves. We're a closer family than ever. Sometimes it takes a tragedy to realize what you have. I hope your papa also comes to understand the gift he has in you and his family.

Think of all the good that grew from two girls from opposite sides of the world having a conversation about the most important gift of all: purpose. I just reread your first letter to Abby. In it, you said your name means "life's purpose." I believe you and Abby will be forever connected through a common dream, a common purpose of using your voice to help others.

May you never forget our Abby, your friendship, and her challenge for you to use your voice and gather your team to make a positive impact. Abby told me you like words. Maybe you'd like to add "impact" to your journal.

Never stop dreaming.

Our warmest gratitude,

The Larson family

One last thing-I know Abby wanted to meet you and see the well she was sure you would make happen. Unfortunately, that won't happen. The rest of our family would like to visit one day and return Malaika's skirt. For now, it lies on Abby's bed, next to her yellow bucket, which holds all your letters.

By the time Bosco finished reading, Neyah wasn't the only one shedding tears. Bibi and Mama wiped away tears, and the boys sat quietly.

Neyah felt numb. Abby always sounded so...alive. Even when she was sick. It didn't seem possible. And all the money given by strangers for—a well? How could something so terrible and so wonderful be mixed together?

Neyah finally spoke. "I am sorry, Mama."

"Sorry? For what?"

"I know you and Papa do not like it when I—when I try to change things."

"Neyah," Mama whimpered. "It seems I have a lot to learn from my daughter and her friend from across the ocean about this thing called change."

Mama shifted and faced her daughter. "I fear change because the only change I know is the kind bringing death or drought or floods. As for dreams, I stopped dreaming years ago. I want to dream again. I need you, my daughter, to teach me how."

Neyah grabbed Mama's hands and whispered to her tearful eyes. "Mama. Someone has to fetch water. Why not dreams?"

FIVE METERS AWAY, Papa sat in disbelief at what he'd overheard. His daughter and a stranger from half a world away had teamed up to change the way things had always been done. And worse yet, it appeared his wife was being influenced by all this talk of change.

I cannot let that happen, Papa thought. *But how do I stop it? How do I stop my daughter from dreaming? It is like asking the moon to stop rising.*

Rubbing his hand across his forehead in frustration, Papa

began to shake. He knew it wasn't from illness. It was the same awful shaking that happened every time fear set in and grabbed him; it was the same uncontrollable dread he'd experienced as a boy when his family had been attacked. It took over his legs, his stomach, his mind. Papa heard it screaming at him, reminding him he wasn't in control of everything or anything, not even his own family.

Once the shaking subsided, Papa took a deep breath and muttered to himself. "Change. Yes. There will be change. I will see to it."

Fatigue crawled through every inch of Papa's body begging him to rest. He curled into a fetal position and wrapped his arms around his bony middle. Mumbled words of prayer led him closer to a much-needed sleep. His final words before he drifted off barely made it past his lips: "May my decision to trade my daughter be the right one. If not, forgive me."

36

BRAVERY

"I feel much better." Papa smiled as the family finished their evening meal of ugali and a few vegetables. Still thin and needing a walking stick, he made an announcement. "The nurse said the cholera is gone." Cheers erupted and the twins nearly knocked him over with hugs.

Neyah heard Papa's announcement and felt a flood of relief as she finished her meal in her hut. Papa might not love her anymore, but she still loved him. And now that he was better, she thought it might be time to ask for more of the moon. Taking a deep breath, she stood and walked out wearing the confidence of Abby Larson.

"Papa, maybe you would like to help me with a small project."

Neyah's brothers stared wide-eyed in silence waiting for Papa's reaction to her boldness. Months had passed since they'd heard their sister and Papa have a conversation.

"You are good at building things," she continued. "You and I can teach others in the village how to build a tippy tap."

"Neyah, stop. Please." Mama's pitiful plea to halt didn't work.

"Papa, you told me silence kills. When that lion stalked Bibi and me, you insisted I be done being a quiet girl. You are right. I am done."

"Neyah!" Mama clutched her chest.

Staring at the ground, Papa asked, "What is a tippy tap?"

"Mr. Sahli taught us how to build one. Follow me."

She led him behind her hut with her head held high. Everyone followed.

Neyah pointed to a contraption made from two forked branches stuck in the ground. Across the two supports lay a straight stick with a plastic water jug and bar of soap hanging from it.

Kato's eyes grew big as he strolled around it. "You built this? It looks as good as Mr. Sahli's!"

Neyah's face grew warm.

Mama inspected it. "What is it for?"

"It is a handwashing station, Mama." Neyah's eyes sparkled. "Watch."

Neyah knelt and touched the stick attached to the water jug with a light rope. As Neyah's foot leaned against the stick, the container tilted and poured water on her hands. After rubbing soap on her hands, her foot pressed for more water to rinse her hands.

Neyah held her breath in anticipation as Papa inspected the tippy tap.

"Papa, you do not have to touch anything so germs cannot spread, and since you control it with the foot pedal, no water is wasted."

Papa looked at Neyah for the first time in weeks. "Child, you are not only dreaming; you are also doing. Anything else you have dreamed up?"

Neyah's face lit up at his interest. "Papa, you can build latrines. Mr. Sahli can show you how!"

Bosco laughed. "You asked for it, Papa."

Papa studied the tippy tap. "With all this building, will I have time to tend to my fields and cattle?"

The twins giggled.

"Only if you are fast!" quipped Neyah.

Papa's face clouded. He clenched his fists and shouted. "I will show you fast." His bare foot met the thick horizontal stick of the washing station at its midpoint causing the plastic vessel to fall and split open as it struck the rocky ground. Water sprayed into Neyah's face and mingled with her shock.

As Papa stomped away, Neyah's wet eyes followed him.

37

DREAM OF A WELL

"Students, the cooler season is here!" Mr. Sahli announced as June breezes soothed the air.

Students jumped from their seats and cheered with delight. They knew exactly what Mr. Sahli's words meant.

The headmaster laughed and punched the air to celebrate the relief from the high temperatures the winter months brought. Students shoved, lifted, and carried every bench and table to a shady area outdoors. Following the morning gathering and singing of the national anthem, Mr. Sahli delivered his first lessons against the backdrop of magical Mt. Melo. For the next two months, the great outdoors would be their classroom.

As her brothers began their first outdoor school days, Neyah sat in her hut finishing her letter to Abby's parents. The shock of Abby's and Nilsa's deaths lingered. The humiliation over Papa's reaction to the tippy tap still burned. But the loss of her cousin and Abby renewed Neyah's commitment to take action, no matter the cost.

Dear Abby's Mama and Papa
  My body and soul weep of the news of your daughter and

my friend I cannot believe this tumor that kills her She was filled with much life and wanted only good She not even know me and she helped me None of that good dies She lives on in my heart I do as Abby did She did not give up I will not give up My small voice now be big voice She told me not to wait I look for way to change what needs change now

To my rafiki Abby who now is in heaven I say asante for your heart of kindness You make me see my dreams and purpose are nothing but a rock until I do something

I be sad to not finish dream of meeting Abby Her picture I keep forever I wrap her Millie Andrew Mama and Papa and her Isaac and Jada and sleepover friends in arms of comfort from my family

I still say your turn Abby Larson Your turn to rest in heaven I take over your job now and keep talking and doing for you my friend

Thank you for being my inspiration.

Neyah

PS Still I dream of a well Water shooting up and soaking Letsokoane people to the skin When that day rises I look into my cup and see clean through to face of Abby And still I dream of my papa holding me again same as Abby's papa holds her

At midday, Neyah changed into her uniform and walked to school with Saida.

Hearing the girls' voices, Mr. Sahli leaned out a window to greet them. As the person in charge of enforcing school rules, he was supposed to discipline tardy students or those with a dirty uniform or no pencil by sending them home. Although he believed in sound discipline and teaching children to be responsible citizens, Mr. Sahli never sent a student home. When they woke before dawn to fetch water, feed animals, or care for younger siblings, he was happy to see them no matter what time they arrived.

"Welcome girls!"

Mr. Sahli noted Neyah's sad face. Wondering if her Papa had fallen ill again, he came to her table. "How are you today, Miss Neyah?"

Without looking at him, she handed him two letters: the one from Mrs. Larson and the one she'd written to the Larsons.

Mr. Sahli skimmed the first letter and squeezed his eyes shut as though in pain. Kneeling beside Neyah, he picked up her quaking hand.

"I'm very sorry to hear about Abby. It sounds like the two of you could move a mountain once you set your mind to it."

Neyah's throat tightened and once again felt her heart splintering.

"You probably could use a little good news then."

Mr. Sahli held up an envelope he picked out of the drawer in his rickety desk.

"Another one came yesterday. *This* could be the one, Neyah!" His contagious smile accompanied his words each time an agency letter came.

Neyah sensed her teacher's efforts to cheer her up and forced an appreciative smile as she wiped away tears.

The agency letter ended up being just another form letter explaining the lengthy process to be considered for a well project. Big words Neyah didn't understand like political congruency, sanitation committees, and financial sustainability popped up throughout the letter. She wrote them in her journal and asked Mr. Sahli to define them.

Neyah sighed. "Abby would never give up, and neither will I. Mr. Sahli, I sent my persuasive letter, but these agencies want more. They need a proposal, whatever that is."

Mr. Sahli smiled into Neyah's hopeful eyes. "Are you

willing to give up your exercise breaks to help me write a proposal?"

Neyah's face glowed. "You have a deal." She stuck her hand out. His deep laugh filled the air as he took her small hand and shook it until Neyah finally pulled away in a pile of giggles.

38

THE WATER PRESIDENT

It was a perfect afternoon to nap or relax and enjoy an early September day of mild temperatures and clear skies. But no one in Letsokoane felt relaxed.

Hassan twisted a stick back and forth until it snapped in two. "When will they be here?"

Bosco and Kato kicked a rag ball with two friends while Neyah paced back and forth. "Soon...I hope."

"Patience," urged Bibi.

Neyah's family waited along with other villagers for the special guests to arrive. Two hours passed.

After Mr. Sahli and Neyah had spent months trying to get an agency interested in considering Letsokoane for a possible well dig, one had actually agreed to come and check it out. Today was the day. Neyah thought a few more hours of waiting wouldn't matter. But, as always, patience wasn't her strength.

Excited about what this gathering meant, Hassan asked, "Where did all these people come from? This is like the rain festival parade, only bigger!"

Neyah patted him on the back. "It seems other villages want

a well as much as we do, Hassan. But today is our day. We are going to find out what our future might bring."

Bibi and Paul leaned on one another for support. Although Bibi had just recovered from pneumonia, she insisted on coming. Her arm motioned Neyah to her side. "Your papa is here, child."

"He is?" Neyah jerked her head up in a panic and searched with anxious eyes for her father. She wanted him to share in the excitement over this day, but she was also keenly aware that it had been six months since Papa had announced his decision to exchange her for cattle.

Bibi touched her pale hand against her granddaughter's chest and then her head. "Neyah, Papa is here and here. His heart and mind are with you. His pride will follow."

Neyah slumped. "Bibi, everyone from the county is here. Everyone, except Papa. For all we know, he is finalizing his deal to make me a wife."

Neyah missed Papa terribly. Now that he felt stronger, he managed to spend short periods working manure into the rocky fields. Cholera had failed to kill him, but it appeared her big ideas might. She recalled Papa's reaction to the tippy tap and sighed. Mr. Sahli is right. Some people aren't interested in change.

"Here they come!" Kato shouted.

Neyah's heart thumped in her chest as she stretched to get a glimpse. Her skin itched, but she tried to ignore it. Instead, she concentrated on the officials who came to decide if Letsokoane met the requirements for their next well-digging site.

Two dusty jeeps crawled between the crowded lines of onlookers and stopped near the village center. Five men and two women stepped out. The men in their dark suits and tight collars wiped the sweat from their faces as they strolled to an open area. Their formal dress made them look official, but quite out of place in the primitive village. Wearing long, colored skirts and wide-brimmed hats, the women smiled and waved at the curious onlookers standing near the grass huts.

"Good afternoon, ladies and gentlemen!" Mr. Sahli's beaming smile and long strides met the guests. Several village elders accompanied him.

"Good afternoon to you," replied a man who appeared to be the spokesperson. "It's our pleasure. I presume you are Mr. Sahli."

Pumping the man's hand with gusto, Mr. Sahli grinned. "Yes, indeed, and you must be Mr. Rono."

Still not believing it, Neyah clasped her hands under her chin. One of the many proposals she and Mr. Sahli wrote finally received an encouraging reply. Representatives from The Water Saves Project stood before her. They came to assess the commitment of the village to this life-changing project. Neyah tried to read their expressions. If today turned out the way she hoped, these people would work with local experts to study their land, conduct interviews, and complete geological tests to weigh the possibility of finding water. According to Mr. Sahli, the determination of whether their village would receive a well wouldn't be made for several weeks. But she had made it this far...and her dream of a village well finally felt possible.

Mr. Rono and the others took turns shaking hands with the elders and, at last, addressed the crowd.

"Good afternoon, everyone!" Mr. Rono's voice sounded important and cheerful.

The attentive and quiet crowd came to life. Whistling and clapping, the villagers rose to their feet offering the guests a jubilant welcome.

Mr. Rono and his colleagues laughed and clapped along enthusiastically.

"Judging from this crowd and your excitement, I can see there is great anticipation here over this thing called water!"

The crowd erupted again with high trilling sounds and lots of banging on iron pots.

"We are thrilled too, for there is nothing more important to your health, your future, and your children's future than to have access to clean water every day. Our visit is the first step in determining whether this project is something you are committed to. For if we dig and find water and build this well, it is not our well. It is yours. Yours to maintain and care for—not just a few days or months, but for years. If our hydrogeologists decide this is a good spot to find water, we only dig if your community is ready for this change. You will need funds to pay for repairs. We expect you to establish a water committee to oversee the entire project from digging and maintenance to ensuring sound sanitation efforts. The water committee job is huge. Each person on it must believe in this 100 percent, and it needs a persistent leader. Are there any questions?"

"Only one," called out Mr. Sahli.

"Yes?"

"We have our committee. Are you interested in meeting the members?"

Mr. Rono stalled. He knew his agency's policy. He was hired to guide the formation of the water committee and explain the roles and responsibilities. It seemed these folks jumped ahead and had chosen their committee.

He twisted to his left and silently surveyed his colleagues. One shrugged with a "why not" gesture. The woman with a straw hat beamed and tipped her head forward.

"All right!" called Mr. Rono. "This is highly unusual to already have a water committee. But let's meet them!"

Seven villagers stepped forward and faced the guests.

Mr. Sahli poured his pride out over the crowd. "Letsokoane

voted these individuals to our committee. *When* a well is built, this will be the best and happiest water committee you have ever met!"

One by one, each member introduced themselves.

"I am Mayor Bazaar, chosen to represent our community and handle the budget and communication."

"My name is Monica, chosen for my honesty as the treasurer. I will read the water meter and collect 100 shillings a month from each family for maintenance and repairs."

"Jambo. I am Julius, chosen as a mechanic. I fixed a well in another community. I know how to make tools, too."

"My name is Gideon, chosen as a builder. Julius and I will maintain the well and recruit villagers to build animal troughs and latrines."

"I am Hadjara. I am a mother and almost like a nurse. I will teach hygiene and sanitation."

"I am Omar Sahli, chosen as a teacher to help Hadjara show villagers how to build and use hand and dishwashing stations."

The last person came forward and took a deep breath.

"I am Neyah Jabari, chosen for my dreams and purpose to save lives and be...the water committee president."

Mr. Rono shifted his weight. The crease between his eyes deepened. His colleagues looked amused.

Mr. Rono finally spoke. "The water president. How old are you?"

Neyah stretched tall and answered promptly. "Nearly fourteen, sir." Her bright yellow shirt from the secondhand market commanded attention.

"And what, uh, what skills do you bring to this project?"

"I read, I write, and most of all, I use my voice. I will track water usage. I will do anything!"

Neyah paused, detecting a sense of hesitancy in Mr. Rono who stood rubbing his neck.

"Sir, if you are not interested in our project, I will keep searching for someone who is. I walked up to six hours a day for water for almost eight years. Mr. Rono, sir, we all have dreams here, and as you said, we cannot achieve any of them without clean water."

Mr. Rono looked into Neyah's youthful eyes as if searching the depths of her determination.

"Neyah, what are your plans as the water president?"

Neyah tilted her chin up. Her eyes drifted to the crowd, distracted by the sight of Papa standing with a group of men who didn't appear too pleased. She held his gaze. Was Papa proud of her or disgusted? Could he be thinking about the words he told her after chasing the lion away? "You are done being a quiet girl. Silence kills." Or was he calculating how many cows he could get if he traded her?

Neyah cleared her throat and began. "As water president..."

Papa turned and walked away. With emotion filling her chest, Neyah watched him make his way out of the crowd. She folded her hands in front of her and turned toward Mr. Rono, the one likely to decide whether to proceed with this project. She swallowed hard.

"As water president, I will hold regular meetings and talk to everyone about taking responsibility for paying their water fee and practicing good hygiene. If they ask questions, I will find answers. I will care for this well as a mama cares for a baby. When it needs something, here I am."

Mr. Rono tilted his head to study Neyah. Was it desperation in her eyes? No, more like a guided purpose. She had done her research into what the responsibilities were. But could he depend on a young girl to pull this off? His eyes tried reading the thoughts of the other committee members. He gazed beyond them to the waiting crowd.

Neyah registered Mr. Rono's doubt. Gesturing to the man

standing beside her, she said, "And Mr. Sahli will help me with everything."

Mr. Rono leaned back on his heels and turned to the crowd. "Is there anyone who questions this young lady becoming your water president?"

Neyah held her breath and closed her eyes in a silent plea. *Please, Papa.*

A pair of birds sang overhead as the officials surveyed the crowd and waited.

Neyah felt lightheaded with anticipation. She let her breath out and opened her eyes.

From a bench at the back of the crowd, Papa mechanically leaned forward and slowly pulled himself to a stand. He took his time walking to the front of the crowd. As Neyah caught sight of him, her body stiffened. Her chest drummed with something between anger and dread. *It has been six months.*

Mr. Rono didn't notice Papa. Hearing no response from the crowd to his question, he motioned to his team members. One by one, they nodded. When he turned back to Neyah, a smile flooded his face. Mr. Rono extended his hand. Neyah squealed with excitement as she grabbed and pumped his hand victoriously.

"Friends of Letsokoane," Mr. Rono called to the crowd, "as representatives of The Water Saves Project of Kenya, it's our pleasure to introduce your water committee members and...your water president!"

The villagers leaped to their feet joyously applauding while Neyah's eyes brimmed with tears.

Papa twisted the heel of his worn sandal into the dirt as his eyes locked with Neyah's. Her mouth opened to draw in air, then she watched him spin and make his way away from the crowd and back to his field.

39

PAPA'S DOUBTING CLUB

The drilling rigs couldn't make it to Letsokoane. Too wide and too steep, the ravine made it impossible.

"We need to bridge that gully so the drilling equipment can safely drive across it. Each family needs to send one member each day to help the construction crew fill it in. Bring a basket or wheelbarrow or your own hands to carry rock and gravel."

Neyah got used to repeating these instructions at the family meetings she held as her first water president assignment. Juggling her fetching and chores with school and committee work stretched her thin, but she never tired.

Once the water committee got the word that the hydro-geological reports showed a high potential for water in the area, Neyah's focus sharpened. Most people listened, hugged her, and offered her food. Others argued and expressed skepticism. Committee members accompanied Neyah to lend their support and answer questions. But it was clear to everyone in Letsokoane that it was Neyah Jabari who was boldly and feverishly leading the mission.

The drilling company felt confident a well could also be dug in Malaika's village once the ravine was gone. No one acted surprised when Neyah suggested Malaika be water president for her community. Malaika immediately began recruiting her own committee with confidence.

"Look at us, Neyah!" Malaika waved her stumped hand over her head. "Here we are trying to persuade our elders to bring a miracle. Who knew Mr. Sahli's persuasion assignment could be used right here in our villages!"

The two young water presidents understood the benefit of having a water source close by. However, convincing their communities wasn't easy.

"Who will pay for all this?" An elderly man with a walking stick demanded. Neyah knew he was Papa's friend. She wondered how many others Papa dragged into his doubting club.

"Remember the story of Abby I told you? Before she died, she asked her school to help raise money, and now over a million dollars has been given to bring clean water to places like ours. Those generous donations plus resources from local agencies, along with our hard work, will pay for it."

Papa's "doubting club" indeed had formed and met often. About a dozen men huddled together in a field a good distance from the ravine. Zuberi, a man who seldom agreed with Papa in the past, now seemed to be Papa's closest confidant. He discussed the notion that a well might end the tradition of keeping girls and women busy fetching water.

"What will our wives and daughters do?" Zuberi asked. "Get an education and leave? Who will build the huts and cook and clean? And how will we get more cattle if our daughters leave? We will be left with nothing to trade."

"How will we pay for the maintenance?" another man asked.

Often quiet at these meetings, Papa added, "Do not worry. A well will dry up in the dry season just like the mudholes."

"Haji, bringing a well to Letsokoane is a big mistake," Zuberi insisted. "The water committee is run by your daughter. You need to put a stop to this."

Papa nodded in agreement. Turning to the man standing beside him, he spoke sternly. "It is time, Silas. It has been more than six months, and it is a perfect time to stop this nonsense idea of a well. Deliver my cattle and I will bring my daughter to you."

"I had some bad luck, Haji. Several cows have died. I will need at least another year to grow my herd and trade for your daughter."

Papa fell into a shaking rage. "I said six months!"

"I did not kill the cattle, Haji. The drought took them."

As Silas walked away, Papa's shaking slowly lessened. He wondered, *is there nothing I can control? What else can I do to stop a girl who is motivated to change the way we have always lived?*

Two MONTHS LATER, with the ravine filled and packed, a gravel road joined the two villages allowing heavy equipment to cross. On a clear December morning, the rumbling machines rolled across the ravine, and workers began setting up the drilling rig.

On the morning of the first drilling day, Hassan and Kato sprang like jumping beans from their sleeping hut.

"We are going to go watch!"

Mama held up her hand. "Whoa! First your chores!"

246 | MARY BLECKWEHL

"Aww, Mama," groaned Hassan.

On the most important day of her life, Neyah woke with a smile she couldn't hide and quickly slipped into her favorite floral smock. Curious about the unfamiliar voice outside her hut, she listened at the entrance.

"She is a headstrong girl, Silas, but my daughter will make a good wife," Papa explained as he wrung his hands. "You will have to let her know who the ruler is, though. She used to be an obedient, quiet girl. Lately, we see a different side. It is time to take her from school and contract her as your wife today."

Neyah gasped. *Today? Papa wants to get rid of me now?*

The man named Silas sighed in exasperation. "Don't worry Haji. I can handle your daughter as I have my other wife. But I already told you. I need time to increase my herd. I give you my word. I will have your cattle in a year, maybe less."

With heat crawling up her neck, Neyah peered out of the hut. She could tell Papa was agitated by the way he paced in a tight circle. The man her father called Silas appeared older than Papa.

Papa shook his finger at Silas. "You have one year, Silas. Or I find someone else who has cattle to trade."

Neyah clenched her teeth as Silas and Papa shook hands. She watched Silas leave as Papa walked to the fields.

Fear paralyzed Neyah. Her best day suddenly turned sour. This was her reward for trying to save lives? She started to dash after Papa and beg him to change his mind. Bosco's shouts interrupted her quest.

"Mama! Paul has the fever and is vomiting. He does not want you to know because he wants to watch the digging."

Any other day, Neyah might have felt afraid for Paul and for Mama. But today, she felt afraid for herself. *Was it too late to ask Papa for forgiveness? To send the digging crew away and be content to fetch and drink dirty water until it killed me?*

As the stormy cloud of Paul's illness and Papa's trade deal hung over her, Neyah pondered the idea of calling the whole thing off. But she didn't want to let her community down. She felt like a slice of rubber being stretched back and forth.

Neyah inspected the crowd gathered near the dig site and paced. The people watched and waited as though attending a grand ceremony. Families camped out with their pots and jerry cans. They were more than ready to fill them to the brim from a new, convenient source. Some carried their corn grinding and babies as well as their optimism in tow. With the school year over, women and girls finished their fetching early and brought dried goat meat for the digging crew and a bit for themselves. People from neighboring villages even trickled in the night before, in anticipation of a miracle. *They are all counting on me,* Neyah thought, *but what help can I be if Papa trades me?*

"You are not quitting."

Neyah jumped at the sound.

"Mama!"

"Neyah, we are all in this now. This is for those who have walked and fetched and—died. For your sick Papa and your dying brother, for the Nilsas and Malaikas, and especially for all the baby girls yet to be born who will have choices beyond fetching."

Tears slipped from Neyah's determined eyes. "And for you, Mama. I will not back down."

"Good."

Neyah went to the site between chores and sitting with Paul. The crew's mammoth machine sat anchored and ready to tear into the ground next to a water truck used to aid the project's drilling process. Noticing a lot of green, she touched her green shirt and giggled. Green hard hats, green monster machines and trucks, and even green water bottles for the crew.

However, the sand spinning out of the ground wasn't green. Sand, sand, and more sand. All of it brown and dry.

After many days, Mr. Omondi, the crew manager, called a halt. Standing in front of the water committee, the crowd leaned in to listen. "There is no water here."

A collective groan filled the space.

"This is impossible," Neyah whispered to herself, tasting bitter disappointment. What more could go wrong? Abby and Nilsa. Papa's plan to sell her as a wife. Now this. All of this preparation. The letters. Abby's campaign. She failed. The water president failed.

Neyah felt all eyes on her.

This could not be the end. I am the water president. Abby would do something. I must do something.

Neyah marched forward to the crew leader. "What does this mean, Mr. Omondi?"

"It means we dig again in a new spot the geology survey identified. This happens sometimes. If there's water around here, we'll find it."

Neyah breathed a sigh of relief even though she didn't like the "if" part.

A bigger rig came in. The crew tried two more locations. Drill bits clogged. Bolts broke. A well can collapsed at the second site. A generator stopped working at the third location. Brakes went out on a truck. Tankers carried more fuel in for the compressors.

"These are all common problems." The crew director tried to reassure Neyah at one of his daily updates. "They delay, but they never stop us."

Neyah did her best to be patient but, after the third dig, she felt hope slipping away. Holding a battered jerry can, she stared at the digging rig and spoke to the man in charge. "Water is everything in this place. Many are counting on it. We must find water."

As she went home, she passed Papa hoeing the corn. His uncomfortable stare made her realize a cold truth. His plan to trade her threatened her purpose far more than any dry dig.

As she milked Bela, Neyah overheard her parents talking.

"They still have not found water," Mama said.

"Of course not," Papa said. "Water is in the river. Not under this." He stabbed the hard ground with a stick.

THE MIRACLE

Paul's condition deteriorated overnight. His symptoms mirrored Papa's cholera. Chills shook his body. The village nurse came, but none of her remedies provided relief.

Neyah squatted outside the hut where Paul lay wasting away and wept at the sight inside. Papa rocked Paul's small, sweaty body in his lap. She knew how Papa favored Paul and caught sight of the misery Paul's illness brought her father. Although she hoped this distraction would cause Papa to forget about his plan to sell her, deep down, she doubted it. To make matters worse, Neyah fought a rising fear that all the people she loved were, one by one, slipping away.

Neyah could see Bibi sitting beside Papa in the hut, mumbling prayers as she held vigil over both her son and grandson.

"It is a terrible thing to watch your child's life slipping away before you." Papa's voice cracked.

"Yes, my son. It is," Bibi whispered. "I have experienced it myself."

Papa curled his body in a fetal position around little Paul. A wounded animal howl grew from the depths of Papa's soul.

Only half his size, Bibi took her adult son in her arms and rocked him with the comfort of a mother's love.

"Haji," Bibi whispered, "I believe prayers and time will heal Paul. But you have another child whose life is slipping away from you. Your daughter is like you. Stubborn. Determined. Smart. What will you do with a daughter like that? Throw her dreams away? Sell her for the best cows?"

"Tradition guides me, Mama."

"Tradition has nothing to do with it. It is your foolish pride. It is your fear of losing control. The fear of losing another daughter to something you and I know little about—the future."

Neyah wrapped her arms around her knees and rocked back and forth in silence.

On a sizzling Saturday in mid-January, the crew began digging at a fourth site. Hopes were high as the noon sun, despite the disappointing previous digs. Although several children still came to watch between chores, most adults no longer took the time to stand around and wait for the possibility of striking water. Some decided it wouldn't ever happen. Others, including Bibi, remained to watch over the young children and pray for this miracle hidden deep under the earth.

Darkness crept in, and villagers headed home. The crew took a break before pressing on through the night, something rarely done on a digging site. Time was money, and they were nearing the end of the funds budgeted for this dig.

The Sunday morning sun welcomed the faithful, the curious, and the skeptics. The water president hurried through her chores and ran to the dig site. Pacing, Neyah's eyes scanned the crowd as she awaited her daily progress report.

"You are wearing a rut in the ground." Kato offered her flatbread. Neyah's stomach turned it down.

Spotting Mr. Omondi, Neyah rushed to him to receive the update.

"Good morning, Ms. Water President." Mr. Omondi's friendly smile encouraged her. "Earlier this morning, the drill bit ground through the sand before hitting clay. This is a good sign!"

"What does it mean?"

"It means we keep grinding."

Neyah nodded and returned to a spot behind the caution barricade. The good sign she believed in would be water gushing out of the rig. Until it happened, she'd pace.

"How is Madam President today?"

Mr. Sahli's voice surprised her. "Nervous. Three digs and no water."

"Ah! Your job is not all glory then," he teased.

"It is not going the way I hoped."

The headmaster looked around and noticed Papa Haji staring at him. "Hmm. Yes. Being a leader is not easy."

THE GIGANTIC MACHINE continued to whine and grind. When it struck sandstone, the exhausted and dirty crew let out a whoop, alerting the onlookers of more progress.

Mr. Omondi came to Neyah and yelled over the loud machinery. "The area we hit is water-bearing sandstone. The crew can practically feel the water beneath them. Here comes the final push!" Giving the anxious crowd the thumbs up, he returned to the rig.

For most of the morning, the drill bit spun and cut through rock. Word spread that a water strike was imminent, causing the crowd to swell. When the rig struck an aquifer, a deafening roar filled the air.

The village of Letsokoane held its breath. At first, sludgy gray mud spewed from the ground, followed by strong gusts of water rocketing upward like fireworks.

Glued to the scene, Neyah's eyes filled. *It is happening! It is finally happening.*

A geyser of water taller than the rig shot skyward. It spurted higher and higher until gravity caused it to rain down across the equipment and workers. Waiting years to be released from the earth for this special occasion, the force looked spectacular. The gush glistened against the blue Kenyan sky like diamonds in a light show.

Kato and Hassan squealed and dashed toward the spray with dozens of other children to get soaked in the life-saving flow. Like a magnet, the geyser pulled villagers from their fields and compounds. They encircled the spray and allowed jubilation to rock the digging site.

"Maji! Maji! Maji!" The Swahili word for water swirled with the wet celebration. Mothers lifted babies high to get the first taste. Toddlers scampered under the cool spray, giggling and raising their arms to catch the magic raining down on them. Old and crippled knees dropped to the wet ground in thanksgiving.

Neyah covered her mouth in disbelief. The idea that clean, naturally filtered water sat right there all this time proved too much. Tears streamed down her cheeks and onto the ground that produced this precious gift.

Malaika screamed and dragged her friend into the wet celebration. "See? I told you water is clear!"

Stretching her arms to touch the long-awaited dream, Neyah delighted at the color spectrum filtering through it. She slid her arm through Malaika's and twirled her round and round, soaking up the moment no one thought possible. As other girls joined their celebration circle, an expression of a boundless future splashed across each face.

Neyah raced back to Bibi and, with Mama's help, carried Bibi into the spray of water. They huddled together laughing and crying, allowing the burden of three generations of fetching to drain from them.

The celebration of body and soul-quenching went on for hours.

ALONE IN THE FIELD, Papa leaned against his hoe. In disgust, he shook his head and watched the other fool farmers drop their tools and run to get a closer view of the wet miracle. As the rainbow formed in the water geyser where it met the sunrays, Papa looked away.

"What is the use for that much water?" he snarled and swung his hoe high and hard into the rock-solid ground. His wooden handle cracked in two, and the metal blade flew like a windblown leaf until it dropped several meters away.

41

TOO LATE

Two days passed since the digging rig struck water, but the joy of finding water barely seeped into the Jabari family compound.

"The nurse says Paul only has a few more hours." Mama's frightening words sliced into Neyah like a knife. "There is nothing more to do." Her flat tone sounded like she'd already buried Paul.

Against Mama's advice, Neyah and Bibi went into Paul's hut. Chills racked his shrinking body. His sunken eyes stayed disturbingly wide open. When Neyah touched him, he bolted back as though she'd shocked him. Bibi sang softly, and Neyah twisted her hands in frustration.

Steaming out of the hut in anger, Neyah crashed into Papa. She wanted to yell at him, accuse him of not allowing boiled water and letting Paul die. But one look at Papa and Neyah knew he was out of his mind with worry over Paul. Mama was right. It was too late.

Bosco and Neyah leaned against a sprawling tree near a neighboring compound. Neither spoke as they awaited the inevitable announcement of Paul's passing. The sound of machinery whirred in the distance as the digging crew placed pipes to complete Neyah's dream. Neyah thought it a beautiful day to die. Blue sky with wisps of clouds, birds chirping their happiness, and water flowing. Paul was missing the whole thing. He'd never know they found water. Paul, the storyteller, and Papa's favorite child.

Suddenly, Bosco clamped onto Neyah's arm and pointed at their home fire ring. In astonishment, she watched Papa boil and pour water into a teacup before carrying it to the hut where Paul lay wasting.

A force beyond her control pressed Neyah forward. Transfixed, she watched from the hut entrance as Papa held tea for Paul to sip. Too shocked and confused to breathe, Neyah's lips slightly parted. Her knees weakened.

As he set his tea down, Papa saw Neyah. Their eyes fixed on one another. "One minute did not seem enough," Papa said. "I boil it for two minutes. This is the fourth week."

Neyah should have been happy. Papa did it! He actually boiled water for Paul. Instead, she burned with anger. *He is too late to help Paul. And why is Papa still cutting me out of his world?* She tore out of the compound feeling a rage that had brewed for months.

42

FINISHING ABBY'S JOURNEY

10 months later

It was a long trip. Nearly eighteen hours in the air. More than thirty hours since they left home. Air turbulence, airline food, and nerves didn't help. Only a day's drive and four hundred and thirty kilometers separated the Larson family from the village of Letsokoane.

After a decent night's sleep in the airport hotel in Nairobi, Abby's family woke at 6:00 am on a warm October morning and headed out on the last leg of their journey. They would drive through part of the Rift Valley, a 3,700-mile trench running from Lebanon to southeast Africa. Their itinerary included a safari through Lake Nakuru National Park.

Delighted to get a front seat by the jeep driver, Abby's brother, Andrew, hopped in. "Hey, Kareem! You guys have a steering wheel on the wrong side! Wait 'til my friends back home hear about this!" He snapped photos of Kareem behind the wheel.

"And we drive on the wrong side of the road too!" Kareem's hearty laugh amused Andrew.

As they entered the park over three hours later, everyone grabbed their binoculars.

"Elephants on your right!" Kareem shouted. "Zebras on your left."

"Look at the big white bird on the elephant!" exclaimed Mrs. Larson.

"That is the cattle egret getting a free ride in exchange for eating pesky insects," explained Kareem.

Viewing the wildlife took their minds temporarily off the reason they flew to Africa.

"Wow, look at the pretty flamingos!" exclaimed Millie as they drove by Lake Nakuru. "There must be thousands!" She jotted a note in her bird journal. Millie loved birds and wondered how many new ones she'd see in Kenya.

"Guess what?" Kareem asked. "There are more than a million flamingos out there. Too bad there aren't a million rhinos."

"Oh, I want to see a rhino!" said Andrew. "And wait, you want a million rhinos running around?"

Kareem laughed. "I guess we do not need that many. But we only have about 150 rhinos living in this park. The poachers are getting the best of them."

Janine, the Larson's travel guide, sat in the back with the luggage. "Millie, you see that black-and-white bird hovering over the lake. It's a..."

"Pied kingfisher!" Millie smiled proudly at her bird knowledge. "Wouldn't Abby have loved to draw all these animals?"

"She sure would have," replied Mr. Larson.

The beauty of the safari and African animals captivated Abby's parents too. They held hands and smiled as their children snapped photos of baby elephants, giraffes eating from treetops, and lions lounging in the tall grass.

Once the Larson's jeep exited the national park, Kareem drove them through Baringo County. An occasional herdsman wearing a bright red robe walked along the roadside with goats or cattle.

"Those cows are skinny," commented Andrew.

"This is bush country," Kareem replied. "Lots of thorny bushes, and not much grass for cattle due to overgrazing."

"Pee-yew!" Millie cried, covering her nose as wafts of manure drifted in through the open jeep windows.

"Most of the herders are young children," Mrs. Larson said. "Why aren't they in school?"

"Children do many chores, and herding is one of them," Kareem explained.

The Land Rover barely squeezed past three herders waving at the jeep. They looked hot and thirsty.

Mr. Larson commented, "It doesn't seem like anyone is in a rush to get out of the way."

Kareem replied, "These tribesmen are Maasai. When you have nowhere to go, there is no need to rush." He gave a short history of the tall and proud Maasai tribal people and their centuries-old nomadic traditions.

The jeep took them by several bomas, a grouping of several thatched-roof huts built in a circle. No green lawns, flowers, or lush landscaping, thought Mr. Larson. Just a lot of brown. And yet, he felt drawn to the peaceful setting. He took photos non-stop with his new camera: gently rolling land, thin cattle herded by barefoot children, and an abandoned coke truck parked in the shade of an acacia tree. He smiled as goats jumped in and out of the back end of the truck.

For two more hours, they bumped along on a twisty, washboard dirt road with no air conditioning and poor springs. Mrs. Larson tried to relax and not clench her jaw. Her husband smiled at her and touched her shoulder.

Mangy dogs barked, and young children rushed to their vehicle, waving and smiling as if witnessing a jeep full of celebrities. Some cupped their hands and reached out for —something.

Kareem took a sharp turn onto a side road with deep, dried ruts. Everyone rocked from side to side as dust drifted in through the windows.

"This is awesome!" shouted Andrew.

Feeling a wave of carsickness, Mrs. Larson pulled her shirt up to her dust-filled nose. She thought about her SUV and paved highways back home as she swayed. She wished for such a convenience here. This trip wasn't about comfort though. Abby had been gone for a year and a half. Her family had planned this momentous visit in her honor for months and knew discomfort would be part of the journey.

Stuffed between her parents in the second seat, Millie held on for dear life to her dad's leg. "I need a bathroom."

Hearing Millie's comment, Kareem called out. "There is one ahead. Fifteen minutes."

A half-hour later, Kareem jerked to a stop and yelled, "Bush bathroom break!" and pointed to both sides of the road. Brush and scraggly trees lined the dusty road. With no building in sight, Millie gave her mother a panicked look. She followed her parents out of the Land Rover. Janine, Millie, and her mother walked to one side of the road and found a bush to squat behind. Andrew and the men went to the other side. "Is this the way Neyah's family goes to the bathroom?" Millie asked.

"We'll soon see," Mrs. Larson said.

More than nine hours after leaving the Nairobi hotel, the jeep drove into Letsokoane.

43

THE NEYAH AND ABBY CONNECTION

"I hope they like the well," whispered Neyah to herself as she squeezed into the dress the missions had sent for her fourteenth birthday. It had fit perfect then, but that was months ago. Her head pulsed with excitement and uneasiness. The last time she felt this unsure, she was on her way to visit Malaika after the bandit attack.

"Abby's family is coming today." Neyah continued to talk to herself to calm her nerves. "They will meet my family and see what Team Neyah and Abby accomplished." She smiled as she reached up and touched her plaited hair. Now that she had plenty of water to wash it, she had let it grow out and enjoyed twisting and braiding it with Malaika's help. She gave her hair a pat before crawling out of her hut.

As Neyah walked toward the ravine bridge with Mama, Bibi, and her brothers, the sight took her breath away. Hundreds of people lined the bridge waiting to welcome their guests. Children held a small black-and-white photo of Abby. Hungry goats pranced among the crowd, poking noses in pockets and occasionally finding a corn treat. Oblivious to the significance of the day, skinny pigs and rambling donkeys meandered on the bridge.

An observant Devison spotted the jeep first and shouted "Ab-by! Ab-by!" Everyone joined in and as the chant grew, it traveled down the dirt road to meet Abby's family.

From 150 meters away, Neyah watched as two children jumped out of the jeep and peered with curiosity at the crowd. When the adults emerged, Neyah could feel her heart pounding. She rocked back and forth in her sandals.

MR. LARSON LEANED back to stretch his body. "My legs are so stiff!"

"Yes, and the noise of the jeep engine is still roaring in my ears," said Mrs. Larson.

Kareem laughed. "Ahh...now your ears can hear a better sound!"

"Ab-by! Ab-by! Ab-by!"

As the sound of their daughter's name met them, Mr. and Mrs. Larson held onto each other as though paralyzed. The girl they cried over. The girl they were so proud of. Her name chanted here in Africa, of all places! The sound of Abby's sweet name massaged their sore muscles and evaporated their fatigue. A tiny, barefoot boy barreled toward them and wrapped his arms around Millie's legs. A drum beat in the distance as the steady rhythm of the clapping hands and chanting grew louder. And then, silence.

A single child's voice cried out, "Welcome to the Abby Larson party!" The chanting, drum beating, and clapping resumed.

Abby's loving smile fluttered before the Larson family as

children waved her photo in their direction. Cowbells clanked. The mood felt festive and inviting.

Mrs. Larson's knees weakened, and her hand covered her mouth. She felt the months of grief and fatigue peel away as new emotions took over. Reading through Neyah's letters, she had a grasp of what drew Abby to this special place so far from her home. Now, seeing the villagers with her own eyes, and hearing the joyous celebration, she could better understand the depth of her daughter's connection. These people were proud and devoted to their community. Taking action to solve a problem had been as important to Abby as it was to them.

"Come on!" called Millie to her parents. She and Andrew ran toward the trail lined with villagers.

Mr. Larson turned to his wife. "Annette, look at all the children!"

Noticing bare feet, shaved heads, and beautiful smiles, Mrs. Larson's eyes overflowed with tears as she took in the number of youngsters. Nodding, she searched the faces of the adults. She had lost a child. She knew many of these parents had lost children too.

Mr. Larson reached out to take his wife's hand. "Abby is probably wondering what we're waiting for."

"Let's go, then!" declared Mrs. Larson.

As Abby's parents made their way between the two welcome lines, they stretched out to touch those who came to greet them so enthusiastically. The shaking of hands and clutching of arms went on and on as they passed by strangers who acted like long-lost friends. Noticing open wounds and sores on their hands, the Larsons touched them anyway. Many villagers hugged them tightly. As Mr. and Mrs. Larson relaxed, they leaned in to return warm hugs to these new friends speaking foreign words.

"Karibu! Karibu! Jambo! Karibu!"

Fingers stroked Millie's shiny blond hair. In return, she giggled and smacked high fives.

Andrew took selfies with anyone interested, and it seemed *everyone* was interested!

WAITING at the other end of the bridge, Neyah wrestled with her skirt hem and her emotions. She smiled and clapped along with the others. But on this day when she wanted to only feel joy, consequences weighed heavy on her heart. She managed to bring clean water to her village but had lost Papa in the process.

Bibi tugged at Neyah's arm. "Help me meet our new friends from across the ocean."

Neyah hooked her arm in Bibi's. "I can do that!"

It warmed Neyah to have Bibi with her on such an important day. She knew it bothered her grandmother that Papa refused to attend. Last night, she heard Papa tell Bibi he couldn't be part of "his daughter's selfish dream" to bring a well to Letsokoane. *At least Papa has not traded me yet,* Neyah thought. But the deadline Silas and Papa had agreed on wasn't far off.

She touched one of the many strands of beaded necklaces Bibi had wrapped around her neck. "Bibi, you win the prize for the most colorful jewelry today!"

Bibi giggled as she hobbled along with other members of the Jabari family. "I want to make a good impression on our guests."

Perspiration trickled down Neyah's back. As the Larsons drew near, Neyah noticed the resemblance of Millie to Abby's picture. *Oh, how I wish Abby had lived to see this day.*

Serving as the interpreter as well as the family's travel guide,

Janine introduced the water committee members to Abby's family.

"Jambo! You are Neyah!" Mrs. Larson cried through tears as she reached for her hands and whispered, "Asante sana! Thank you for everything."

Neyah choked out, "Karibu, you are welcome." It baffled Neyah to think she had done anything the Larsons needed to thank her for.

Mrs. Larson watched Neyah's tears spill down her cheeks and struggled to keep her voice steady. "It's wonderful to meet you finally. And this is your family?"

Neyah sniffed and nodded. Seeing Mama smiling and looking proud in her colorful Christmas dress, Neyah's shoulders relaxed.

"This is my beautiful Mama." Mama giggled nervously. "And my loving, patient Bibi." Both women gazed at Mrs. Larson with wet eyes and grasped her arms in gratitude.

"We have much to talk about," Bibi grinned her impish grin.

Neyah motioned to her right. "And here are my brothers, Hassan and Kato." The twins wiggled and strutted like roosters, drawing a laugh from the Larsons. "And this is my oldest brother."

Bowing in an exaggerated fashion, Bosco declared, "I am the Great Bosco, Neyah's business partner."

"Nice to meet you boys," chuckled Mr. Larson. "And your other brother—it's Paul, I believe? I think you wrote he'd been ill."

"Yes, you are right. Paul," said Neyah, her voice thick with emotion. "Paul became very sick last year..." Neyah's eyes swept the crowd. "I wish he..."

Suddenly, a strong-looking boy, with eyes and a grin that matched Papa's, popped out from behind Mama. "Jambo! I am Paul!"

"Oh, yes. Here he is!" Neyah smiled. "Paul is my fourth brother and a little late today as he was babysitting some baby goats."

44

CHANGING HEARTS AND OPPORTUNITIES

K areem carried a large, flat box from the jeep. Handing it to Neyah, Mrs. Larson spoke with warmth. "Abby insisted you have this. I'm hoping it didn't break on our trip here!"

Neyah carefully opened the box. Her face brightened as she peered inside at her reflection.

"It's the mirror Abby hung in her closet," smiled Mrs. Larson. "She didn't know how you could possibly live without a mirror!"

Peering into the magical looking glass took Neyah's breath away. Tears spilled from her bright eyes. She had only seen a wavy outline of herself in the murky mudhole. The mirror not only revealed her wide smile but her new hairstyle.

"I have never seen myself," Neyah said. "Asante."

"You're welcome."

Andrew took an envelope from his cargo pocket. "This is Abby's last letter she wrote to you a year and a half ago. We saved it to give it to you in person."

Neyah bit her lip and swatted away fresh tears as she accepted the letter. "Thank you."

"You can read it later," Andrew whispered with a smile.

Neyah removed a folded paper from her dress pocket and replaced it with Abby's letter. Glancing at Mr. Sahli standing behind her family, she felt reassured by his presence. He helped her write and practice her welcome speech in English. He gave her a gentle nod of encouragement. Taking a deep breath, Neyah's eyes took in each member of Abby's family before beginning.

"We welcome Abby's family from Minnesota to Kenya and to Letsokoane, the place we call home. You came a big distance. We have been looking forward to this day for months. When we say thank you for your visit and kindness, we know you are here to not only rejoice in the water project but also due to great sadness of losing your daughter, your sister, and my good friend.

"We wish to show our big dream of what Abby's big heart helped us achieve. We are happy you came to celebrate this dream come true. We have clean water near us now, and much more. Choices. Choices for girls, women, and families. Choices for healthy lives and growing businesses. Choices give us hope that more dreams can come true. Asante sana from every villager. Asante sana from me. Thank you so much."

Relieved she made it through with only a few tears, Neyah peeked at a smiling Mr. Sahli before folding and handing the paper to Mrs. Larson. A group hug to Neyah from Abby's family brought applause from the crowd.

Leading the way to the well, the mayor explained the challenges of bridging the ravine and drilling. He stepped onto the cement landing surrounding the well's tubing and made an announcement as the crowd circled the well.

"As mayor of Letsokoane, I declare today Abby Larson and Neyah Jabari day, for together with their purpose and young voices and letter writing, they not only helped bring us safe water, but a brighter future."

Following applause and much hooting and hollering, the mayor invited Hassan and Valencia to the well. They took turns pumping the metal handle up and down and giggling over the new-fangled machine. As they pumped, village children ran and stuck their heads under the spout. Others splashed in the puddles forming beside the cement. Valencia's twisted limbs proudly handed water mugs to Abby's parents. Hassan followed her lead, pumping water for Andrew and Millie.

The mayor pointed out a plaque cemented onto the well wall and read it with gusto.

"Here stands the Neyah and Abby Project, a bore-hole well dedicated to the memory of Abby Larson of Cedar Grove, Minnesota, USA. She and Letsokoane's first water president, Neyah Jabari, showed us nothing stands in the way of dreams. Not distance, not age, not money, not even dry land. Water was first tapped here earlier this year, January 14th, on what would have been Abby's 14th birthday."

Holding his cup of water high, Mr. Larson called out to those gathered, "Cheers!"

With a background of cheers, the Larson family drank their first sips of water from the well.

Abby's father stepped forward. "It came as a shock to see our Abby researching how wells were dug and starting a fundraiser—especially for someone she never met who lived halfway around the world. Our daughter hadn't thought of others much until she started writing to you."

Mr. Larson paused to clear his throat. "Honestly, we often had to remind her to not be so selfish. Abby liked nice clothes, attention, boys! and things with a big price tag. She never hesitated to ask for more, and now...we see how her insistent personality paid off. As an independent thinker, Abby was also a doer and took action when she saw something that needed fixing. In fact, she fixed my bike chain at age four!"

Mrs. Larson interrupted with a laugh, "Uh, she didn't exactly fix it!"

Abby's father shrugged and nodded. "Once, Abby redecorated our bedroom with her paint box before we knew what she was up to! What I'm saying is, our daughter didn't wait around for adults to take the lead, and she seldom took no for an answer. As parents, we always hoped Abby might direct that energy toward things beyond herself. We are standing here looking at the person and community who helped her do that."

After shooing some flies away, Abby's father took a deep breath and gestured toward the well. "Neyah, you helped Abby find her purpose. Together with your voice and purpose, you helped shape Abby's wild schemes into this! Your village and parents must be very proud of you."

As Neyah choked back tears, Mr. Larson realized he hit a nerve. Neyah's mother was there but not her father. He recalled Neyah's letters about her sick father. *Had he died?*

Mr. Larson, sensing the awkward moment, tried changing the mood. "Abby would love all this. With all my heart I wish she could see this. But I know what she'd say. 'This is great, but where are the other wells? And what about hospitals, electricity, and cell phones!' Because, that's Abby. Once she accomplished one project, she was on to the next. Something tells me that you, Neyah, are wondering the same thing!"

Mr. Sahli stepped to the front of the crowd. "As a matter of fact, Neyah and Malaika have suggested a few new projects!"

Mr. Sahli's comment brought some applause and laughter.

"Some of the money from the yellow bucket campaign will be used to build a well in other villages and provide piping for our school to carry water from the spring. This will mean better attendance, not only for girls, but for all children because they won't be home with sick bellies anymore. We plan to maintain the wells and teach children to find ways to help others as Abby and Neyah did. As for hospitals and electricity, we don't have a plan for that...yet!"

Mr. Larson grinned. "Sounds great! Abby would love knowing kids are getting to school and working toward their dreams. And speaking of hospitals, we have a surprise! I'm a photographer for a large health organization, and they're assigning a mobile health clinic to your county."

"Ah! Wonderful!" Mr. Sahli exclaimed. "I taught students to boil water and use the water purification packets, but the traveling clinic will educate everyone, not only those in school."

Neyah peered at Abby's parents. She saw the pride and joy in them. It was a relief to see how much they loved the well.

Mrs. Larson turned to the crowd. It took her a minute to brush away tears. "Life is full of opportunities where we live, but sometimes we overlook what is sitting right in front of us." She glanced at her husband and took his hand.

STANDING in the shadow of a tree, Papa listened to Mrs. Larson's words through the interpreter. Doubt and a renewed sense of what he must do tangled inside his chest. He noticed Neyah staring at him. Guilt, mixed with a sense of honor, made him turn away.

Abby's mother continued to speak. "In Abby's last days, she never stopped talking about her crazy wonderful plans and ideas for you to build a brighter future. Thank you for letting us see what *you* have started here to show Abby's true colors and Neyah's incredible courage to stand up for what is needed and take action. This is what can be accomplished when we listen to one another."

Mrs. Larson gazed at Neyah affectionately. "See what you've done, Neyah? It couldn't have been easy to convince others how change can bring good things. You've given your community and yourself more choices now. We look forward to learning where your dreams will take you."

Papa walked away. He'd heard enough about change and dreams, and he needed to get to his meeting.

"Hello, Silas."

"Hello, Haji. It has been a year."

45

THE WORTH OF A DAUGHTER

Bosco handed Andrew a worn jerry can and motioned him to the pump to give the handle a try. After pumping with all his might, Andrew spun with a devilish grin and doused his family with cold water causing them to run away squealing.

As Mr. Larson squeezed the water from his shirt, he walked to the two oversized suitcases Kareem rolled up.

"We heard you guys might need something to go with all this water!"

Millie shook herself off like a wet puppy and unzipped one suitcase. "Abby's school thought you should smell good!"

As she opened the suitcase, hundreds of bar soap fell out. Even though most members of the crowd didn't understand her words, everyone understood the purpose of soap and cheered.

The water committee and Mama took their guests on a tour of the vegetable gardens behind the new well. Neyah scanned the crowd wondering where Papa went. Maybe he returned to the field to avoid the celebration.

"Wow! This looks better than our garden in Minnesota!" said Mr. Larson.

The recently tilled, moist ground surrounded hardy

vegetables. Rocks lined each plot of gourds, kale, beans, potatoes, and onions. Mama smiled with pride at how organized and healthy it all looked.

"No more dry, cracked ground, and no more plain porridge," Mama grinned as she pulled up an onion. "Now we add vegetables!" She glowed as she clasped Mrs. Larson's hands in hers and handed her the onion. Neyah beamed at Mama's excitement. She admired the fresh flower Mama wore in her hair. She thought it looked as though it had been picked from Mama's flowered dress.

"Now that Neyah and I do not have to carry water from a great distance, my children and I have time to plant and care for this garden. Our children bathe in a reed shower room we built behind our hut instead of in the dirty river. And I no longer ask myself, 'Do I need my water for cooking, or do I save it for animals?'"

Reaching for Neyah's hand, Mama continued, eyes filled with tears. "My daughter's dream of never missing school has come true. Your Abby, along with Neyah's friend, Malaika, achieved something no one in this village could do. She encouraged Neyah to use her voice to bring change. And look what the great result is! We cannot do enough to thank you, but we want to try. We have a big celebration meal planned. You can taste some of our sweet tomatoes and beans!"

"What about bread?" asked Hassan. "Mama makes the best mandazi in Kenya!"

"I'm starving!" said Andrew. "Can I taste it now?"

"Yes. If my hungry boys did not eat it all! Come, follow, and we shall feast!"

Other families in the crowd scattered to their compounds to participate in celebration meals of their own. The water committee members, along with Neyah and Abby's family, did as Mama directed and followed her. As Neyah and Bosco helped Bibi to the table, Neyah nearly collided with Papa. Her face faded to pale as she watched in shock when he took a seat at the table. She chose a bench as far from Papa as possible and tried her best to appear joyful and choke down a few bites.

After a meal of Mama's bread, fresh vegetables, and roasted goat legs, the Larsons asked to see more of the village. Mr. Sahli showed them the new latrines and hand washing stations built by village boys and their fathers. He proudly demonstrated how the new shower stalls and dish-drying racks worked. Uncle Aman entertained the guests by singing as he ground corn. Mama showed how to make ugali, and the twins demonstrated everything from goat milking to soccer skills.

The remaining goat leg hung over the open fire. Millie declined to taste it at dinner. Bosco sliced off a piece with the machete and handed it to her. "You do not want to go back to America without a taste!"

Cautiously Millie accepted it between two fingers. After chewing it a long time, she swallowed and grinned. "It's no worse than spinach!"

Mr. Sahli laughed. "Spinach isn't my favorite either, Millie."

"Neyah!" Millie begged as she grasped Neyah's hand. "Show me where you sleep!"

Neyah brought Abby's family inside her sleeping hut where they saw Abby's photo hanging. Andrew's eyes bulged with surprise. "I can't believe you share these two little rooms with your grandma and two brothers!"

Mr. Larson laughed. "Andrew, I think you and Millie would fit nicely in our bedroom with us!"

"No way! You snore!"

After infectious laughter, Neyah ushered her guests from the hut. When she crawled out, she nearly collided with a man she had seen only once before, but definitely knew who he was. The sight of Silas sent a cold fear racing through her veins. A waft of manure met her nose as she passed in front of him. She could feel his eyes follow her as she made her way to the table where the remainder of the evening meal buzzed with flies.

Ignoring the other guests, the man greeted Papa in a gruff voice. "Good evening, Haji."

Papa swallowed hard. "Hello, Silas."

"I brought your cows, as you requested."

Panic flooded Neyah's face. She stumbled back.

"Papa!" Bosco sounded surprised. "I did not know we were getting more cattle."

Papa nodded as he turned and glared at Neyah. "We have plenty of water for them now."

Neyah understood his message. Papa was blaming her for pushing his hand to trade her.

Papa continued. "And it is a good time to grow our herd."

Silas tipped his head upward and grunted. "And it is a good time to collect my new wife. I take it your daughter's necessities are together, and she is ready."

Mama gasped and sank to the ground.

Mr. and Mrs. Larson exchanged questioning glances. Millie, sensing tension, ran to cling to her mother.

The water committee members stared at the stranger in confusion.

"Haji, don't—" whispered Bibi.

Papa cut his mother off. "Collect what you need from your hut, Neyah."

What I need is not in that hut, thought Neyah.

Bibi tried to walk to her and tripped on the uneven ground. Bosco caught her and held on tight.

The Larsons huddled together, uncertain what they were witnessing.

Too angry to worry about what Papa thought, Neyah didn't

move. When it was evident she didn't intend to cooperate, Papa directed Bosco to retrieve her belongings.

Bosco hesitated and shook his head.

"Now!" demanded Papa in a trembling voice.

Bosco pursed his lips and finally moved. He disappeared into the hut and came out with an armload of Neyah's clothes and her woven mat.

Papa looked at the man waiting for his future wife.

"Silas..." Papa's voice broke. He began to shake. As if in a daze, Papa scanned the faces surrounding him. When his gaze fell on Mama, her pleading eyes said more than words ever could.

Papa tried to steady his voice. "Silas, Neyah is no longer a girl."

"I can see that," Silas sneered.

Neyah covered her ears and shook her head in disbelief. This had been such a wonderful day.

Papa pointed at Neyah with a shaky arm and steadily raised his voice. "She is no longer quiet and shy and bendable."

Silas laughed. "I will fix that!"

Neyah shuffled further back and prepared to run for her life.

Papa clasped his hands together to control the shaking.

"This young woman is strong, and loud, and daring beyond my imagination. She will be a wife who works until she can no longer work, and she will care for her family with all her might!" Papa's thick voice wavered on his last words.

Neyah watched Bibi rock back and forth, hands folded in a silent plea. In horror, she heard Mama moan the way she did the day they buried Lulu. Neyah couldn't bear anymore of this. She dropped her head onto her chest and allowed her eyes to close as she focused on how to escape.

Papa took a deep breath and dropped his voice to a bare whisper. "She will be ready."

He looked at Neyah as if in pain. His shaking slowed. Digging his fingernails into the back of his neck, Papa threw his arms skyward and groaned, causing alarm among those gathered.

"She will be ready!" Papa shouted. "Someday!" Then his voice went to a whisper. "But that day...that day...is not today, Silas. And maybe it will never come."

Neyah's eyes flew open as she grasped her chest.

Papa, in an ocean of pent-up emotion, struggled to remain standing. "It is her choice. There are ideas she dreams of today. Ideas to make a difference."

Neyah felt faint and sank to the ground. Bibi's arms flew wide as she chanted a prayer of gratitude.

Papa stretched his neck and strode up to Silas. His eyes were clear, and his voice was even. "My daughter is not for sale. Her dreams and future are not mine or yours. Only hers."

Silas protested loudly. "Haji, in bad times, everyone sells their daughters!"

Mrs. Larson gasped in disbelief.

Papa nodded. "But I am not everyone. I am her father. And I will never make a difference if I do things the same as everyone else. Take your cattle and go home."

Silas yelled. "We had a deal!"

"And the deal is off. Go." Papa spoke calmly but sternly.

Neyah glanced at Silas from where she knelt. The way he scowled at her caused her stomach to lurch. He muttered under his breath before marching toward the field where his cattle grazed.

Neyah's lips quivered.

Papa took the clothes from Bosco and kneeled before Neyah. Clearing his throat, he carefully chose his words.

"Neyah, please look at me."

He waited.

"Bibi, Bosco, and Paul will keep their hut. I will build a new hut for you. It seems a water president deserves more space."

No one, not even the birds, made a sound.

"My daughter, because I spent my childhood with no dreams, I grew to be a man with no purpose, until now. You taught me why I was spared all those years ago. I was granted a chance to live, and to grow a new family." Papa gestured toward them. "My purpose is not to stand in the way of my children, but rather to clear the path so you might find your own way."

Not sure whether to trust her ears, Neyah scooted back. Hesitant, she lifted her face to her father. Half expecting Papa to strike or scream at her, she braced and held her breath. What she saw were tears and open arms.

"Neyah, forgive me," he whispered.

Neyah fell into Papa's arms, squeezing him with all her might.

Papa was back.

46

FETCHING DREAMS

The celebration—a much quieter one—went on for a second day at the water well. As Mr. Larson rubbed the dedication plaque, Papa softly touched his shoulder. The interpreter sat near them. "We have not officially met. I am Neyah's father."

Mr. Larson looked into the eyes of a man who, no doubt, had many stories to tell. Happy ones, tragic ones. Perhaps someday he would hear some of them. He extended his arm, and the two fathers embraced. "It's great to meet the father of the water president!"

Papa nodded timidly. "Our girls. Your Abby. My Neyah. So much alike. Strong-willed, determined to do good."

Papa motioned for Mr. Larson to sit with him on the concrete barrier encircling the pump. He spoke solemnly. "Our Neyah never said much. She seemed afraid. I admit to being part of the problem. I thought it was my job to be in charge of her future. Luckily, she followed her own heart and not my advice."

Abby's father laughed softly. "Sometimes fathers learn from their children."

Papa choked on his words as he pointed at the well. "And our girls, see what they accomplished in spite of us."

Mr. Larson smiled through his misty eyes. "They set their sights on a purpose."

Papa shaded his eyes with a hand and pointed at his field. "Why did I fight this? Why could I not see how water could improve my crops, water my cattle?"

"I don't know what you call it here, but in America, we call it stubbornness!" laughed Mr. Larson.

Papa smiled and touched Mr. Larson's hand. "I know what it is like to lose a daughter. Your angel daughter grew old enough to make a difference; she lives still in Neyah's voice. For Neyah not only speaks now; she also does something. The result is good."

The rest of the Jabari and Larson families came clamoring toward them with Malaika's family close behind.

Mr. Larson laughed when he saw Neyah leading the clan. "And something tells me Neyah's just getting started."

"Hey Mom!" shouted Millie. "What did you do with the skirt?"

"Oh, I almost forgot!" Mrs. Larson opened her backpack.

"My skirt!" Malaika shrieked when she saw the red-flowered fabric.

"You must be Malaika!" Mrs. Larson smiled as she handed her the skirt.

"Oh, asante!" Malaika hugged it like an old friend and rubbed the poinsettias gently. Holding it to her waist, she frowned. "It looks a little small now." Malaika smiled at Millie. "Would you like to keep it?"

"Sure!" Millie squealed. She ran and grabbed it. Everyone laughed as she nearly lost her balance hopping around on one foot in an effort to step into the skirt. The skirt hung loosely on her hips. Millie twirled and danced around in it until the skirt dropped completely off, causing everyone to roar in amusement.

Millie picked it up and cradled it in her arms. "I will take good care of it, and when I outgrow it, I'll send it back for Neyah's little sister to wear."

Neyah grinned at Papa who held the newest member of the family. Abigail Subira Jabari, a plump and happy one-year-old, squirmed until Papa set her down. Hugging her maize husk doll Mama made, she wobbled over to her big sister.

Kissing her sister's delicate forehead, Neyah cooed. "One day, Abigail, I will tell you all about the girl you are named after."

Papa gathered his two girls into his arms. "And I will tell her the story of why she will never have to spend her days walking for water."

Mama joined the embrace. "Yes, and someday all of us dreamers—we will sail across Lake Victoria together, and find what is on the other side."

EPILOGUE: ABBY'S LAST LETTER

Dear Neyah,

I'm finally home. Mom is writing this, and I made sure she uses lots of ! Dad is sitting in bed with me rubbing my head. Bieber (my dog, not the singer!) is beside me, and I'm rubbing his head ☺ My hair is growing again-kind of prickly yet. Is that how yours feels?

It's great to hear your papa is better! I hope Malaika and Paul will be okay. Being sick stinks! I feel a little better but can't see so good. I sleep a lot because of all the medicine.

When I get back to school, I'm going to read your essay to the student council and persuade them to do more for you to get a well. You can't drink dirty water forever!

I have a lot of time to think now and figure you're a lot like me after all. I didn't think so when we first started writing. Now I feel like you have big dreams as I do. I like to get things moving. It sounds like you do too.

Another thing, maybe all this medicine is freaking

me out, but what if it was me who was born in Kenya and you were born here in Minnesota?

Anyway, I will see you someday and we can rub each other's heads and make a toast with a glass of cool, clean water. Until then, Cheers! Here's to yellow buckets and DIY girls! (DIY isn't a word but you can still write it in your journal.) And thanks for teaching me some Swahili words!

Rafiki yako forever,

Abby Larson

P.S. I'm going to send you a little mirror Grandma gave me. It was hers when she was little. I have two others. You need this one. Grandma said it reveals the real "you" when you look in it and smile. Try it!

One more thing about Grandma. She read me a book of quotes yesterday. I'm not into quotes, but it was Grandma! I love this one since it pretty much sums up what you and I have been writing about. I don't know who this Paulo Coelho dude is, but he hit "the nail right on the head" as Dad would say.

"Go further than you planned. Ask for the moon: you will be surprised how often you get it."

I hope you get your moon, Neyah Jabari.

Your turn!

AUTHOR'S NOTE

We all face problems in our lives. Some we can solve on our own, and others we need help to solve. Big problems like water scarcity affect hundreds of millions of people and require many hands and hearts to solve. But no matter the size, a problem won't get fixed unless someone takes a first step. Sometimes that simply means listening and doing our part to help because we're all better together.

On the family farm where I grew up, we hauled water from the electric-powered well for farm animals and household use. The water was safe to drink and, although it was a time-consuming task to retrieve it, no one missed school to collect water, or became ill from drinking it. Following a trip to East Africa a few years ago and discovering the danger and health risk involved with fetching and drinking contaminated water for everyday survival, I learned the water crisis is tragically real. But it is also one of the more solvable world problems.

I wrote *Fetching Dreams* as a conversation between two girls of vastly different cultures with the hope that others may be inspired to step in, speak out, and partner up with classmates and neighbors—whether they're across the aisle, across the street, or across the world—to better understand each other's challenges, and help where they can.

Just as it "takes a village" to solve big challenges, it takes many people to bring a book to readers. With gratitude, I wish to thank Holli Anderson and the entire Immortal Works Press team for seeing a place for this story, written to empower young people to gather courage, tackle problems, and gain a sense of purpose; World Vision, charity: water, and other organizations working diligently to end the global water crisis and whose amazing stories inspired me to write this one; Aaron and Donna Eicher for sharing contacts; Brian Frazier for logistic details of accessing water in the neediest regions; Rebecca Koech and Rose Ringeera of Kenya for fine-tuning content and generously sharing personal stories; Amanda Huiker and John M. Olsen for editing; Les Huth for an amazing Africa trip; Wanzita Ally, Bethany Friberg, and Mary Laiser of Tanzania for sharing water-carrying experiences; and sensitivity readers in Kenya and the United States for time and valuable input. A special thank you to my husband for his patience with all my writing craziness.

BEYOND THE YELLOW BUCKET

- 2.2 billion people in the world do not have access to safe drinking water.[1]
- Each day, nearly 1,000 children die due to preventable water and sanitation-related diseases. Most are under five years of age.[2]
- Women and girls are responsible for collecting water in 80% of households without access to water on the premises.[3]
- Women and girls spend an estimated 200 million hours hauling water every day.[4]
- The average woman in rural Africa walks 6 kilometers (3.7 miles) every day to haul 40 pounds of water.[5]
- 443 million days of school are missed every year due to preventable water-related diseases.[6]
- 2.6 billion people gained access to improved drinking water from 1990 to 2015.[7]
- The United Nations has a goal of providing clean water and sanitation for all by 2030.[8]

1. https://www.unwater.org/water-facts/water-sanitation-and-hygiene/
2. https://www.un.org/sustainabledevelopment/water-and-sanitation/
3. https://www.un.org/sustainabledevelopment/water-and-sanitation/
4. https://www.worldvision.org/clean-water-news-stories/global-water-crisis-facts#facts
5. https://www.worldvision.org/clean-water-news-stories/global-water-crisis-facts#facts
6. https://www.charitywater.org/global-water-crisis/education
7. https://www.worldvision.org/clean-water-news-stories/global-water-crisis-facts#facts
8. https://www.un.org/sustainabledevelopment/water-and-sanitation/

DISCUSSION GUIDE

1. Why do you think Neyah didn't talk very much? Have you sometimes felt like not talking?
2. Do you know someone who is quiet or afraid to speak up? What can you do to help them feel comfortable to speak and share their thoughts?
3. How were Malaika and Abby alike? How were they different?
4. Bibi seemed to understand Neyah's longings better than other family members. What do you think is the reason for this?
5. In one of her letters, Abby said...*what if it was me who was born in Kenya and you were born here in Minnesota?* Have you wondered how your life would be different if you were born in a different place or time?
6. What are some words to describe Papa? Mama? Mr. Sahli?
7. How did Neyah's situation create a sense of purpose for Abby?

8. Describe the bond that formed between Abby and Neyah? Did their cultural differences make the bond difficult to form, or did it help to develop it?

9. Have you (or someone you know) stood up for an injustice or something you/they believed in, even though there were negative consequences?

10. Abby got the Every Drop Counts campaign going. Is there a cause you feel a strong desire to support?

11. Who or what was the biggest influence for Neyah in her transformation from a quiet girl to a confident spokesperson?

12. Do you think about your purpose? How do you come to form a purpose?

ABOUT THE AUTHOR

Mary Bleckwehl is a midwest farmer's daughter who learned how cows and corn grow but decided growing young minds suited her best so she became a teacher, a mom, and a writer. *Fetching Dreams* follows her debut middle grade book, *The Worry Knot,* four picture books, and five nonfiction books. She and her husband live in Northfield, Minnesota where cows, corn, and young minds prosper.

This has been an
Immortal Production

9 781953 491558